Unethical Practices

ANNE M. HOLMES

Shoestring Books
5100 Capital Drive – Suite 304
Burnaby, British Columbia
Canada V5B 4S7

Unethical Practices
Copyright © 2010 by Anne M. Holmes

Anne M. Holmes has asserted her moral right
to be identified as the author of this work.

This novel is entirely a work of fiction.
Names, characters, places and incidents are the product of
the author's imagination. Any resemblance to actual events,
locales, or persons, living or dead, is coincidental.

ISBN 978-0-557-72299-0

All rights reserved. No part of this publication may be
reproduced, stored in a retrieval system, or transmitted, in
any form or by any means, electronic, mechanical,
photocopying, recording or otherwise, without the prior
permission of the publisher.

This book is sold subject to the condition that it shall not, by
way of trade or otherwise, be lent, re-sold, hired out or
otherwise circulated without the publisher's prior consent in
any form of binding or cover other than that in which it is
published and without a similar condition including this
condition being imposed on the subsequent purchaser.

To the Jack Conquests of the world for keeping
an eye on the guys in lab coats.

CHAPTER ONE

"You've got to help me!"

Alec hesitated before looking up from his paper. Dammit, he thought, this sort of thing just doesn't happen. People simply don't demand help on the 8:17. There he was, sitting, minding his own business, reading his *Guardian*. The entire rest of the train was full of dressed-for-success stockbrokers reading their bloody *Financial Times* and *Telegraphs*. Why him?

The woman slipped into the seat opposite him and Alec finally looked up at her, surprised, when he did, that she didn't look at all the sort of person who said, "You've got to help me!" to complete strangers on trains. Not that Alec had any terribly clear idea what women who said such things should look like, but surely not like this?

This was probably the most beautiful woman Alec had ever seen in his life. She looked as if she could have been a model from *Vogue* – well, maybe not *Vogue*. In these days of heroin chic, *Vogue* models all looked like starving refugees and there was nothing anorexic about this woman. Even without a trace of make-up her eyes, an unforgettable aquamarine, were large and luminous. Her white gold hair, pulled tightly back off her face, emphasised the sort of strongly defined cheekbones and jaw line most models paid a fortune to achieve. The wide, generous mouth, Alec was prepared to bet, owed nothing to collagen injections. Despite the bizarre situation and the demands for help, even in blue jeans and a T-shirt underneath a Burberry, its belt tied casually around her slim waist, this woman positively screamed poise and confidence.

Alec glanced around the carriage at the stockbrokers and cleared his throat. "Is someone bothering you?"

"No," the woman said, "but someone is going to be bothering me at the next station."

"Oh?" Did she, he wondered, consider herself to be some

sort of psychic pervert spotter in need of potential protection? "I see," he added, not seeing at all.

"Look," she said, "I don't have time to explain. Take this." She thrust an envelope at him. "Get it to Tilly Arbuthnot."

"I say," Alec began, but before he actually could say anything, she had dropped the envelope in his lap, jumped to her feet and fled from the carriage. The train pulled into a station. As commuters poured into the carriage, threatening his seat during the remainder of the journey, Alec hesitated. Just as he'd decided he really would have to get up and find the woman, he spotted her on the platform, involved in a heated discussion with two men. One of the men, silver haired, tall, slim and immaculate, grabbed the woman's bag and peered into it, while the other, a burly bruiser, looked on. As the whistle blew and the train began to pull away the silver haired man threw the bag down on the platform in apparent fury.

Alec craned his neck. The last glimpse he had of the woman, before the train rounded a bend in the tracks, was the defiant look she gave the silver haired man as she stooped to retrieve her bag.

Bloody hell, thought Alec, instinctively covering the envelope on his lap with a section of his paper, as the seats around him filled and less successful commuters took up positions in the aisles. He pretended to read the G2 section for the remainder of the journey, although he failed to absorb a single detail. The package on his lap seemed to be increasing in temperature, which, given its location, was rather alarming. Alec carefully slid a hand under his newspaper and fumbled with the envelope, only to withdraw his hand rapidly at a loud "Tut, tut" from a middle aged woman sitting opposite him. Bloody, bloody hell, thought Alec, I see that woman on this train every other day and now she thinks – literally – that I'm a wanker. Wonderful.

The train finally pulled in to Waterloo, after what seemed like several hours, although it had, of course, been the same thirty-eight minute trip he took every week day. Alec hurried down the platform and made his way to the gents toilet, where he locked himself in a cubicle and examined the package which so recently had felt as if it was burning a hole in his lap.

Unethical Practices

It was a normal manila envelope, designed to hold A4 paper. A yellow post-it note had been attached to the front, upon which was written: Tilly Arbuthnot, 17 Kenwood Mews, Hampstead NW3. There was also a telephone number. Underneath the post-it note, the envelope had been stamped: VACO INDUSTRIES - CONFIDENTIAL.

Well, I'm buggered if I'm going to go traipsing off to Hampstead in my lunch hour, thought Alec, not realising he'd spoken out loud until a voice from the next cubicle replied, "You don't have to go to Hampstead to get buggered, dear. For a tenner, I'll do you right now."

Alec shot out of the gents and made his way rapidly to the station coffee bar, glancing over his shoulder to make sure he hadn't been followed by the accommodating fellow in the next cubicle. After purchasing a cup of greyish liquid which purported, despite all evidence to the contrary, to be coffee, he sat down.

The word CONFIDENTIAL in big, bold letters was, of course, enough to compel anyone to immediately open the envelope. Alec did so, lifting the two bits of metal on the flap and extracting the contents. Sheets of paper contained line after line of complete gibberish. He tried looking at them upside down and sideways, in case there was some kind of optical trick, but its meaning remained a complete mystery. Further inspection of the envelope revealed its contents to include a compact disk.

Industrial espionage, Alec decided, was the only possible answer. He considered simply dropping the envelope on the floor, minus the yellow post-it note, in the hope it would be found and somehow make its way back to VACO Industries, whatever and wherever the hell VACO Industries was.

Just as he was about to do exactly that, a number of things struck him. Top of the list was the fact that he certainly had liked the look of the young woman on the train. And he hadn't liked the look of the man who'd grabbed her bag. Somehow he couldn't imagine how anything destined for someone called Tilly Arbuthnot, which was such a jolly hockey sticks sort of name, could be all that serious. Perhaps most important was his uncertainty about fingerprints. He wasn't sure whether they could be lifted from paper, but he suspected they could.

Although Alec had never had occasion to be fingerprinted for anything, so it was highly unlikely the police could trace the envelope back to him, he had inordinate faith in the ability of the Old Bill and no interest whatsoever in ever having to "assist them in their enquiries".

So, he wrapped the envelope once again in his *Guardian*, hurried out of the station and down Stamford Street to his office in the Creed International Publishing office tower with its commanding view of St Paul's and the Thames.

Following his failed careers as an actor, a rock musician, an artist and a journalist, Alec had finally found his niche in life. He was, and had been for the three years since his thirtieth birthday, the chief sub-editor of *Sweetie,* a magazine for teenage girls.

Once upon a time, *Sweetie* had employed honest to God journalists to write the articles which filled the space between the adverts, but those days were long gone. Now articles were supplied by a series of incredibly trendy "freelancers", who may have fit right in at rock concerts and nightclubs, but could not, for the most part, string an intelligible sentence together if their lives depended on it.

Even when there had been real journalists around, before Creed decided journalists, their union and the annual round of rancorous collective bargaining were, and therefore would be made, redundant, there had been sub-editors and chief sub-editors teeming about the building. Before the computers C.I.P. invested in after divesting itself of the journos, subs were important to catch spelling mistakes and typos, not to mention reducing five thousand word treatises to the five hundred word articles they were supposed to be.

Now, with semi-literate trendoids turning in stories on bits of bog roll, subs were enormously important and chief subs, as Alec firmly believed they should, completely ruled the roost. Of course, technically *Sweetie*'s editor Roger Wilcox was higher up the pecking order than Alec, but, as everyone knew, Roger seldom left the Stamford Arms between eleven in the morning and eleven in the evening. Roger was rumoured to only be in employment at all because he had something big on someone in management.

"I used to be in Fleet Street," was a regular refrain of Roger's during his brief morning appearances in the seventeenth floor office. It had been the refrain of many a drunken magazine editor and deputy editor, before the corporation streamlined them into early, unwanted retirement. The fact that there hadn't been a daily paper published there in years didn't prevent these old hacks from regularly congregating in Fleet Street boozers regularly to relive their glory days. Quite often Roger, the only one of them still in semi-gainful employment would hail a taxi or lurch over Blackfriars Bridge to join in a nostalgic session in El Vino's or the Cheshire Cheese.

Alec felt a bit sorry for them, but he, whose brief career in journalism hadn't brought him within twenty miles of Fleet Street, knew these old relics had brought much of their present day misery upon themselves. They'd flagrantly fiddled their expenses, spent three hour lunches in the pub (and only staggered back into the office at all because the pubs still shut for two and half hours in the afternoon in those days) and generally swanned about leaving everything to their long suffering chief subs. Somebody in management, dense as they were, was bound to notice eventually.

So, the boozy editors were long gone, replaced, with the exception of Roger, by smartly dressed marketing executives, who let the chief subs get on with producing the magazines.

This particular morning, Alec was far too distracted by the envelope poking out through the folds of his *Guardian* to get on with much of anything.

He considered chucking the envelope in the bin, but couldn't quite get over the feeling he'd had ever since he'd very nearly given up his seat on the train to go to the assistance of that damsel in distress, that perhaps this was some sort of opportunity to redeem himself for cock ups past. Certainly he was never going to see said damsel again if he did nothing and presumably she would be grateful and might even agree to go out for a drink with him, perhaps even to a play.

He picked up his telephone receiver and dialled the Hampstead phone number. After two rings, a deep, no nonsense voice said, "Obviously, I'm not here, leave a message." Alec immediately rang off. He hated answering machines, never knew what to say. He mentally composed and rehearsed a message, then dialled the number again.

At the sound of the beep, he began, "Hello, this is Alec..." As always, he hesitated before saying his last name. It was a source of never ending amusement to the trendoids and the clerical staff that Alec shared the same name as a famous American actor. Alec suspected they went out of their way to write far more stories about this particular actor than could possibly be necessary simply to wind him up. Well, he might not be as dishy as his American counterpart, but he at least had three months of RADA under his belt, so was probably a better actor.

He cleared his throat and began again. "This is Alec Baldwin. I ran into a friend of yours on the train. She asked me to drop off a parcel for you. I'm afraid Hampstead isn't terribly convenient for me. Could you possibly give me a ring and see if we can arrange something else or if it's possible to pop the package in the post or send it round by courier?" He left his phone number and rang off.

Curiosity again got the better of him. He removed the CD from the envelope, slipped it into his computer and attempted to view its contents. There was only one file on the disk. Alec clicked on it. *Enter Password to open file* said a little box on his computer. He ignored this and hit Enter. *The password is incorrect Word cannot open document* said another box on his computer. Bollocks, thought Alec. There must be some way to get into this file. He copied the contents of the CD onto his hard drive and tried accessing it that way. *Enter password to open file* said the same box on his computer. After a moment's consideration, he typed "VACO". Password incorrect. He tried "vaco". Password incorrect. Bollocks, bollocks, bollocks, he thought, slipping the CD back into the envelope and the envelope into his desk drawer. It was time to turn his attention to the pile of copy on his desk.

Excellent, thought Alec, when he saw that the very top article in the pile was by Mandy Evans. Unlike all the other bloody trendoids, Mandy could actually write. In fact, despite her match stick figure and flaming red, improbably rag dollish curls, she wasn't really a trendoid at all. She was an honest to God journalist, who provided *Sweetie* with most of the "serious" articles they ran on depressing topics like race relations and youth unemployment. Trendoid copy Alec generally left to his three sub-editors, knowing they were more than capable of turning it into sentences which all sounded as if they'd been written by the same person.

Mandy's copy was different. Mandy's articles were succinct and to the point. Mandy's articles were a joy to read. Mandy's articles were his. No *Sweetie* reader was ever able to share Alec's joy in Mandy's prose, because, by the time Alec finished hacking it to bits and regurgitating it, an article by Mandy read as if it had been written by the same hackneyed hack who'd churned out the stories on fashion, make-up and celebrities. Ruining Mandy's articles was a challenge, which Alec felt only the chief sub-editor was able to meet.

Needless to say, Mandy Evans detested Alec. He didn't mind. If she'd wanted her work treated with respect, she should have taken it to the *Observer* – that or accepted his invitation to go out for a drink, which she'd so roundly rejected last year. As Alec mentally sharpened his literary hatchet, he smiled to himself. The latest edition of *Sweetie* would be on the newsstands that day. He couldn't wait to hear Mandy's reaction to what was left of her interview with the former Soviet general and his warnings about global arms build ups. She'd barely recognise it.

"*Baldwin?*" a voice barked in his ear an hour later, just as Alec was putting the final touches on the destruction of Mandy's article.

Alec almost jumped out of his seat. Turning to look up, he met the piercing cobalt blue gaze of a tall, gaunt woman of indeterminate age, whose clothing – such that he could see – comprised a pair of ancient cowboy boots, a cape-like Mac and a battered fedora.

"Yes," he admitted with some hesitation.

The woman thrust a hand towards him. "Tilly Arbuthnot," she said, adding, as Alec even more hesitantly allowed his hand to be crushed by her grip, "I believe you have something for me."

Alec snatched his hand away. He remembered the message he'd left on her answering machine quite clearly. All he'd left was a phone number. "How did you know where to find me?"

Tilly Arbuthnot shrugged, as if finding Alec had been the easiest thing in the world. "The phone number was obviously part of the Creed exchange. I just called the main switchboard and asked who you were."

"I see," said Alec, not seeing at all. Why hadn't she just returned his call?

"I believe you have something for me," Tilly repeated.

Again Alec hesitated. "Look," he said in what he hoped was a forceful manner, "this envelope says VACO Industries, Confidential on it."

Tilly's eye widened, as if to indicate her surprise that Alec could actually read. She tapped her foot impatiently. "So?"

"So," said Alec, "I'm not at all sure I should be giving it to a complete stranger. Perhaps I should ring VACO Industries?"

Tilly made an impatient snorting sound. "I work for VACO Industries, you dolt," she said.

"Really?" Alec wasn't at all happy about being called a dolt, nor was he sure he believed her. "What exactly does VACO Industries do?"

Another impatient snort. "Oh, for God's sake," Tilly said, "we run the UK arm of the space programme."

"What space programme?"

"The *European* space programme."

"Oh," said Alec, surprised. "Is there one?"

The Arbuthnot woman was clearly at the end of her limited patience. "Yes, there is a European space programme, yes, I work on it. And, as I have now said three times, I believe you have something for me."

Alec began to open his desk drawer, then shut it again. He looked curiously at Tilly. "What exactly do you do on the space programme, Ms Arbuthnot?"

"*Doctor* Arbuthnot," she corrected. She looked at Alec as if he were some mysterious specimen and said, "I'm a rocket scientist." Her tone clearly implied: What else?

"Oh," said Alec once again.

Tilly Arbuthnot did not look like a rocket scientist. Not, he was forced to admit, that he had any more idea what rocket scientists should look like than he had about what damsels in distress should look like. Perhaps she wore a lab coat? Alec tried to picture it, but it still didn't seem likely. "I say," he said, "what was the young woman on the train doing with these confidential documents?"

Tilly sighed dramatically and spoke, one word at a time, to ensure he understood, "She. Was. Bringing. Them. To. Me."

"Oh," said Alec yet again. He should, he thought, just hand the bloody envelope over and have done with it, but he couldn't let it go. "Why?" he demanded.

"So the Libyans wouldn't get them."

Libyans? Space programme? Rockets? This was definitely out of his league. He snapped open his desk drawer and removed the envelope.

"Thank you," Tilly said, snatching the envelope from his hand. With that she turned on her heel and stomped out of the office.

A moment later he heard the ping which signalled the lift doors opening, followed by his editor's voice booming, "Tilly Arbuthnot! I don't believe it!" then the Arbuthnot woman's barked, "Roger Wilcox, you old rogue. How the hell are you?" If further conversation passed between them Alec couldn't hear it.

A minute or so later, Roger shambled around the corner, heading for his office. After a moment's hesitation, Alec followed him.

In the three years since Alec had begun working for *Sweetie*, he had never set foot inside Roger's office. Aside from the fact that Roger took virtually no interest in the day to day or even year to year operations of the magazine – other than insisting they had at least one *real* story, usually assigned to Mandy, per issue – Roger's office billowed smoke. During his brief morning appearances, Roger did nothing, at least nothing Alec could see, except chain smoke – this despite supposedly stringent no smoking rules. People who wanted to venture into Roger's office – not that anyone except Mandy, a chain smoker herself, ever did – needed a gas mask.

Alec knocked timidly on the door and went in. Roger already had a fag dangling from the corner of his mouth, which nearly fell to the desk when he saw who was standing in the doorway. He stared at Alec for a moment, then said, "Baldwin! What can I do for you?"

Alec very much doubted Roger was capable of doing anything for anyone and hoped his expression said so. He waved a hand in front of his face to remind the editor that there was *no smoking* in offices any longer, then asked, "How well do you know Tilly Arbuthnot?"

Roger, who'd merely grinned at Alec's waving hand, now beamed. "Tilly? Known her years. One of the best."

"Best what?"

"Best bloody journalists I've ever met. She used to work in Fleet Street, you know. Ace investigator for the *Grauniad*. Lovely woman. Great legs."

"What? You mean she's not a rocket scientist?"

Roger, in the process of inhaling deeply on his Silk Cut, began to laugh at Alec's question and ended hacking so badly it sounded as if he was going to cough up a lung. Alec finally took pity and gave the editor a few slaps on the back. When Roger's colour faded from purple back to its normal bright red, he was still chortling. "Rocket scientist? Who on earth told you that?"

"She did," Alec informed Roger huffily. Hell's bells, he thought. He'd just given European space programme secrets to someone who clearly had no right to them whatsoever. Could that possibly be deemed treason? Surely not. Surely treason only counted during times of war. Didn't it? What to do? Alec bit his lower lip and considered. *Do nothing*, his subconscious whispered. As this was exactly the course of action Alec had always favoured, he did not find it difficult to follow the advice. He backed out of Roger's polluted office, shut the door and returned to his desk.

It was late afternoon before Mandy Evans stormed into Alec's domain, waving the most recent issue of *Sweetie*. "Baldwin, you bastard," she said, enraged, "you unspeakable bloody bastard." Mandy slammed the magazine, opened to her article, in front of Alec. "Didn't Roger tell you to keep your filthy hands off my stuff?"

Alec smirked. Of course, Roger had told him, complaining as he did, that they might lose the only decent journalist they had writing for the magazine, and of course Alec ignored him.

"Something wrong, Mandy?" he asked, all wide-eyed innocence.

"Wrong?" Mandy repeated, staring down at him as he sat at his desk smiling. "Baldwin, there are so many things wrong I don't even know where to start." She glanced at the magazine for a moment, then pointed at a paragraph. "Let's start here, shall we? There is absolutely no need to take this sentence, which begins 'Flashing his fourteen carat fillings, Averin says' and insert the words 'gold' and 'tooth'. 'Flashing his fourteen carat fillings' is called alliteration, you cretin. 'Flashing his fourteen carat *gold tooth* fillings' is not."

Alec was mentally rubbing his hands together gleefully. Of course he knew the sentence read better before. Of course he knew what alliteration was.

He smiled blandly and said, "But, Mandy, people might not have understood that you meant gold tooth fillings. It's very important to make your meaning clear, although I understand that when you're dashing things off in a hurry, it's not always possible." His bland smile became quite magnanimous. "That's what subs are for."

"Oh is it?" Mandy's eyebrows shot up. She didn't even deign to comment, as Alec had hoped she would, on the suggestion that she ever "dashed" anything off. "I've always wondered what the hell subs were for," she said. "I always thought you were a sub species of teachers. You know the old saying: Those who can, do; those who can't, teach. I always thought there was an extra line: Those who can't teach, sub-edit."

Alec's rapid response surprised even him, "Mandy, my dear, it has been my experience that those who do, seldom can."

"Baldwin," Mandy said, her eyes widening in surprise, "that was very good. Have I been underestimating you? Is it possible you aren't quite as gormless as I thought?"

Rather difficult to preen about being asked if one wasn't quite as gormless as supposed, but Alec did sit up straighter in his chair. "Yes, Evans," he said, mimicking her tone, "I rather think you have been underestimating me."

Half an hour later they were sitting in the Stamford Arms, Alec having accepted Mandy's unexpected invitation to go for a pint. Part of Alec's brain registered the fact that Mandy was looking particularly winsome and that he really should be concentrating on being as charming as possible. Unfortunately, that wasn't the particular part of his brain which was engaged at the time. Out of the corner of his eye he glanced around the pub looking for detectives from Special Branch waiting to collar him for giving away space programme secrets.

"Earth to Baldwin," said Mandy eventually. "Come in, Baldwin." Alec snapped his head around and stared blankly at Mandy. She gave him an encouraging smile. "Something on your mind, Baldwin?" she asked.

"Um, yes." Alec wondered if he dared trust her with this story or whether she would go straight to the police. Or, worse yet, not believe him. He decided to go slowly. "Have you ever heard of VACO Industries?" he asked.

"VACO?" she repeated her tone contemptuous. "Oh, yes, I've heard of them. Swine." Alec, surprised by the disgust in her tone, asked her what she had against the space programme. It was Mandy's turn to stare blankly. "Space programme? What is this, Twenty Questions? What's the next question? Do I know what time it is in Timbuktu?"

The fine hairs on the back of Alec's neck stood up on end. "VACO isn't involved in the European space programme?" he asked.

"Not that I know of, although they might consider it sometime in the future after they've finished screwing up this planet."

Ah, Alec thought, beginning to see light at the end of the tunnel. VACO was obviously a polluter of some sort. Mandy, a staunch supporter of the environmental movement, hated polluters more than anything else. "So," he asked, "what exactly is VACO?"

"VACO Industries," Mandy informed him, "is Victor, Arthur and Charles Ormond, three brothers who've made a lot of money killing things. They make products that kill bugs and kill germs and kill pain. The fact that these things also kill people and fish and birds is of no interest to them whatsoever, because the link cannot be proven *scientifically*. They have blokes in lab coats who will swear blind that not a single VACO product ever did anything but benefit the human race, same as the tobacco industry has blokes who will swear on their mother's grave that these – " she pulled out a pack of Marlboros and lit one " – are actually helping my lungs – never mind the fact that their mothers all died of lung cancer. VACO has a finger in every dirty chemical pie going. They're bastards."

CHAPTER TWO

Several miles north of the Stamford Arms and insofar as she was able, Tilly Arbuthnot paced around her tiny Hampstead flat. The cramped lounge of the mews flat reflected the eclectic nature of its owner. Whilst it may have been true that the large oak Art Deco desk underneath the window was from the same era as the overstuffed red velvet settee, the same could certainly not be said of the delicate Queen Anne chair, or the art nouveau lamps on a Victorian sideboard. Scattered about the walls and on various surfaces were mementoes of the many places Tilly's career as a foreign correspondent had taken her.

She'd purchased the flat with the surprisingly large proceeds of *Oh, What A Stupid War*, an astonishingly, to her, popular book she'd written in the early 1980s. In her time, Tilly had covered a number of wars, starting in Central America and moving on to Asia, Africa, the Middle East and the Balkans. She hated everything about war and that had been reflected in the stories she'd filed. Not for her the human interest stories about plucky young soldiers missing Hartlepool in the heat of the Gulf. Tilly's articles pulled no punches, starkly conveying the brutality of war and laying the blame where it belonged – firmly at the feet of the leaders, often democratically elected, who were responsible for the carnage yet never got so much as a wrist slap, let alone the war crimes trial they deserved. She had, over the years, made herself exceedingly unpopular with a number of those leaders, including every US President since Reagan and every Prime Minister since Thatcher.

It was not, however, war in general which was causing her to pace that night, but a corporation with which she had been waging her own covert war for years.

In the wooden filing cabinet beside her Art Deco desk were

folders filled with information about VACO Industries. The information she'd been able to verify from the requisite number of sources had gone into the various newspaper and magazine articles she'd written about VACO over the nearly two decades since the company and its chairman, Sir Victor Ormond, had first caught her attention.

The other stories, gleaned from workers at or communities near VACO facilities around the globe, the stories she couldn't prove, but knew beyond doubt to be true, those stories were neatly filed away, along with her research into the history of the company and the family who ran it, all awaiting the day a publisher's advance or her own bank balance would allow her the luxury of writing an exposé of this particular enemy. She'd even decided on the title – *Very Awful Chemical Outlaws*.

Tilly had nailed them on a number of occasions.

She'd nailed them in the early eighties for their appalling labour practices in Mexico, where VACO's expedient solution to the problem of a union being formed had been to fire all the organisers and everyone else who was related to or, indeed, had ever been seen talking to them.

She'd nailed them again a few years later for permanently contaminating the ground water near VACO's polyvinyl chloride plastic plant in Spain.

The year after *Time* magazine's suppliers chopped down a large forest and discharged thousands of gallons of toxic chemicals into various waterways bleaching the paper for an issue which would declare the environmentally-embattled Earth "Planet of the Year", VACO took an early lead in corporate green washing by building a recycling plant in Burma for all the plastic packaging, containers and bottles the western world's guilty citizenry were saving for collection. Tilly's nose for news began twitching wildly. She found an editor who agreed with her and gave her a plane ticket.

In Rangoon, in the heat of noon, humming the Noel Coward song under her breath, Tilly toured this plastic recycling plant, where she found women working without any protective masks or clothing in crowded, unventilated rooms, separating poor quality and highly contaminated plastic from reusable plastics. Huge piles of plastic bags, bottles, food wrappers and jugs bore familiar logos: VACO, Dow, DuPont, Monsanto. The plant manager freely admitted that well over a third of the stuff ended up in local landfills. And Tilly, of course, got the photos to prove it.

The last time she'd nailed them had been several years earlier, an article written in the aftermath of an explosion at a VACO pesticide plant in India. The article, to Tilly's tremendous satisfaction, had prompted Sir Victor Ormond to lay and just as hastily withdraw libel charges against her and the Sunday paper which had commissioned and published it.

Far less satisfying were the atrocities she could not lay definitively at VACO's corporate feet: the cancers and infertility afflicting VACO workers, the birth defects, illnesses, and learning and reproductive disorders afflicting the communities with the misfortune to be located within polluting distance of VACO plants.

Even more disturbing were the rumours she'd begun to hear in her travels, stories of autopsies performed on dead street children in Asian and Latin American countries in which VACO pharmaceutical plants were located, autopsies which revealed drugs doctors could not identify in the children's bodies. One doctor in Brazil had told her outright – and completely off the record – that he thought VACO had found an inexpensive way of bypassing drug testing laws. After all, he pointed out, inadequate human testing on a VACO diabetes drug some years earlier had led to three deaths, the withdrawal of the drug from the market, and an expensive law suit. Much better to find dispensable subjects and uncover all possible side effects in advance.

Filing that piece of information away, Tilly had thought she'd heard it all about VACO, that there was nothing else this company could do to shock her.

That, of course, was before her anniversary tea at the Savoy had been interrupted two days earlier.

"I beg your pardon, but aren't you Tilly Arbuthnot?"

The young woman's words had brought Tilly back to the present with a snap. Tea at the Savoy was an annual event, something she did every year on the anniversary of the death of her friend David, killed during the Serbian shelling of

Dubrovnik – a journalist in the wrong hotel bar at the wrong time. Tilly had been sitting beside him when the shell took out his chest. It was hardly surprising that it had affected her deeply, although quite how deeply she'd been unable to admit – to David's family at the funeral, to her editor back in London or to herself. Any war correspondent who claimed to have never been terrified was a liar. Gut wrenching fear was part of the job. But somehow it was manageable. Tilly had managed it for years, but her ability to do so died with David. She'd lost her edge. She'd covered her last war.

Her editor understood. No one could do that job indefinitely. She'd come home, been reassigned to domestic stories, done well enough for a year or two. Even her best friend Stella thought she was over it. Then one last self serving, on the take, bastard politician had tried to shut her up. He'd failed and had fallen from grace, but the effort to bring him down had cost Tilly her job. It had taken her years to claw back to the far from enviable position in which she now found herself: a respected freelancer eking out a precarious existence.

She couldn't really afford the now staggering price for tea at the Savoy, but she still came, just as she and David had met there once a year for the twelve years prior to his untimely demise. They had, in their cups, been occasional and amiable lovers, but had decided early in their acquaintance that they were much better suited to being friends.

She looked up at the silver blonde with extraordinary aquamarine eyes who seemed quite oblivious to the fact that the gaze of every man in the room was fixed on her and admitted that she was indeed Tilly Arbuthnot.

"I know this is awfully rude," the young woman said, "but might I join you?"

It had been a long time since Tilly had taken tea at the Savoy with anyone. Initially she hesitated, feeling this would somehow be a betrayal of David's memory. However, this girl looked as if she might have an interesting tale to tell and David, Tilly decided, assuming he was actually there with her in spirit, might enjoy eavesdropping on their conversation. Tilly nodded and the young woman sat down in the chair opposite. An attentive waiter hurried over with a fresh pot of tea and an extra cup.

"May I," Tilly asked, "be allowed to know who you are and how you knew who I was?"

"Oh, that's easy. I recognised you from the photo on the jacket of your book." Tilly, unable to believe that at forty-five years of age she could still possibly look twenty-eight, sighed inwardly at the realisation she had probably looked middle aged in her twenties. A nicely manicured hand was proffered. "My name is Helen."

"Helen what?" asked Tilly.

Helen hesitated, her smile tentative. "If you don't mind, I'd rather not say."

Intriguing, thought Tilly. "Not at all, my dear," she said. "Although I would appreciate knowing how you recognised me from the jacket of a book which must have been written when you were seven years old."

"I read your book a few years ago when I was studying political science," said Helen. "It was highly recommended by my tutor."

"Really?" Tilly wasn't sure whether she was more flattered to be recommended university reading or thrilled to discover that universities were actually teaching students about the bloodiness of war and not just surfing the bloody net. "Is that what you wanted to talk to me about?"

Again the hesitation. "Not really," said Helen, taking a sip of tea before continuing. "You were threatened with legal proceedings by VACO, weren't you? For an article you wrote?"

Tilly nodded, smiling at the recollection. How that bastard Victor Ormond could have thought the paper would run a story about VACO deliberately selling nerve gas as a pesticide without proof was beyond her. As soon as Ormond's brief saw the documents she had, Sir Victor had high tailed it. The smile turned into a chuckle. Tilly reached for a pastry, before turning her curious gaze back to Helen. "Is that what you wanted to discuss with me?"

"Sort of." Helen glanced around the room, then leaned forward and said quietly. "I work for VACO. They're up to something very unsavoury." Tilly waited patiently, asking nothing. Eventually, Helen continued. "It's something in the biotechnology division, a seed coating they thought would make them a fortune. They invested a huge amount in its development. Their tests showed some fabulous results on the final product. They were getting ready to ship the seeds out to farmers all over Europe and then – " another hesitation "– Arthur Ormond got hold of it. It wasn't his project, he's not really involved in biotech. But he was intrigued. He decided to run some tests and found out that, yes, the seed coatings did guarantee huge crop increases in the first year. But what no one else at VACO had bothered to find out was that after the first year the soil would be barren, possibly forever, certainly for hundreds of years."

"Christ," said Tilly, dropping her half eaten pastry on to her plate. "When did this happen?"

"About three years ago."

Tilly felt an old, familiar adrenaline rush. "Can you prove this?"

"Yes." Helen leaned even closer to Tilly. "Look, that's not the worst of it."

"Really?" Tilly found it hard to imagine what could be worse.

Helen shook her head. "VACO invested millions of pounds in this and Sir Victor isn't the type to just shrug and write that off. He wants at least some of that money back and he's found a way to get it."

"How? If VACO sold one batch anywhere, they'd be ruined when the truth came out."

"What if the truth didn't come out? What if the buyer was someone who wanted to destroy the food supply in part of his country, to deliberately cause a famine?"

"Oh, my God." Tilly had been leaning forward to listen to Helen. Now she sagged back against her chair. As much as she detested VACO and its chairman, she couldn't believe even Sir Victor Ormond was capable of something this vile. A thought struck her, a thought she didn't particularly like. Is this, she wondered, some sort of wind up? Now *that* was something of which she would consider Sir Victor more than capable. "Pardon me asking, my dear," she said, surveying Helen through narrowed eyes, "but security around VACO must be pretty damned lax if this is common knowledge."

"Believe me, security at VACO is far from lax and I certainly should not know about this. I was somewhere I shouldn't have been and I overheard some people talking."

"Did they catch you?"

"No, thank God. If they had, I doubt I'd be here telling you about it."

"And why exactly are you telling me about this? Assuming you can actually prove what you're saying, any number of newspapers would be interested in the story."

Helen reached across the small table and placed her hand on top of Tilly's. "I don't know anyone at any of the papers. I've read your book. I've read your articles. I feel as if I can trust you." She gave Tilly's hand an urgent squeeze. "Will you help me?"

Tilly sighed. She was still a name, a force to be reckoned with, still wrote regular features for the Sunday papers, but it was all pretty tame stuff. She hadn't had a coup, an honest to God, get-the-bad-guys scoop since her last big VACO story several years ago.

"My dear," she said, fervently hoping she wasn't being set up for something, "what on earth makes you think *I'd* be helping *you?*"

They arranged for Helen to ring Tilly later that evening to finalise plans, then the younger woman departed. Tilly signalled for her bill, after topping up the tepid tea in her cup. She popped the last of the pastry in her mouth and chewed reflectively. *Well, David,* she asked her absent friend silently, *what do you make of that?* She answered her own question, although she could hear David's voice offering the advice: *Call Jack.*

Dr Jack Conquest was the only scientist Tilly knew well and one of the few she trusted to be completely unbiased. He was a big bear of a man, six and a half feet tall, bushy black hair, bushy black beard, brooding brown eyes and a filthy laugh as deep as the ocean's floor.

She and David had met him in Kuwait in the aftermath of the completely stupid Gulf War. He'd been commissioned by an environmental group to catalogue and analyse the damage done by the burning oil fields and had provided her with documentation for some of her best copy. In the past year she'd seen him quoted a number of times on the idiocies of biotechnology and figured that if anyone could tell her whether Helen's story might be true, it was Jack.

While her call was misdirected from one university department to another and the minutes ticked away on her phone card, Tilly was remembering one day she'd spent out in the scorching desert heat with Jack. As he surveyed the devastation from the still burning fields, Jack had shaken his head, grunted and said, "Fucking Henry Ford."

Tilly, attempting to mop the sweat off her forehead with an already sodden handkerchief had smiled and asked him what he meant.

His response had been a passionate lecture about the woes inflicted on the planet by Henry Ford's automation of the motor car industry and the increased demand for petrol, the use of which was responsible for climate change, unbreathable city air, an epidemic of childhood asthma, the destruction of countryside everywhere for omnipresent motorways, and, increasingly, wars to feed the whole mess. Some years later when Tilly read *Gridlock* she couldn't help suspecting that Ben Elton had had a pint or two with Jack before writing his novel.

"And then there's bloody PCBs," Jack had thrown in.

Tilly had given him a blank look. "PCBs?"

"Polychlorinated biphenyls," Jack had responded with exaggerated patience.

"I know what PCBs are," Tilly had replied, although, in truth, the knowledge was vague – a chemical compound, now banned, once widely used as insulation. "I just don't know what they have to do with Henry Ford."

Jack had taken a large pull from his water bottle before answering. "Basic chemistry. When you extract petrol from crude oil, you have a lot of other chemicals, including benzene left over. Shame to waste it, right? So, some clever dicks in lab coats start messing about, trying to find some use for all the leftover stuff. Eventually, they discovered that if you heat benzene right you can glue two benzene rings together and if you then throw in some chlorine gas you can make some stuff that isn't soluble in water, doesn't burn, but does conduct heat well. With no idea what this chemical cocktail of theirs might do to humans or wildlife other clever dicks started throwing the stuff into everything from electrical transformers to bloody carbonless copy paper. Now we're stuck with the bloody stuff. A third of it's already escaped into the environment and if much more gets into the oceans we can probably kiss marine mammals goodbye – their immune systems are already screwed. We've got stockpiles of the stuff and no way to destroy it without producing and releasing chemicals that are even worse."

Tilly, fascinated, had further researched the subject when she got back to London. The article which resulted, "Henry Ford's War," had won her an award and Jack's friendship – he claimed – for life.

Just as both her phone card and patience were expiring, the university switchboard finally succeeded in transferring her through to the lab, where she connected with Jack, swore him to secrecy, then ran the salient facts past him.

"Jesus Christ," was all he said over the line.

"So, this could be true?" she prompted.

There was a moment's pause. She could almost see him shaking his head and rolling his eyes. "Oh, yes, Tilly, it all too possibly could be true. This is an industry full of clever dicks in lab coats running amok and saying, 'Oh, look what we can do!' Most of them have no idea what they're playing at. They're so thrilled to have a fully fitted lab and an unlimited research budget that it's short circuited half their brains. Frankly, there are probably filing cabinets full of fuck ups at VACO and Monsanto and Novartis. This is stuff they're not going to send out a press release about."

Tilly cradled the telephone receiver on her shoulder and ran her hand through her frizzy brown hair. If she was going to be able to convince Gus MacPherson or some other editor to run with this, she going to have to get her information verified by someone who knew what they were talking about.

"Jack," she said, "someone's offered to get me some documentation on this. Will you have a look at it for me and let me quote you?"

"Not unless it's in the next twenty minutes," Jack told her. "I'm just heading off to Brussels to cast pearls of wisdom before the swine at the EU."

"Shit." Who else could she get?

"Look," Jack offered, "I'll give you the fax number for my hotel. If you feel safe sending it on, I can have a look at it for you there. Can't promise a fast turnaround, 'cos I'm going to be in and out of meetings, but I'll do what I can."

"Do you have a mobile?" she asked. Everyone except her seemed to these days. The streets of London were teeming with pedestrians wandering about, elbows bent, hand pressed to ear, yelling at someone miles away. This spectacle was, she was sure, one of the main things about the human race at the end of the century which would amuse extra terrestrials no end – assuming they didn't bypass Earth altogether on their way somewhere less messed up.

One of Jack's low rumbling laughs came down the line. "You are joking, aren't you? Those things fry your bloody brains. Sorry, you'll just have to take a chance on finding me."

As soon as she got back to her flat that afternoon, she'd dug out and begun sifting through her VACO files, making occasional notes on background information she might want for her story.

Now a major multinational corporation, VACO Industries had begun life humbly in 1940 as Ormond Pharmaceuticals. Its chemist founder, Robert Ormond, was considered by many to be a genius. Certainly he was portrayed as such in the company history section of VACO's glossy annual reports.

What the annual reports didn't say, but Tilly had managed to dig up in one of her various spurts of research, was that the start up money had been provided by Robert's profligate younger brother, James, who'd amassed quite the pre-war fortune in numerous dodgy ventures, including brokering arms shipments to both sides in the Spanish Civil War. Tilly's interest in James Ormond had been piqued by one of the few references to him she'd ever come across – a notation in the diaries of Nancy Astor, who'd had the younger Ormond brother as a weekend guest and had summed up her impression with the words: "Devilishly good looking seems an apt description of Robert Ormond's brother James. One could, I suppose, live with the fear that by the time he departs the maids will be pregnant or the silver disappeared (or both), if it weren't for one's certainty that, underneath that charming, polished exterior, beats the heart of a truly evil, quite possibly deranged, man."

If anyone other than Lady Astor had thought James Ormond mad, there was no suggestion of it in the various obituaries bemoaning the still youthful playboy's demise in an avalanche in the Alps in 1946.

Within three months of James Ormond's death, the *Times* had announced first the "unexpected" (for which Tilly read "unplanned and probably unwanted") birth of Robert and Amelia Ormond's third son, Charles, and then the patenting by Ormond Pharmaceuticals of an antibiotic which, in the space of a year had made Robert a very wealthy man. In the midst of post-war austerity, Robert Ormond used his newly acquired riches to purchase a hundred acres in Kent and build for himself a mansion which many considered to be one of the worst architectural monstrosities of the twentieth century.

By all accounts, Robert Ormond had very much fancied himself as lord of the manor. Everything Tilly'd read about him suggested he was a completely self centred autocrat, given to unpredictable fits of rage. This impression had been confirmed some years earlier when Jack Conquest had introduced her to Bill Williamson, a now retired colleague, who'd once worked as a lab assistant at Ormond Pharmaceuticals.

"Oh, aye, he was a bastard, all right," Bill had agreed. "Trained his eldest to be a bastard, too. How that nice wife of his ever put up with either of them, I don't know."

Victor, of course, as the eldest, had been brought up to take over the company. He had, according to Bill, been the only human being of any interest to Robert – until it suddenly became clear that it was Arthur, not Victor, who'd inherited Robert's genius in the laboratory.

"After that it was all Arthur this, Arthur that and to hell with Victor as far as the old man was concerned," Bill had told Tilly. "If he hadn't been such a prize pillock, I might've felt sorry for the bastard."

In 1963, a short article in the *Financial Times* announced that day to day operations of Ormond Pharmaceuticals had been taken over by Victor Ormond while founder Robert recovered from some unspecified illness. Try as she might, and tried she had, Tilly had never been able to discover the nature of this "illness".

There was no reference to and, as far as she could ascertain, no sighting of Robert Ormond from the time that article appeared until his obituary was published in the *Times* two and a half years later.

The anticipated power struggle between Victor and Arthur Ormond failed to occur. Neither challenged the surprisingly fair terms of Robert's will which divided his personal wealth and the shares in Ormond Pharmaceuticals equally between "my sons Victor and Arthur, my wife Amelia, and our youngest, Charles."

Was she, Tilly wondered when she unearthed a copy of the will, the only one to have noticed the separation of Robert's "sons" Victor and Arthur, and the "youngest" – no reference to relationship – Charles. Hmm, she'd thought at the time. Some question, perhaps, about the sire of Amelia Ormond's "unexpected" third child?

The name change from Ormond Pharmaceuticals to VACO Industries had been almost immediate, as had the branching out into pesticides, plastics and other chemical research and products.

It seemed that, like his father before him, there wasn't much Arthur Ormond couldn't come up with in the lab. He was a bit of an invisible man. Other than one grainy newspaper photo of the family at Robert's funeral, Tilly had never even seen a picture of him. There'd been a messy and surprisingly under-reported divorce in the seventies, which was the first and last time Tilly had found his name in any publication until a year or so ago when he'd flabbergasted the biotech industry and, word had it, outraged Sir Victor, by writing a letter to the *Daily Telegraph* in support of the Prince of Wales' denouncement of genetic engineering.

After talking to the young woman from VACO, it no longer surprised Tilly that Arthur Ormond had felt compelled to sound the warning about the unknown dangers of tinkering with nature. Of course, if he'd really wanted to sound a warning, he could have described the near catastrophe with VACO's damned seed coating, but that was a bit too much to expect.

Two days after pulling all her old VACO files out, Tilly was trying very hard not to pull all her hair out. It was eleven hours since Helen had left a message on Tilly's machine, saying she'd had to pass the material to a man on the train, that everything would be fine, and that she would ring as soon as she could. But she hadn't rung and Tilly had no idea where she should even begin to look.

Helen had confided no more than absolutely necessary, but she had succeeded in convincing Tilly there was minimal risk involved in removing the material. All Tilly had to do was meet her at Waterloo. Dead easy, Helen had said. Tilly, because she'd wanted to, had believed her. Now, belatedly, she rebuked herself. She was an old pro. She should have demanded more information, but she hadn't. She'd thrown caution to the wind, because the wind was carrying such a strong aroma of a long overdue scoop.

And now, here she was, alternating between pacing around her flat, dialling, with no result, the mobile phone number Helen had given her last night, and trying to make sense of an incomprehensible sheets of paper which were supposed to be proof that VACO's seed coating was an ecological disaster, but certainly made no sense to her.

She had, despite his predictions of unavailability, managed to track Jack down in his Brussels hotel and fax him the printed material, but all he'd been able to do was confirm her suspicion that whatever was printed on those pages was complete gibberish. His suggestion that she e-mail the contents of the CD to his laptop was particularly unhelpful. Although her ancient computer had a modem – of sorts – and the world's most basic – and frequently useless – e-mail system, there was no way she would be able to forward the contents of the CD to anyone. Her computer didn't even have a CD drive. She'd known for a long time that an upgrade was needed, had been fantasising about a fancy laptop to replace her antiquated system. Unfortunately, her hand-to-mouth existence as a freelance journalist meant the closest she'd got to a laptop was carting around the battered portable typewriter she'd been using on foreign assignments since the 1980s.

By the time she got off the phone with Jack, Tilly was furious with herself. She should have demanded more information from Helen – something, anything that would give her a hint where to start looking for the girl.

She was fairly sure those bastards at VACO wouldn't actually harm Helen, but she wasn't completely sure. Even though the young woman had come to her, Tilly felt responsible for this cock up. She'd been so excited by the thought of a front page splash, by the thought of sticking it to VACO again, she'd forsworn her usual attention to detail and agreed without hesitation to everything Helen had said.

Damn, damn, damn. If she hadn't agreed to meet the train at Waterloo, she would have been in her flat when Helen rang. Instead, when the call came, Tilly was sitting in a stalled Northern line train. The line, a disgrace for as long as she'd lived in Hampstead, had that morning, come to a grinding halt for twenty bloody minutes between Leicester Square and Charing Cross. She'd missed the arrival of the train from Kent completely, and then wasted another forty minutes going back to her flat, where she found a message from Helen and another from that idiot at *Sweetie*.

What on earth had possessed Helen to give the envelope to him? And why on earth hadn't Tilly asked him more questions when she'd had the chance? It was night time now and there was no way to reach him again until he got to the *Sweetie* office the next morning.

A smile fleetingly crossed her face. God, what a prat that Baldwin was. She couldn't believe it when he'd asked what VACO did. And then to swallow her line about the European space programme. And the look on his face when she'd said "Libyans"! She'd thought he was actually going to wet himself. How she'd managed to keep a straight face was beyond her. And then fancy running into Roger Wilcox.

Tilly stopped her pacing and gave herself a smack on the head. Of course! Roger Wilcox! That was how she could track down the Baldwin prat! She grabbed her voluminous handbag from the settee where she'd tossed it and ferreted around until she found a dog eared address book. She found Roger's number and, hoping he hadn't moved in the past ten years, dialled.

At the other end of the line the phone rang several times before Tilly finally heard a barked, "Wilcox" followed by a crash, then "Shit!" Tilly held her breath, hoping the crash hadn't been his scotch glass breaking, which might send him lumbering off to the decanter and cause him to permanently forget the phone call he'd just received.

"Roger," she said after a lengthy silence, "are you there?"

"Eh? What? Just a sec." She could hear the sound of ice clinking in a glass, then, "Who is this?"

"It's Tilly, Roger."

"Tilly? Good God. Twice in one day, after all these years. Suddenly realised how much you fancy me?"

"Oh, for God's sake, Roger," Tilly said, exasperated. "Listen to me. Are you sober enough to drive?"

"Me? Shouldn't think so, old love. Even if I was, I'm banned at the moment."

"Well, then get into a taxi and get over here. And, before you say one word, no I haven't suddenly decided I fancy you. This is important, Roger. Extremely important." She made sure he had a pen, gave him the address and rang off. She could, of course, have tried to get the information about Baldwin from him over the phone, but she suspected it was going to take some strong black coffee and possibly a good shaking to get his attention.

Tilly had first met Roger Wilcox about fifteen years earlier on a flight from New York to London. She'd been there to cover a breaking story at the United Nations. He was returning from a freebie junket to Florida. After plying her with whisky for two or three hours, he'd tried to convince her to become a charter member of the mile high club and had been disappointed to discover that she could hold her booze rather well and wasn't the least bit interested in a knee trembler.

Although she never would have admitted it to him at the time – in fact she'd started out pretending she had no idea who he was – Tilly was very impressed with Roger's work. Despite being employed by the tabloid press for several years, he'd never allowed himself to be lumbered with naughty vicars and 'Ave A Go Grannies and had over the years produced some very meaty pieces. Talented, tenacious and totally without tact, he had been known the length and breadth of Fleet Street as "Roger by name, roger by nature".

Perhaps his well known inability to keep his fly zipped was how he'd made the acquaintance of Polly, the "French Polisher". Perhaps, as he claimed, she just turned up at his office. Despite his position as a veteran of the tabloid press, Roger was shocked by the black and blue face of the young prostitute who approached his desk that day. She had, she told him, been beaten to a pulp by a wealthy bastard and she wanted to nail him. Roger did exactly what he should have done. He took her to the police, but not until after he'd interviewed her himself and had a staff photographer take several pictures. The next morning, as charges were being laid against the industrialist in question, Roger's paper came out ahead of anyone else with the story, including the chilling photographs.

Unfortunately, the industrialist had a patrician QC representing him and twenty people prepared to swear he was somewhere else at the time of the assault. The QC made mincemeat of Polly and the charges were withdrawn.

The next day, the industrialist brought libel suits against both the newspaper and against Roger personally. The paper settled out of court, but the suit against Roger, who had by then been abandoned by his employer, continued. Roger lost his job, his house, his wife and, most important to him, his edge. He moved into a seedy furnished bed sit which, rumour had it, he'd been sharing with Johnny Walker and Jack Daniels ever since.

The ravages of this long standing relationship were clear when Roger rang Tilly's bell half an hour later. Never a particularly handsome man, there had once been a quite magnetic intensity about Roger Wilcox. However, his ability to confuse a compass was long gone. The telltale red veins which spread across his face matched the colour of his once brilliantly blue eyes. He lurched into Tilly's lounge, reeking of booze and cigarettes, and flopped his now considerable weight down so heavily on to her Queen Anne chair that she was afraid of the splintering noise she might hear. Before he could say a word, she handed him a mug of strong black coffee.

Roger peered at her offering, suspiciously at first, then disapprovingly. "Got a drop of anything to put in this, old love?"

"No," she told him firmly. "Drink it."

Roger made a face at her, but obediently took a sip. "All right, Tilly," he said, narrowing his eyes, "what's this all about?"

She couldn't see any point in preamble. "I need Baldwin's phone number."

"Baldwin?" he repeated, then laughed. "Oh, yes, that's right. Baldwin. What exactly were you playing at this morning, telling Baldwin you were a rocket scientist?"

"I was pulling his leg, Roger. And I want to do it again. Do you have his phone number?"

"Why on earth would I have Baldwin's phone number? Why on earth would I want to talk to him? The fellow's an ass." Roger took another tentative sip of his coffee, then looked at Tilly. "Are you sure you don't have a drop of something I could put in this?"

"Yes, I'm sure. Roger, please help me out. If you don't know his phone number, do you know where he lives?"

"Christ, I don't know. Some village in Kent. Long Pissington or Upper Piddleton or something like that."

His eyes widened in astonishment when Tilly leaned over, grabbed him by the shoulders and shook him. "Think, Roger. Where does he live? This is important!"

Roger nodded slowly. "Yes, Tilly," he said, "I can see it is." He took a deep breath. "Find me a map of Kent. I'll remember the name when I see it."

Tilly fetched her atlas and opened it to the appropriate page. Roger removed a pair of spectacles from his breast pocket, put them on and began running his thumb slowly over Kent. After a surprisingly short time, he said, "There it is! I knew it had something to do with bogs." He pointed at the page triumphantly. "Lower Wipington."

Tilly snatched the telephone receiver off its hook and punched in the number for directory enquiry. Fortunately, Baldwin's number wasn't ex-directory. Unfortunately, after three rings she heard a mechanical voice saying, "Hello, this is Alec. I'm afraid I can't come to the phone right now. Please leave your name and number and a short message after the tone and I will get back to you as soon as I can. Thank you for calling."

"Baldwin," Tilly barked as soon as the tone sounded, "this is Tilly Arbuthnot. I have to talk to you as soon as you get in, no matter what time it is." She left her number and slammed the receiver down. "Damn!"

She glanced at Roger, who was eyeing her curiously. Before she had a chance to say anything, the telephone rang. Thank God, she thought, grabbing the receiver, the prat was home after all. "Baldwin?" she demanded.

"Sorry to disappoint you, Ms Arbuthnot," said a voice she

did not recognise. "I'm ringing on behalf of your friend Helen. She says you have something that doesn't belong to you."

Tilly, who'd read the phrase in numerous thrillers and had, until that moment, dismissed it as ludicrous, felt a chill run down her spine. "I do, do I?" she asked.

"I sincerely hope you do, Ms Arbuthnot, because I assume you'd like to see your friend again."

The chill ran all the way down to her toes. Oh my God, she thought, this sort of thing just doesn't happen. "Now, see here," she began forcefully, but was interrupted.

"No, you see here, Ms Arbuthnot. I want you to take that envelope, walk to the end of your road, place it on top of the pillar box, then turn around and return to your flat. You are to leave your guest where he is and walk to the pillar box alone. You have five minutes to do as instructed, after which I will assume the well being of your friend does not concern you."

"I want to speak to Helen," Tilly said, but before she'd finished the sentence, the line went dead.

Think, Tilly, she commanded herself.

Her frantic glance around the room alighted on the fax machine. She grabbed the VACO envelope, pushed the Copy button on the machine and began to feed in the sheets of gibberish. Pausing only long enough to assure herself that the copies were legible, she shoved the pages back into the envelope and closed the metal flap. There was nothing she could do about the CD. Not pausing for a coat, she grabbed the door handle.

"Tilly," Roger's voice echoed the concern in his gaze, "what the hell is going on?"

She gave him a despairing look. "No time to explain, Roger. Just look out the window and watch me walk to the post box and back. If anything happens, ring the police."

"And tell them what?" he asked her disappearing back.

Tilly opened the street door and walked as purposefully as her trembling legs would allow to the post box at the corner. As she carefully balanced the envelope on top, she glanced quickly up and down the street. There didn't seem to be a soul about. She walked back to the street door of her flat, turned the handle and stepped inside. As soon as the door shut behind her, she heard a car start up. She yanked the door open, but, by the time she peered outside, the dark saloon was already rounding the corner past the post box. The envelope was gone.

She wearily mounted the stairs to her flat. What if surrendering the envelope did no good? What if, in addition to all the other names she'd called Victor Ormond over the years, the name murderer should be added?

When she entered the flat, Roger handed her a piece of paper. "What's this?" she asked.

"The registration number of the black car that just shot around the corner," Roger told her. He then handed her a stiff cognac, from which Tilly took a large swallow, noticing as she did that, while he'd managed to unearth the cognac bottle she'd hidden, he had poured nothing for himself. "Tilly," he said, "don't you think you'd better tell me what's going on? What exactly are you working on?"

Tilly considered him thoughtfully for a moment. Like everyone else in Fleet Street, including the cowardly proprietors of Roger's former newspaper, Tilly knew that Polly the French Polisher had been telling the truth, that a rich bastard had beaten her savagely and got away with it. That rich bastard had ruined Roger's life and if anyone deserved to know what she was working on it was Roger, because that rich bastard was Sir Victor Ormond.

"VACO, Roger," she said. "I was trying to nail them once and for all, but I'm starting to get worried that I may have got someone killed instead."

She could see the light ignite in his eyes and, although they were standing some distance apart, she could feel him experiencing the same adrenaline rush she'd had when she first spoke to Helen. Roger's hand wavered towards the cognac bottle, then pulled away. He walked over to the coffee table, picked up the mug he'd abandoned, drained it quickly and handed the empty mug to Tilly. "Pour me another one of those, love, and then tell me all about it."

Half an hour later Tilly finished her tale. "So, you see," she said, "that's why I have to find Baldwin. He's my only hope."

"Our only hope," Roger corrected, "and if that's true, all I can say is gawd 'elp us."

In Kentish Town, not many miles away from Tilly's flat and far from Lower Wipington, Alec's only hope at that particular moment was that the second chance an understanding Mandy had graciously given him would last a damned sight longer than the embarrassingly short first.

Fortunately for him – and Mandy – this particular hope was fulfilled.

CHAPTER THREE

When the door opened and Sir Victor Ormond re-entered the dusty cellar, Helen was struck by a description of him she had once read in a trade journal: 'The Cary Grant of the chemical industry'. Clearly the writer did not known Sir Victor well, for a less charming character Helen could not imagine. Still, she had to admit he did have the looks and bearing of a somewhat ageing matinee idol. As much as she loathed the man, she could, in her most objective moment, understand women finding him attractive – at least from a distance. Up close, of course, they would have met those heavily-lidded, lizard-like pale grey eyes, their colour a match of his once raven, now silver hair. Helen defied anyone to meet that gaze and not be chilled to the bone.

The staff at VACO Industries referred to him as the Ice Man. They considered him emotionless and completely devoid of humour, which was not exactly true. Helen, who knew him better than most, knew that some things made Sir Victor Ormond smile. She had seen satisfaction part his lips into a smile of triumph when he was certain his enemies, be they business rivals or helpless children, were cornered with no hope of escape.

He was smiling a repulsive, self satisfied smile as he sat down opposite her and said, "Who is Baldwin?"

Helen Ormond gave her uncle a look of sheer detestation, before returning her gaze to the ceiling, "I have absolutely no idea."

"No? I thought perhaps he might be one of your little helpers. Your friend Tilly Arbuthnot seemed awfully eager to speak to him." Got you, his look said as Helen's eyes widened in alarm. "My dear, you didn't think it would take me long, did you? It was very considerate of you to use a mobile phone that displays the number of the person ringing. Once I had a telephone number it was no trouble getting a name and address. I suppose," he added, leaning back in his chair and surveying her through narrowed eyes, "you chose that bitch deliberately, just to provoke me?"

Helen attempted to regain her bored demeanour. "I don't know what you're talking about. I've told you. I had no idea that phone was in my bag until you found it. If someone was ringing that number, why don't you ask them who they were trying to contact? It certainly wasn't me."

"Listen to me, Helen," Victor said with exaggerated patience, "I know someone at HQ handed some confidential material over to you this morning. Its disappearance was discovered almost immediately. I know someone at HQ rang that mobile number soon afterwards and that you used it to ring the Arbuthnot woman."

Helen knew her expression must have betrayed her surprise. Victor's smile deepened. "My dear," he added, "there's a call log on mobile phones. Rather stupid of you not to have deleted it. And I do know you somehow got that stolen material to Ms Arbuthnot, because I have now retrieved it from her."

Helen could see the satisfaction mounting in his eyes. "Oh, yes," he said, smiling and withdrawing a folded envelope from the pocket of his jacket. He emptied its contents on to the table which sat between them. "Recognise this?"

Helen, unable to take her eyes off the computer sheets and disk, merely shook her head.

"No? Look at me, Helen." She forced herself to raise her gaze to meet his cold grey eyes. "I'm sorry you've developed this obsessive desire to destroy your family. You're not at all well. I can find half a dozen specialists who will swear to that, and by the time they have, you won't have much credibility, even with a fool like that Arbuthnot woman."

Victor pushed back his chair and stood in front of his niece. "You know I'm enormously fond of you, Helen," he said, running his fingers gently down the side of her cheek. She flinched from his touch and saw immediately the pleasure her discomfort gave him. "But I am not prepared to tolerate the corruption of my employees."

Unethical Practices

He leaned forward suddenly, his hands grasping the arms of her chair. His face was so close she could feel the warmth of his breath, smell his musky aftershave. Helen shut her eyes. "Somebody at VACO helped you. I know it wasn't your father, because he's in Singapore. I'll find out who it was eventually. You know I will. So, why don't you make it easier for both of us?"

Helen forced herself to open her eyes and look at him. "I don't know what you're talking about."

Victor straightened abruptly, although he still loomed over her. "You can't possibly think your father will get you out of this, can you? Believe me, he can't. You've gone too far this time. If you don't tell me what I want to know right now, I promise you, you will regret it." He folded his arms across his chest and waited.

Helen repeated, slowly and clearly, "I... don't... know... what... you're... talking... about." Victor's arms dropped to his side. He turned his back on her and took a step away. Helen began to exhale the breath she seemed to have been holding for an hour.

The blow, when it came, snapped her head back against the chair. Another blow followed. She felt his signet ring rip her cheek. His face was once again inches from hers. "I've been waiting a long time for this, princess," he hissed, his spittle landing on her face. "And I'm going to enjoy it." Suddenly he was at the door, unlocking it, flinging it open. He turned to look at her momentarily. "Think about that for a while," he suggested, before slamming and locking the door behind him.

Helen looked around the cellar in which her uncle and Johnson, his chauffeur cum bodyguard cum thug, had deposited her that morning, after dragging her past the trained-to-be-oblivious-when-required servants. A naked bulb hanging from the ceiling illuminated old pieces of furniture, trunks, boxes and crates.

Helen waited, knowing what was coming. On the other side of the door Victor flicked a switch. The light in the storage room went out, leaving her in absolute darkness. She knew what Victor was relying on and she was determined to prove him wrong. Sitting in the dark, she thought of Jamie and smiled. Somehow, between them, they would find a way to stop Victor.

You will not beat me, you will not beat me, you will not beat me, she repeated, over and over to herself. The mantra, she found as her heart beat slowed and her breathing steadied, was better than meditation.

Helen Ormond, though she would never have admitted it to anyone – least of all herself – was an emotional basket case obsessively woven by her uncle, Victor. He'd poisoned her childhood and even when she'd escaped his physical presence he'd stayed with her, buried in her psyche, leaving her fearful of men and ashamed of the beauty she'd inherited from her mother.

The first five years of her life had been happy and uneventful. An eighteenth century cottage, lovingly restored by her mother, surrounded by a beautiful garden, replete with a swing, a slide and a tree house, had been the enchanted home she'd shared with her parents. There had been many week day visits to her adored grandmother in the large house in which her father had grown up. There had also been the special occasion visits, birthdays and Christmases, when not only her grandmother but also her uncles were in attendance. Helen had doted on her father's younger brother, Charles, who lived in New York and was seldom seen. Charles who did magic tricks. Charles who taught her to ride. Charles who made her beautiful mother laugh. Seeing Charles had always been a treat.

Not so Victor, her father's elder brother. From her earliest memory Victor had made her uncomfortable. Victor who crept up on you silently. Victor who scowled. Victor whose very presence in some indefinable way made her normally merry mother nervous and apt to snap if Helen wandered out of her sight.

Her contact with Victor had been mercifully infrequent until Nana Ormond had a stroke and her parents decided to go and stay "for a while". The "while" seemed to last forever. Although only a child, Helen could sense how increasingly miserable her mother was becoming. Why couldn't her father

Unethical Practices

see? Why hadn't he done something? Helen had known Victor was the problem. More than once she'd seen her mother visibly blanch when Victor made one of his sudden, silent appearances.

She'd come across them once in the hallway, Victor cornering her mother, twisting her arm, making her plead with him. Helen hadn't thought twice about it. She'd run across the hallway and kicked Victor in the shins. He'd repaid her two days later, while her mother was up in London, by locking her in this very cellar and turning out the lights, waiting hours until the house was in an uproar to suggest someone try the cellar. Her father hadn't believed her when she'd told him Victor had locked her in. Her mother most definitely had believed her and two days later announced she was going to London to find them a flat.

Her mother had been gone a week. When she returned, she'd barely had time to hug Helen and tell her she'd found them an adorable flat before the door to Victor's study opened and her uncle and father told her mother to come inside. When she did, they shut the door. Helen had waited and waited in the hallway, trying unsuccessfully to hear what the raised voices on the other side of the door were saying. An hour later her mother had emerged, her face ashen. She'd scooped Helen into her arms and carried her up the stairs. In her parents' room, her mother had hastily begun throwing clothing and jewellery into a suitcase.

"I have to go away again for a bit, darling," she'd said, trying to wipe away her tears before Helen saw them. "I'll be back for you soon. I promise." After one last hug, she'd turned, lifted her suitcase and walked out of the room.

Helen had followed as far as the landing and watched through the banisters as her mother descended the stairs and crossed the foyer, head held high like a fairy tale princess. She'd paused momentarily near the door where Victor and her father stood, but only long enough to spit in Victor's face. Then the front door had opened and closed. Outside a car door had slammed, an engine started, there was the sound of tyres on gravel, then nothing.

A fortnight went by. Helen spent entire days at the bay window in the attic nursery – the only room in the house which afforded a view over the estate wall – staring down the road and willing her mother's car to appear. The only thing that appeared, creeping up behind her, was Victor, who placed a clammy hand on her shoulder and informed her that her mother wasn't coming, that she no longer wanted Helen, had left her with him.

Helen knew he was lying, knew that her mother would never willingly leave her with Victor. Her father was impossible. He'd tell her nothing, merely confirming that her mother would not be returning. She didn't believe him either and screamed the house down. Her father accused her of hysteria and hired a tight lipped and stern governess to move into the nursery with her. Miss Whatever Her Name Was, the first of many, didn't last long. Her father hired them, her uncle fired them.

"Charles isn't coming," he said, refusing again to look her in the eye.

"Why not?" Helen demanded to know. Charles always came for Christmas.

Her father and Victor exchanged the sort of shifty glances adults somehow fail to realise are as obvious as fireworks to the child from whom they wish to keep a secret. Something was up. But what? Her father sighed before saying, "Charles got married. He's spending Christmas with his wife's family in New York."

She was about to ask why he hadn't told her Charles was getting married, but stopped herself. What was the point? He didn't tell her anything. Why should he tell her that?

Helen kept her head down – literally. She would walk about the place staring at the floor, her eyes sweeping about the rugs and parquet for any sign of Victor lurking, refusing to raise her gaze when she spotted his feet anywhere, instead changing direction and making off hastily in the opposite direction.

"Lift your head, child," was the frequent refrain of her frequently replaced governesses and tutors, all of whom despaired of her posture. Helen kept her head down.

She was ten years old the day Victor caught her off guard in the hallway. It was a sunny summer day and her eyes hadn't properly adjusted to dull light when she came back from riding her pony. She was late for one of her lessons and had run back all the way from the stable. Her cheeks were flushed, her long, white blonde hair tangled and wild from her recent gallop. She didn't see him standing in the hall, didn't realise anyone was there until she heard him gasp and say, "My God."

Despite her usual precautions, she looked up and was surprised when she did that he was actually smiling at her. She couldn't remember ever seeing Victor smile before. He sat down on the bench under the coat rack and held his hand out to her. "Come here, Helen," he said. His voice, although it seemed to hold no threat, didn't sound the same. It was soft, almost, she thought, kind. Keeping her eyes fixed firmly on his, she took a step towards him. He reached forward and touched her hair. Helen held her breath, ready to flee if he raised his hand to strike her.

He didn't hit her. Instead he lifted his hand, filled with her hair, to his face and inhaled its smell. Then, more gently than she would have imagined it possible for this detested man to do, he ran feather light fingers down her cheek. His lizard lids blinked rapidly over his cold silver eyes and he sighed, the smile returning to his face.

"Such a beautiful little princess," he said.

Helen, frozen to the spot, her eyes locked on to his, made no reply. Something was very wrong. Victor always acted as if he hated her. Why was he being so kind, so gentle? And why on earth was he calling her a beautiful princess?

"The boys are all going to want you, aren't they?" he asked, tilting his head slightly, an almost playful note in his voice.

Helen couldn't imagine what he meant. The only contact she had ever had with boys were the ones she'd seen on television or read about in books. Generally, they didn't seem to want to have anything to do with girls. Why would they want her?

Victor shook his head and slid his fingers back into her tangled hair. "But you won't let them, will you, princess?" Helen's eyes widened in mystification. Let them? Let them what? When she made no answer, his fingers in her hair tightened into a grip. "Will you?" he repeated, giving her hair a tug. Helen, still without the least idea what he was talking about, shook her head. Victor nodded with approval and leaned forward, so close that she could feel his breath in her ear as he whispered, "That's right, because you're mine, aren't you?"

Whatever spell smiling Victor had temporarily cast over her was broken. "No," she said.

Victor's head snapped back. He stared at her, no trace of humour or kindness in his face. "What?" he demanded, yanking painfully on her hair.

She was saved from answering by a voice calling her name. She and Victor looked up to see Mrs Frazer, Helen's most recent tutor and governess standing on the landing. "You're late for your lesson," the Scottish widow said, speaking to Helen but staring at Victor.

He let go of her hair immediately, attempted an unconvincing smile, and, patting her on the backside, said, "Off you go, princess. You shouldn't keep Mrs Frazer waiting."

Victor decided that day that Helen was old enough to eat her evening meal in the diningroom. Overriding Victor's objections, her father acquiesced to Helen's pleas that Mrs Frazer also be invited to take her meals with them. Her father, she knew from past, special occasion meals, was apt to be interrupted by telephone calls from his laboratory, which would cause him to wander off and not return until the meal was over. Under no circumstances did she want to be left alone with Victor.

Mrs Frazer, a no nonsense but nonetheless kind hearted woman, lasted longer than the combined total of all the other guardians of Helen's education and well being. She arrived shortly before Helen's tenth birthday and saw immediately how lonely and troubled her young charge was. Unlike her predecessors, who'd questioned nothing, Kathleen Frazer demanded to know why on earth Helen was not attending the local school and mixing with other children. When Victor informed her that Helen, as a member of a wealthy family, was a potential kidnapping victim, she'd snorted derisively in his face, although she made no headway in her fight to get Helen out of the nursery and into the real world. Appeals to Arthur elicited the same ridiculous response.

Victor made one attempt to sack Mrs Frazer, three months after her arrival. Instead of submissively packing her bags and departing with a fortnight's salary, she'd stared him down and said, "We'll see what Helen's father has to say about that, shall we?" Arthur, however incapable he may have been at showing it, genuinely loved his daughter and could see that the Scottish widow was drawing the child out in a way no previous caregiver had. There was no further talk of Mrs Frazer returning to Edinburgh.

It took Mrs Frazer two days to draw out of Helen a full description of the scene she'd witnessed in the hallway. When she had, her lips compressed into a determined line and she went off in search of Jenkins, the butler, demanding he summon a locksmith to install a dead bolt on the nursery door. Confronted later by Victor for what he claimed to be an act of gross insubordination, the widow had simply smiled sweetly and claimed it was an added precaution against potential kidnappers.

It took two years for Helen to draw "the facts of life" out of Mrs Frazer. She'd been expecting these mysterious "facts" to be some sort of list like the ten commandments, some hard and fast rules to help the uninitiated navigate their way through the mine field of adult life. Instead she found out that men had the same "things" that stallions and bulls had, that men put their thing, called a penis, into a woman's vagina, which was apparently not the same as the pee hole, when men and women wanted to make babies.

This was very disturbing news to Helen, who'd never stopped puzzling over Victor's comments in the hall that summer afternoon. Ever since that day she'd found it more and more difficult to avoid him. Aside from the nightly dinners, it seemed to her that he went out of his way to seek her out, appearing in the kitchen, in the stables, places she'd never before seen him. Wherever he found her, there was that knowing smile, a "Hello, princess", a pat on the head, a squeeze of the shoulder. His touch terrified her, although she didn't know why. Not once since the day he'd pulled her hair in the hall had he harmed or threatened her in any way, and yet... Just seeing him appear in the kitchen doorway was enough to make her feel physically ill.

Cook told her she was lucky to have such a doting uncle.

Mrs Fraser told her to make sure the dead bolt was locked on the nursery door whenever she had a night off.

For some time after her mother left, Helen had eavesdropped whenever she could at the other side of the drawing room door, hoping something, anything in the pre-dinner conversations of her father and uncle would give her a clue about her mother's whereabouts. No such luck. All they ever seemed to talk about was work. In the end she'd given up. It certainly hadn't been her intention to eavesdrop when, one evening, on her way down to dinner, she heard Mrs Frazer's voice coming from her father's study.

"He touches her," the widow was saying. "Constantly."

"He's very fond of her," her father replied. He sounded distracted, as he frequently did. "She's his niece."

There was a moment's silence, then Mrs Frazer's reply, "It's not *natural*."

Now her father sounded irritated. "Oh, come on, Mrs Frazer, you're exaggerating."

Another, longer pause, then, "Mr Ormond, in case you hadn't noticed, your daughter is twelve years old. The lass is *developing*. In my opinion, it's not healthy for her to be in this house."

A silence, even longer than the last, spread out. Helen desperately wished she could see into the room, see her father's facial expression, but she knew that to move, to see him would allow him to see her and she did not want that. She wanted to know what he would say, not knowing she was there. She held her breath.

"Mrs Frazer," her father said eventually, "you are going too far." Another pause, and then a sigh. "Perhaps you're right. Perhaps Helen should go away to school. She needs to make friends."

"Yes, Mr Ormond, the lass would benefit from having some friends, but that's not what she needs." There was a thumping sound, as if Mrs Frazer had pounded her fist on Arthur's desk. "You know as well as I do, that what that girl needs is *her mother*."

Inside the study, her father's chair was pushed back from the desk. For the first time in her life, she heard him yell. "That's *enough*, Mrs Frazer! If you want this job, never mention that whore to me again."

Realising the conversation was quite definitely closed and

that she was about to be caught lurking outside the door, Helen bolted down the hall and practically flew down the stairs. She was sitting at the diningroom table, her breath just about recovered when a red-faced Mrs Frazer entered, followed immediately by her equally scarlet-faced father. Victor was not in that evening. Conversation at the dinner table was non-existent.

When the meal was over, Helen fled back up to the nursery and pounced on the dictionary. When she found 'hoar' she was none the wiser. She couldn't see what frozen vapour had to do with anything and, even if her mother had in the intervening years gone grey, she couldn't imagine why her father would talk about it so venomously.

As Helen's thirteenth birthday approached, even her father could see that while his daughter might be emotionally immature, there was nothing immature about her body. He began to talk to her about going away to school. Helen, afraid to raise the subject of her mother, welcomed any opportunity to escape the oppressive presence of her uncle. The school year had already begun and it was decided that she would start at St Aidan's in the January second term. She and Mrs Frazer were dispatched to the school for a battery of tests to establish Helen's educational requirements in the intervening months. The uniform and sports equipment were purchased. All she had to do was get through Christmas and the New Year and then she could escape.

It was Mrs Frazer who pointed out there would be occasions at the school when Helen would need clothing other than her uniform. Arthur provided the money for a shopping expedition, Helen's first trip to London, taken in Victor's car, accompanied by Victor's chauffeur. One of the purchases they made was a teal blue velvet dress, Empire line, with a scooped neck and bell sleeves. It was the first really grown up frock Helen had ever owned and she loved it.

She wore it when she went down for dinner with her father and Victor on Christmas Day. The redoubtable Mrs Frazer was in Edinburgh, visiting her sister, and would return in two days to help Helen prepare for boarding school. As she joined them in the drawing room, her father, clearly somewhat taken aback, told her she looked lovely.

"Yes," Victor chimed in from the wing chair in which he sat sipping a dry sherry, "you look beautiful, princess. I'll miss having you around."

She knew there had been arguments between her father and Victor about her going off to school. She'd heard the raised voices, knew Victor was dead set against it. But Arthur had prevailed. She smiled at her father now, and he, with a bemused shake of his head, smiled back at her, offering his arm to escort her into the diningroom.

Throughout the lengthy meal she was uncomfortably aware of Victor's eyes on her. She kept stealing sideways glances at her father, willing him to notice, but his attention was entirely devoted to the food in front of him and outlining plans for new research in the coming year. When the coffee was brought in, Victor told Jenkins to give the household the rest of the night off. After the butler had departed Arthur noticed there was no cream in the jug.

"I'll go," said Helen, pushing back her chair and grateful for the opportunity to escape Victor's staring grey eyes. In the kitchen, she crossed to the refrigerator, removed the cream and filled the jug. She heard the door open behind her. "It's all right, Dad," she said, "I'm just coming."

She turned to find Victor right behind her. In a moment he had pressed up against her, pinning her against the countertop. The cream jug crashed onto the slate tiles. Victor raised his hands to either side of her face, his fingers lacing into her hair. He leaned forward, staring into her terrified eyes. "You don't really want to leave me, do you, princess?" he whispered. He bent his head even lower and Helen realised he was going to kiss her on the lips. In that awful, stifling second she remembered the scene years before, Victor in the hallway, pressing himself against her mother, who was pleading with him to leave her alone. Thirteen year old Helen remembered exactly what six year old Helen had done, and did it again. She kicked Victor in the shins. He stepped back with a curse. She tried to push past him, but his hand shot out and encircled her wrist.

"You little bitch," he said. "You're just like her."

Neither of them heard the kitchen door open. They were both frozen, staring at one another, Victor with loathing,

Helen in fear for her life but unable to make her mouth open or force out a scream for help.

"That's enough!" Arthur's voice, echoing the first words she'd ever heard him yell, broke the spell. Victor let go of her arm and Helen threw herself at her father. He wrapped an arm around her, kissed the top of her head, then said, "Go to your room, sweetie. I'll be up in a minute."

Several minutes went by before Arthur knocked on her door. He came in, sat on the side of the bed with her, and slipped an arm around her shoulders. Helen slid her own arms around his waist and rested her head on his chest. He began to rock her gently, saying, over and over again, "I'm so sorry, Helen, I'm so sorry, sweetie."

She looked up, astounded to see tears flowing down his cheeks. "It's okay, Dad," she said, reaching up to wipe his cheek with her handkerchief, "I'll be going away soon."

Arthur managed a tentative smile, then withdrew his arm and stood up. "There's something I have to do, sweetie. I'll see you in the morning." He kissed her forehead, then crossed to the door and pulled it open, glancing over his shoulder at her. "Don't forget to lock the door."

In the morning he returned with three large suitcases, which he began to fill haphazardly with her clothing, her books, her stuffed animals. Helen watched his angry movements, unable to fathom the meaning of all this frantic packing. She wasn't due to leave for St Aidan's for over a week.

"Come on," he said, when the last stuffed case was forced shut. "Get your coat on."

Helen glanced at her school uniform, still hanging on the back of the wardrobe door. Had her father arranged for her to go early? "Should I wear my uniform?" she asked.

Arthur shook his head. "You don't need it," was all he said before lugging the cases out of the room. Helen pulled on her coat and boots, then followed him down the stairs, out the front door and to the garage. After depositing the cases in the boot of his Rover, he opened the passenger door for Helen, then got behind the wheel and fired up the engine. Arthur seemed disinclined to talk. Helen didn't know what to say. As soon as they got to the motorway, she knew they weren't going to St Aidan's. They were heading towards London.

"Where are we going?" she finally asked.

"Shush, sweetie, I need to concentrate," was all he said.

An hour later there were crossing the Thames. Fifteen minutes after that they pulled up in front of a white terraced house in the middle of a Regency square. Before Helen could ask where they were, the pillar box red door of the house flew open and there she was.

"Mummy!" shrieked Helen as she ran up the stairs.

It wasn't until hours later, after Helen's bags had been unpacked and her belongings put away in the second bedroom of the spacious flat, after they'd feasted on pâté and cheese and tinned lobster bisque, that Helen finally asked the question her mother had been dreading.

"Why, Mummy? Why did you leave? You said it would only be a little while. You said you'd come for me. But you never did." She couldn't keep the accusation out of her voice.

Her mother looked away, unable to meet Helen's gaze. She made a great show of folding up napkins and stacking plates on a lacquered Oriental tray. Helen waited for her answer. Eventually her mother turned to face her, their two pairs of aquamarine eyes meeting. She reached over and enclosed Helen's hand in both of hers.

"I made one ghastly mistake, darling," she said quietly, "at a time when your father and I were very unhappy." She let go of Helen's hand, picked up her wine glass and took a swig, then forced herself to look back at Helen. "To put it delicately, darling, I let someone cheer me up for a few days. It didn't occur to me that Victor might have hired a private detective to follow me. The afternoon I got back to the house in Kent, I was summoned to Victor's study. There he was, with your father and with that odious solicitor of his. He had photographs of me with my friend and a report detailing things, stupid things that went back to my teens when I was a little wild, but put together the way it was, it made me look like some sort of nymphomaniac drug fiend."

Helen, who had no idea what a nymphomaniac might be and only the vaguest idea what her mother was saying she'd done, shook her head uncomprehendingly. "I don't understand. Why did you leave?"

Her mother sighed. "I lost my temper. I was humiliated, mortified, but mostly furious with Victor and furious with your father for believing a pack of lies. I told them I was leaving, taking you with me and they could both go to hell. Victor said I could go whenever I wanted, but not with you. He assured me no court would let a woman like me have custody of a young child. I didn't believe him. I knew what a bastard he was and I thought I could use that against him, to get you back. But I was wrong. I went to six solicitors and all of them told me I would lose. Of course, they were all willing to represent me – for a hefty fee – but they were quite confident I would never get custody and they were right. I fought for you, Helen, you must believe me, but by the time that swinish QC of Victor's was finished with me, I couldn't even get visitation rights."

And then, said her mother, she resigned herself to waiting until Helen turned sixteen and could make up her own mind. She smiled at Helen, as if she still couldn't believe they were there together. "Then last night, completely out of the blue, your father rang and said he was handing over custody to me." Her mother shook her head, smiling lovingly at Helen. Then she laughed, a delightful sound Helen well remembered despite the intervening years. "Darling, this is the best Christmas present I could have ever had."

Helen wasn't ready to laugh or to believe this was really happening. "No," she protested. "He'll go to court. He'll get me back again. I know he will." Both knew she meant Victor, not Arthur.

"No, darling, you're wrong." Her mother's arms closed around her tightly. "Daddy's done it. He's rustled up his solicitor. It's all legal. I'm your guardian. Victor can't touch you. He's not even allowed to try to contact you. If he ever comes near you, ring the police and they'll take him away. You never have to see him again. You're safe."

Well, thought Helen, sitting in the dusty cellar of the Ormond estate, eyes moist as she recalled that long ago tear and laughter-filled reunion with her mother, I *was* safe.

CHAPTER FOUR

Sally Carpenter also thought she was safe – safe from making any money on this godawful night. She could not believe her luck when she spotted the car making its way slowly down the street. It had started pissing an hour ago. The girls who'd made any money had already buggered off. Sally recognised the car. This one only went for blondes. And Sally, unable to credit her foresight, had put her blonde wig on before she came out, later than she'd intended, tonight.

The word was out about him. He liked it rough. She'd seen the bruises on Meg after she went with him. But he paid well for it. Meg hadn't had to go out on the streets for over a fortnight afterwards. The rent was due and Sally was fed up with her swine of a landlord wanting it in trade. She'd fix him. She'd pay him cash. Maybe even use what was left over to find herself somewhere decent to live. She was tired of the street. She wanted to be able to set up somewhere for herself. Have a card with her phone number in some newsagents' window, be selective, but she couldn't have customers round to that hellhole she lived in. No doubt about it. The decision to huddle under her umbrella had paid off. This was her lucky night. She'd have some bruises tomorrow, but they'd be well healed before she had to start work again.

The car pulled up and Sally sashayed over, crossing her arms and resting them on the door frame to display her cleavage to best advantage. "Hallo, love," she said with a bright smile. "Fancy seeing you tonight."

"Get in," the driver told her tersely. Sally obligingly circled the car and slid into the passenger seat. She reached over and placed a hand on his thigh. He pushed it away. "Where's your room?" he asked.

Sally hesitated. "To be honest, love, my place is a mess.

Haven't had a chance to clean for a while. Know what I mean?" She rubbed her hand over the soft leather upholstery of the car seat. "This is a lovely motor you've got. Couldn't we just go for a nice drive somewhere?"

"No," came the monosyllabic reply.

"I see," said Sally. "Well, there's an hotel round the corner. It'll cost you an extra twenty, but it's clean."

Clean was stretching it a bit, she thought as she led him through the door into the room she'd rented for them, but the overhead light was so dim he'd never know the difference. The room contained a lumpy bed, made up with threadbare sheets, a lumpy chair, and a sink in the corner. While the hotel's patrons frequently wanted to wash up, they never stayed the night, so there was no point in providing a chest of drawers. A single hook screwed into the back of the door was the only concession made to hanging up one's clothes.

Sally's customer removed his jacket, hung it on the hook, then sat down in the chair. Removing his wallet from the back pocket of his trousers, he extracted six fifty pound notes and tossed them on the narrow bed.

Sally's eyes widened. Three hundred pounds! And here she'd been hoping for two if she was lucky. Right, that decided it. She was out of that hell hole tomorrow and the swine could sing for his rent. This was definitely her lucky night.

"Say you're a whore," he demanded, breaking into her dream of a flat with central heating.

Sally gave him what she hoped was a winning smile. "Well, I wouldn't say that, love. Times is hard, ain't they? A girl's got to make ends meet, hasn't she?"

"Say it!" he demanded.

"What?" Sally stared at him. "Oh, I get you." Some of them liked it that way. "Yeah, I'm a whore."

"Why?" he asked.

Why? she wondered. Now what does he want me to say to that? She gave him a considering look, trying to figure out how to play this.

Meg hadn't told her about this bit. He was staring at her breasts. She could see a vein standing out on his temple. This one wants it all right, she decided. Maybe I can get the money and avoid the beating. She sat down on the side of the bed, hiking her already short skirt up high enough to ensure there was no doubt in his mind about whether or not she was wearing knickers.

"Why?" she repeated, sliding her hand between her legs, rubbing and smiling, she hoped, seductively. "Because I don't see why I shouldn't make money doing what I love best." He was still staring at her breasts. Sally decided it was time to show him more of them and reached up to unbutton her top.

"Not yet," he said with an impatient wave of his hand. Sally dropped her hands to her side. "And what is it you love to do best?'

Hmm, thought Sally. That was a bit of a poser. What the hell did he want her to love to do best? Have him come on her face? Take it up the ass? Normally she wouldn't, but for three hundred pounds she'd be willing. She had a feeling it wasn't going to be that simple. And then she remembered something Meg had told her.

Sally smiled and stood up. "Oh, come on," she said. "You know what Cynthia loves best."

"Yes," he agreed, the vein on his temple beginning to throb. Sally reached for her buttons again, but before she had undone one, he was on his feet. One hand ripped her top open, then he threw her down on the bed and was on top of her, scratching and biting.

Oh sweet Jesus, Sally thought, he's going to have me nipple off. She bit back a scream. And then, almost as soon as the savage assault began, it was over and he was back in the chair, head in his hands, sobbing. Sally surveyed the bites and scratches on her body. Not too bad, really, although she'd have to let them heal a bit. Still. Three hundred pounds. It was worth it.

He looked up at her then, tears streaming from anguished eyes. "Why?" he asked. "Why do you do this to me?"

"I'm sorry," she said, fancying she might actually mean it. Never in a fairly hard life had she seen so much pain in another human being.

"Why can't you love me?" he whispered.

He stood up and for the first time Sally saw the stain on the front of his trousers. Blimey, she thought. He never even got his fly undone. He came in his pants. Sally began to think there might be a considerable advantage in making this obviously rich bastard feel better.

"I do love you," she said, holding her arms open to him. "Come here. Let me hold you."

Surprise registered in his face, although the vein still throbbed. He turned away from her and began to undo his tie. Right, thought Sally, he's getting undressed. He's going to come to me. I am going to make him so grateful I'll be the only one he wants to see and then I am going to be set up nicely. After what I've gone through in my life, I can take a few bites and scratches now and then.

She smiled expectantly, but she was expecting the wrong thing. When he turned back to face her, his expression had not softened. The anguish had been replaced by a hatred so burning Sally understood her mistake instantly. This one really was crazy. She tried to scramble off the bed. Too late. He was on her again, turning her over, tying her hands behind her back with his tie.

"Oh, God," she said, looking over her shoulder and seeing the belt he was drawing free of his trousers. "Not the buckle end," she pleaded. "Please."

"Whore!" he shrieked as the silver buckle lashed into Sally's back. "Bitch! Whore!"

Sally no longer tried to bite anything back. She screamed her head off, praying for salvation. "Oh, sweet Jesus," she thought, "he's going to kill me."

Several minutes later, her customer had collapsed back into the chair and was once again sobbing. By that point Sally was beyond noticing or caring.

"Come on, Sal," called the hotel proprietor, banging on the door an hour later, "time's up. I need the room." He tried the door. It wasn't locked. He pushed it open. "Oh, sweet Jesus," he said when he saw the slab of bleeding meat on the bed. "Oh, sweet Jesus fucking Christ."

CHAPTER FIVE

The light, when it eventually came back on, almost blinded Helen. At the same time, relief swept over her. The old terror had been held at bay. Neither the cellar nor her uncle had beaten her – at least not yet. She had no idea how long she'd been sitting in the dark. An hour? Two? Three? Impossible to judge. She squinted, trying to focus.

When the door opened, it wasn't Victor, but Johnson, his "yes Sir Victor, no Sir Victor, three bags full Sir Victor" thug, peering cautiously at her. For a brief moment Helen considered trying to escape, but quickly realised there was no chance. Even if Johnson hadn't been built like a concrete bunker, pins and needles were shooting through her legs, which had been curled up underneath her for so long. How long? Mentally she cursed herself for never wearing a watch. Then she cursed herself for never breaking the childhood habit of sitting with her legs folded beneath her.

She smiled at Johnson with as much condescension as her dubious position allowed.

As he pushed the door open further, his enormous body filling the entire frame, she saw he was carrying an elaborately laid tray. After locking the door, Johnson placed the tray on a crate in front of her.

"Yer uncle wants you to eat," he informed her. Helen sniffed disdainfully, then immediately wished she hadn't. The smell which seduced her nose and rumbling stomach was unmistakable. She didn't even have to look at the plate to know it contained prawns simmered in butter, garlic and lime juice. "You'll like it," Johnson added unnecessarily.

Helen glared at him.

Johnson shrugged. "Suit yerself," he said, reaching down to pluck a prawn from the plate and pop it into his mouth. "Your loss," he said before leaving the room and locking the door from the other side.

Helen waited for the light to go out, but the bulb stayed illuminated. She eyed the tray which had been placed in front of her. The tray and cutlery were ornate silver, the dinner and side plates, the salad bowl were from Nana Ormond's treasured Bird of Paradise set, the lead crystal wine glass and carafe had also only been seen on Nana's dinner table on special occasions.

What on earth could the cook have been thinking as she prepared this meal and set this tray, complete with linen napkin and a single rose in a silver bud vase? Enough of the servants had seen Johnson and her uncle drag her into the house – they must all know she was locked up in the cellar. Enough money, she knew, bought unquestioning loyalty, but this? It was a long time since Helen had lived here. Most of the servants probably hadn't the faintest idea who she was. That bastard butler would know, but he was even more loyal to her uncle than Johnson. She tried to remember, was it the same cook? Was Mrs Cray still there? No, she remembered her father telling her a few years ago, Mrs Cray had retired. It was a new cook, no one who might just take the initiative to pick up the phone and ring Arthur in Singapore to tell him his daughter was locked up in the cellar.

And what message was Victor sending her with this meal? That she was treasured? Hardly. More likely he was telling her the condemned woman deserved a decent last meal. She wasn't entirely convinced the food wasn't drugged – or even poisoned – but Johnson popping one of the prawns in his mouth seemed to suggest otherwise. Besides, Victor wouldn't poison her. All he wanted was to frighten her into telling him who at VACO headquarters had helped her. The meal was simply to throw her off balance. The lights would go out again soon and later there would be another barrage of questions, perhaps more blows.

But if he'd planned her real harm, he would never have brought her here. He didn't know she'd concealed her identity from Tilly Arbuthnot, so he must assume his old nemesis would come banging on the door eventually – perhaps go to the police if Helen was out of contact for too long. He had most of what he wanted. He had the information she and Jamie had so carefully planned to steal. Tilly wouldn't be able to prove any accusations she made against him and no paper would run the story without proof. All Victor wanted now was Jamie and that was the one thing she was determined he would not get, because Jamie was the first and lately she'd realised most important friend she'd ever made.

They met at the bus shelter outside Chelsea Grammar, the school in which Helen had been enrolled after her reunion with her mother. She'd just completed her first fortnight. As thrilled as she was to be back with her mother, away from Victor's suffocating presence, school was turning out to be hellish. The cliques had all formed long before the beginning of the second term of second year. Helen was not the daughter of a pop or film star, had no particular claim to fame which would cause the bolted doors of those cliques to open for her, nor did she have the social skills or self confidence needed to knock at those bolted doors. Although it was still early days, she was already feeling lonely and excluded.

"So, tell me," she heard a voice behind her in the bus queue say, "are the girls as awful as the boys at this school?" Not quite sure if the question had been addressed to her, Helen turned to see a gangling youth peering down at her from a height which seemed to be well past six feet. A school cap did little to control his wild and very woolly flaming red hair. All Adam's apple and elbows, his face positively alive with freckles, the young man smiled lopsidedly at her.

"I beg your pardon?" she said, not knowing quite what to make of this apparition.

"You just started this term, too, didn't you?" he asked. "I saw you and your mother leaving the head's office just before me and mine went in. God, you're mother's beautiful. Is she an actress? Or a model? She should be. One or the other, I mean. Or both, I suppose. This school's hell, isn't it? Stuck up bloody lot. How are you finding it?" He thrust a large, bony hand in her direction. "Sorry. My name's Jamie Mortimer. And you are?"

Helen, who'd never had anyone offer to shake her hand

Unethical Practices

before, hesitated before allowing her right hand to be engulfed in his. "Helen Ormond," she said. "What year are you in?" she asked, unable to think of anything else to say.

He looked surprised that she should ask. "Second, same as you. I've got Batty Bates. I gather you're in the much to be preferred Peterson's class." Helen, dumbfounded by the discovery that this giant was the same age as her, could only stare in astonishment. "Oh, yes," Jamie nodded, understanding. "You could say I've got a head and shoulders start, couldn't you? It would certainly be more original than 'How's the weather up there, Mortimer?' or the stunningly observant 'You're tall for you age, aren't you?'"

"How tall are you?" The boys in Helen's form were all either her height or shorter than her. New to mingling with anyone her age, let alone members of the opposite sex, she had taken this to be the norm.

"Six foot two," Jamie informed her. "Four complete changes of wardrobe from cap to shoes in the past year. My mother despairs. And my father refuses to move to America where I could at least be the star of the school basketball team."

"Are you still growing?"

"Not for the past two months," Jamie said, "touch wood." He rapped his knuckles on his forehead.

Helen smiled. The bus pulled up to the stop and they clambered on board. "Yes," Helen said when they were seated.

"Yes what?" asked Jamie.

"Yes, the girls are as awful as the boys."

"I suspected as much. I suggest we start an extremely exclusive group of our own."

Helen found she liked the idea of forming an exclusive group very much. "Would you like to come to my home for tea?" she asked.

"Yes, please," said Jamie.

Her mother heartily approved of Helen's new friend, making it clear he was welcome any time. Jamie, the younger offspring of a couple who'd mistakenly decided it was best to stay together for the sake of the children, took to spending as much time as he could at Helen's home.

One day in February, during that bizarre week when the

Gulf Stream magically causes the rain to cease, the clouds to scatter and an unbelievably warm sun to shine, Helen and Jamie decided to skip the bus and walk home. As they rounded the corner into the square where Helen lived, she came to a dead stop and gasped. A silver grey Jaguar was parked in the road just ahead of them. The back door opened and a tall, slim, elegantly attired man emerged.

"I've come to take you home, Helen," Victor Ormond informed his niece. As he spoke, Johnson, Victor's recently hired mountainous chauffeur climbed out of the driver's side of the car.

Helen shrieked as Victor grabbed her arm and tried to drag her towards the car. Jamie grabbed Helen's other arm and a tug of war ensued. "Help!" yelled Jamie at the top of his still cracking young voice. "Murder! Rape! Police! *Help!*"

Moments later front doors all the way around the square had opened and people were craning their necks to identify the source of the commotion.

Victor released Helen's arm and returned to the car, slamming the door shut after he'd clambered into the back seat. The Jag had pulled away from the kerb before Helen's mother had yanked open the street door of the flat. She dashed down the pavement to where Helen stood, sobbing on Jamie's shoulder.

"He did *what?*" she demanded when Jamie had finished telling the story. "Come on," she said, leading the way back to the flat. In the foyer, she picked up her handbag and turned to Jamie. "Lock the door behind me and don't open it to anyone until I get back. And, Jamie," she reached up to kiss his cheek, "thank you so much." A moment later the street door slammed behind her.

When they were alone, Jamie, who'd recently and, he hoped, rakishly, begun peppering his conversation with oaths, asked, "What the bloody hell was all that about?"

Helen promptly burst into tears. Jamie produced a handkerchief and, having ascertained that it was reasonably uncontaminated, handed it to Helen. He smiled uncertainly and said, "Clark Gable always had a clean hankie for his leading ladies."

Helen blew her nose into the white linen, appalled by quite

how much liquid had left her body and entered Jamie's hankie. "Sorry," she muttered.

"Don't apologise," said Jamie. "Tell me why you're crying."

Much to Helen's surprise, she did. She told him everything about her life to date – except about her mother and the private investigator's photographs, which, even if it hadn't been a confidence, she wouldn't have wanted him to know.

"Your uncle's a complete and utter bastard," Jamie announced when she was finished. No argument from Helen.

Her mother returned three quarters of an hour later with a WPC in tow. The stocky, cheerful young woman carefully recorded first Jamie's, then Helen's version of events, before departing to canvass the neighbours.

The policewoman came back to inform them that several people in the square had confirmed Helen's story, including one observant individual who had recorded the registration number of the Jaguar. Helen's mother demanded to know if Victor was going to be arrested. "He's in clear violation of the court order not to come near Helen – never mind trying to bloody kidnap her."

The WPC looked uncomfortably at Helen, then at her mother. "May I speak with you in private, Mrs Ormond?" she asked.

Her mother winced slightly at the use of her married name, but didn't correct the policewoman, nor did she deny her request. She led the way into the kitchen, returning several minutes later, alone and grim faced.

"Are they going to take him to gaol, Mummy?" Helen asked, shivering.

Her mother sighed. "No, darling, not at this point. As the very nice WPC has just pointed out to me, your uncle is a rather influential man." She reached for and squeezed Helen's hand. "However, the 'incident', as she called it, has been recorded. Victor will receive a warning that any further 'incidents' will lead to his immediate arrest and prosecution."

"Don't worry," said Jamie, reminding them both of his presence. "I'd never let anything happen to Helen."

Her mother managed a smile for him. "No, Jamie," she said, "I know you wouldn't."

Whatever warning he received from the constabulary,

Victor Ormond abided by. Thirteen years would elapse before Helen laid eyes on him again.

She and Jamie remained inseparable throughout their years at Chelsea Grammar. By third year she'd worked out that everyone thought they were an item. That was fine with Helen. With the exception of her beloved Jamie, boys – even drop dead gorgeous Jason Phelps from fifth form for whom she'd developed some funny feelings – terrified her. They leered at her. They made excuses to rub up against her. And, when she responded in ill disguised frozen horror to these unsubtle approaches, they – including drop dead gorgeous Jason – called her a stuck up cunt. When she subsequently overheard Jason telling his mates, amidst great sniggering, that what she needed was a good fuck, her response was horror. She did not want to be fucked by anybody and she didn't want anyone wanting to fuck her. What she wanted was to be left alone. She insisted her mother buy her a new school uniform which was at least two sizes too big for her and, when she wasn't in school, swamped herself in baggy jumpers.

Camouflage and Jamie were the protection to which she clung. She dreaded the day when Jamie would begin to show an interest in girls and abandon her, but the day never came. In her heart she knew there was something wrong with her, that this fear of sex was not natural. She was grateful for but also puzzled by Jamie's complete lack of interest in girls. When the only possible explanation for this finally came to her, she decided not to tackle Jamie on the subject, but wait for him to choose his time to tell her he was gay.

It came as no surprise when Jamie, the science wizard, was offered a scholarship at Oxford. Helen whose marks would never have attained her a place in either Oxford or Cambridge, went off to Sussex to study modern history and political science, with some vague thought of becoming a journalist but no real plan to do anything in particular after graduation.

She and Jamie kept in touch for quite a while, rang one another every weekend at first, once a fortnight after a bit, then once a month, then whenever they were drunk. They saw one another during the holidays.

Without Jamie to act as a buffer, she found herself the focus of much male attention at university. Eager young men jostled one another to squeeze into the seat beside her at lectures given by self important lechers keen to offer her private tutorials. Helen's lack of interest in any of these would be lovers was a complete mystery to the three girls with whom she shared a Brighton flat and tentative if somewhat insubstantial friendships.

The only man within her circle of acquaintance who did not exude either blatant or vague sexual overtones in his dealings with her was Sheldon Abrams, a forty-five-year-old political science prof. Little more than average height, rather more than average weight, his thinning brown and grey hair worn long and pulled back into a pony tail which only served to emphasise his weakish chin and bulging hazel eyes, Sheldon Abrams was no one's idea of love's young dream. His biting wit and generally contemptuous attitude towards undergraduates as a species made his courses less than popular with the large segment of the student population who were more interested in pints than Pinochet. This group included Helen's flatmates Jessica, Elizabeth and Theresa – or Jess, Bess and Tess, as they had become known by third year. When, over a bottle of rough red wine, they demanded to know one evening if there was a single man in all of southern England who remotely interested Helen and she, after some consideration, suggested that possibly Sheldon did, they howled with laughter. Sheldon, they informed her, looked like a toad. Yes, she had to admit, he did look a bit like a toad, but better an intellectual amphibian than a snake in the grass.

Helen wasn't sure who was more surprised, Sheldon or herself, when she asked him one day if they could meet up for a pint to discuss her essay. Toadish eyes blinking, Sheldon had agreed to the drink, but thought a pub was likely to be far too noisy for any intelligent conversation. He proposed his flat the following Saturday evening. Helen, after only the briefest hesitation, agreed.

She arrived with a bottle of wine. He already had one open and poured her a glass. They sat for an hour on the lumpy sofa in his lounge, the walls of which were lined with books, Sheldon offering prescient suggestions on how to most effectively make the case for the topic she had proposed. Although Helen quickly stopped taking notes, some time passed before Sheldon noticed. When he did, he raised an eyebrow and asked what it was, if not his academic advice, which had prompted her request for a meeting? Helen considered her choices. She could feign surprise, claim that she'd merely lost her concentration and ask him to continue or she could tell him truth.

"I was rather hoping you'd seduce me," she said.

He blinked several times before drawing in his breath and leaning away from her. "Is this your idea of a joke, Miss Ormond? Am I supposed to get all hot and sweaty at the prospect of slathering over your gorgeous young body, at which point," he paused and glanced vaguely around the room, eyes alighting on the French doors leading to the garden, "your spotty and tiresome friends burst through the doors and a riotous half witted laugh is had by all at my expense?"

Helen was mortified. Once you said you were willing didn't men just undo your blouse, produce a condom from their back pockets and get on with it? She had assumed, erroneously it seemed, that all she had to do was voice an interest and then Sheldon, older and surely therefore worldlier Sheldon, would know what to do to put her at ease and help her resolve the problem of being the only twenty-one-year-old virgin in the country. Wrong, wrong, wrong. Too late she realised there was a perfectly obvious reason why Sheldon Abrams was the only man she knew other than her father and Jamie who didn't make her totally uncomfortable – like Jamie, Sheldon must be gay.

"I'm so sorry," she said, stuffing her papers hastily back into her bag, before standing up, scarlet faced with embarrassment, and grabbing her jacket off the back of a chair. "I'll go now."

As she was turning to do just that, Sheldon said, "Wait!" His tone was insistent. She stopped mid-stride and turned to look at him. His expression was incredulous. "You were serious, weren't you?" Helen nodded mutely, miserably, unable to speak. A smile spread across Sheldon's face. He reached for and captured her hand. "My dear," he said, pressing his lips against her palm, "how miraculously flattering."

Unethical Practices

When Sheldon realised some time later that she had presented herself to him *virgo intactus* he went from flattered to a condition which seldom overcame him – speechless. Helen didn't have much to say either. It would be some time before she came to realise quite how bad a lover Sheldon was. While he had certainly seemed to enjoy himself mightily and noisily, she had been left numbly wondering why on earth Jess, Bess and Tess went to the pub every Friday and Saturday night with the express intention of having this *thing* inflicted on them by some lout or other. It beggared belief.

The next morning a beaming Sheldon brought her a cup of tea in bed, along with every single Sunday paper. Not sure how soon she could graciously leave, Helen accepted the tea with a smile and no complaint about the lack of sugar. Sheldon climbed back under the duvet and reached for the *Times*. Helen, although she could have done with a *News of the Screws* giggle, opted for the *Observer*.

Ten minutes later Sheldon nearly snorted his tea out his nose. "Now I know Her Majesty is completely gaga," he sputtered, tossing his paper on her lap. "Fancy agreeing to knight that bastard uncle of yours."

Helen peered down at the page in front of her and suppressed a shudder at the sight of Victor receiving his knighthood – delayed, the caption suggested, for some years by that unfortunate incident with the prostitute. When asked in class the previous year, Helen had acknowledged her relationship to the 'VACO brothers' as Sheldon had called them. The admission made, the conversation had gone no further. She looked at him curiously. "How do you know he's a bastard?" she asked, surprised that anyone outside her family should speak of him with such contempt.

"My dear girl," Sheldon said with a tolerant condescension Helen found immensely irritating, "everyone knows what a bastard your uncle, the chairman of VACO, is."

Really? thought Helen. And what exactly did everyone know? "Do tell," she said.

Seldom requiring an excuse to listen to the sound of his own voice, Sheldon did as requested and told. Helen learned more from him in the next hour than she had from all his lectures over the past year put together. Of course, those lectures hadn't been about a member of her family being involved in bribery, corruption, human rights violations and every other manner of dirty dealing on five continents.

As a child, Helen had given little thought to what went on in the place her father and uncle went every day. Her father, she knew, spent his time in the VACO lab, while Victor ran the business end of things. Until Sheldon began his lecture, it hadn't occurred to her just what the "business end of things" at a chemical corporation might entail.

Helen, willing to believe the rumours she'd heard that sex improved over time, spent every Saturday in the following two months in the ever increasingly besotted Sheldon's flat and bed. The sex did not get better – at least not for her. Sheldon got noisier and noisier every week, screaming her name at the top of his voice and telling her she was the most amazing fuck he'd ever had. Helen was not flattered. Shortly before Christmas she dropped Sheldon and his course.

While she was home in London for the break, an explosion at a VACO pesticide plant in India resulted in the deaths of dozens of workers. "A tragic accident," VACO's newly knighted chairman called it.

"Criminal Negligence" the *Observer*'s investigative journalist called it some weeks later. The lengthy and graphically illustrated colour supplement article revealed that it had been company policy to lock fire doors during working hours to prevent staff taking unauthorised breaks, that the explosion, far from happening with no warning, had been the result of a fire – itself caused by a chronic lack of safety precautions – that there had been ample time to vacate the premises, had a supervisor not fled the building without unlocking the doors. There were also painful details about the many hundreds of people from surrounding villages who had been treated after the explosion. Some had suffered permanent respiratory damage from chemical exposure, others were temporarily blinded, suffered from nausea. There had been numerous spontaneous abortions. It was clear that no one in the medical community could even begin to guess what the long term consequences might be. All this could be and was blamed by VACO head office in Kent on inept local managers, some of whom did face prosecution after publication of the article.

What headquarters couldn't so easily explain was the canisters of nerve gas shipped out from the UK, the labels of which had been removed and replaced by labels for the agricultural pesticides manufactured in the Indian plant. The article stated without equivocation that the order had come directly from head office.

As she considered Victor Ormond capable of anything, Helen wasn't surprised. Nor was she surprised when he almost immediately dropped the libel suit he'd commenced against the paper and the article's author, Tilly Arbuthnot. It seemed *Sir* Victor had got his title just in time.

Despite the protests of Jess, Bess and Tess, Helen went back to keeping her head down, eschewing pubs and parties for her studies. She graduated with a respectable upper second in modern history. Jamie's first in chemistry came with every award imaginable and offers to do post graduate studies pouring in from universities around the world. He chose Stanford as much for the Californian climate as for the quality of the programme.

"Come with me," he astonished Helen by saying. "For a visit," he added hastily. "In the New Year, when the weather's horrible here."

Helen agreed that would be wonderful.

On a hot summer's day which would change her life forever, she saw him off at Heathrow. She didn't visit him in the New Year, didn't see him again until four years later when he arrived back in England with a doctorate and the news that he'd been offered a wonderful medical research job – by VACO.

"Oh, God, Jamie, please don't take it," Helen said. "I can't stand the idea of Victor getting his hands on you." She knew it sounded melodramatic, but she couldn't stop herself adding, "He's evil. The whole damned company's evil."

Jamie, as she suspected he would, laughed.

"Oh, come on, Helen," he said. "I know you hate him and I don't blame you after what he did to you and your mum, but he's only the V in VACO. There's Arthur and Charles, too. And your dad really is a genius. I can learn a lot from him." When she made no comment, he tried again. "I'll be in the pharmaceuticals lab, working with your dad. I'll never even see Victor."

Helen could see his mind was made up, knew he'd already accepted the job, felt irrationally betrayed.

It wasn't, however, the sense of betrayal that caused her to prevaricate every time he'd rung her in the past year and a half, suggesting a pint, a night out at the pictures, an afternoon in the country. Jamie knew her too well. She'd never been able to keep a secret from him. And, while he'd been away, she'd acquired a secret she could never tell.

Sitting in the cellar, waiting for Victor to leave her in darkness again, Helen realised the smell of the prawns was making her feel faint. She hadn't eaten since the morning, however long ago that had been, and then she'd only managed half a slice of toast. As much as she would have dearly loved to leave the tray untouched, to wait until Victor returned, then throw the entire thing in his face, she was simply too hungry.

The first prawn seemed to melt in her mouth. The second and third followed quickly. Helen broke a piece of bread off the roll and mopped up some of the sauce. Then she tried some of the salad. The dressing was delicious, both tart and sweet. Charles, the gourmet chef, would have been able to identify each and every ingredient. Helen simply savoured the taste. Whatever else one said about Victor Ormond, one couldn't fault the standard of cook he employed.

Helen reached for the carafe and filled her crystal glass with white wine, chilled to perfection. As soon as the first drop crossed her lips, she smiled, despite the position she was in and everything else that was going on. Gewürztraminer. The taste was unmistakable. Whatever else he may have done, Victor had inadvertently provided her with her very favourite wine. Helen drank it back thirstily, wishing as she did so that the cook had also provided some water. She couldn't afford to get drunk, not that the half bottle of wine was likely cause inebriation. But she would need her wits about her when Victor returned, as he certainly would.

What, she wondered, was Jamie doing? Had he thought, when he failed to hear from her, to ring Tilly Arbuthnot?

Perhaps it hadn't been too late. Perhaps he'd managed to get on to the VACO computer again and had been able to get the proof to Tilly. Perhaps Victor would return, enraged, to announce that the story was running in the paper. As much as she hoped this would be the case, she realised the danger in which this would place her. If foiled, Victor would want revenge and she knew with a nauseating and terrifying certainty what form that revenge would take. He'd said it himself: He'd waited a long time for this and he was planning to enjoy it. The slap he'd delivered earlier would be a mere appetiser. Helen shuddered. She must be ready for him, ready to somehow escape.

She realised that, without thinking, she'd curled her legs up underneath her again. She couldn't afford to be afflicted with pins and needles when she needed to make a bolt for it. She uncurled her legs, aware that they were already beginning to feel numb, and began tapping her feet on the floor. It didn't help. Her legs still felt numb. Annoyed, she tried to stand up, only to fall back against the chair. A second attempt proved equally futile.

"Shit," she said out loud. Her voice sounded weak. Exhaustion, hardly surprising after the intensity of the last days, seemed to engulf her. Not now, she thought, for God's sake, she couldn't fall asleep now. This was insane. She couldn't let Victor catch her unawares.

She had to stay awake. Had to. Had to...

When the door opened half an hour later, Helen was slumped in her chair, head tipped back, snoring gently.

"Has she finished the wine?"

Johnson peered at the carafe. "Yes, Mr Ormond."

"Good. I knew she wouldn't be able to resist. She'll be out for quite a while."

Somewhere in her subconscious Helen felt hands reaching around her, strong arms lifting her off the chair. She tried to struggle, but her limbs felt as if they'd been weighted down with lead. "Shh, it's okay, sweetie. You're safe now."

Sweetie. Only her father ever called her sweetie. He'd come for her. She was safe now. Helen snuggled against him and let sleep claim her.

CHAPTER SIX

"You'd better go home, Roger," Tilly said at three o'clock in the morning "You can't go to work tomorrow looking like that."

Roger surveyed his crumpled suit, stained tie and mismatched shirt, and assured Tilly there was nothing at his flat likely to be the slightest improvement over what he was wearing. She offered him the use of her sofa and Roger, no heart left for suggestive banter of any sort, accepted her offer. Tilly dug out a pillow and some blankets then retired to the big brass bed which filled most of her minute bedroom.

Six hours later Roger led Tilly into his office at *Sweetie*. It was the first time he could ever remember entering the room completely sober. He immediately lit a cigarette to compensate for his feeling of disorientation. Somewhere on the floor he knew there was a coffee maker some enterprising person had purchased when the beverage dispenser provided by Creed, following the sacking of all the tea ladies, turned out to be incapable of differentiating between the coffee, tea, hot chocolate and chicken soup it was supposed to provide and instead produced a liquid which tasted vaguely and revoltingly of all four. Unable to remember the whereabouts of this coffee maker, he astonished a junior sub by asking her politely to rustle up two cups for him. When the sub returned with the requested mugs, Roger further astonished her by thanking her profusely and telling her she was doing a great job.

"Roger," Tilly said, sipping her coffee and finding it surprisingly good, "how on earth did you land a job as the editor of a magazine for teenage girls?" Out of force of habit, Roger tapped the side of his nose. "Oh, for God's sake," Tilly admonished, "don't give me that rubbish. You've been drunk since you finished with Fleet Street. It's a miracle you're not dead. You're unemployable. How the hell did you get, let alone keep, this job?"

One of the things Roger had always liked about Tilly was the fact that she didn't give a damn what she said to anyone. Some of the stories he'd heard about her meeting with the then Shah of Iran still filled him with awe. Fancy any woman, confronted with the old Peacock King, pulling out a Gitane and saying, 'Look, you and I both know there isn't a lot of Islam practised around here, so what do you say to a gin and tonic?' And, if rumour was to be believed, not only had the old boy ordered her a G&T, but he'd presented her with the solid gold Dunhill he'd produced to light her cigarette.

"Do you still have the Shah's Dunhill?" he asked.

"What?" Tilly squinted at him.

"You know what I'm talking about. Do you?"

Tilly, whom he'd never before known to look the least bit uncomfortable, squirmed in her chair before answering. "Yes."

"So, it's true? What about the rest of the story?"

"No!"

Despite her denial, Roger could see her flush. "No?"

"No. And stop avoiding my question. How on earth can you be the editor of a teen magazine?"

"I've got two teenage daughters, haven't I?"

"Yes," said Tilly, "and as far as I'm aware, they've both been living in Australia with their mother and stepfather for a number of years, so, unless they're e-mailing you regularly or you're running quite a phone bill, I can't imagine they're providing you with much editorial input."

Roger sighed and lit another cigarette. At this point, he couldn't see any reason not to tell Tilly the truth. If, as he fully intended, he went much further with this VACO business, he couldn't see the editorship of *Sweetie* lasting long.

"Do you remember that Who's Who list of tossers Ormond produced for his alibi when he was arrested for beating up Polly?" he asked.

"Vaguely," said Tilly, "although I have no idea who was on it. I don't remember it ever being published."

"Oh, it wasn't. I never saw it myself until the day before I was supposed to go to court. I don't know about the other nineteen bastards, but I did know about the twentieth."

"And?" prompted Tilly, after Roger's pause for effect had gone on quite long enough.

"The twentieth was Sir Geoffrey Bloody Middleton, the chairman and CEO of Creed International, who I knew wasn't with that bastard Ormond when Polly was beaten half to death, because I saw him myself in El Vino's, dispersing champagne to a crowd of hangers on. And he paid for it with a credit card and I got a copy of the receipt and the bill with the time of purchase from one of the barmen who owed me a favour."

"Why didn't you take that to the police?"

"Do me a favour, Tilly!" Roger stubbed his cigarette out in the overflowing ashtray. "The police didn't give a damn. The inspector who took Polly's statement and booked old Vic the next day was bumped back down to sergeant a fortnight later. The only place the detectives assigned to the case were looking for evidence was up their own arses. Nobody was going to reopen the investigation."

"But, Roger – "

"Look," he interrupted, "I did go to Polly. I told her maybe I could get some other paper to kick up a fuss – God knows my old rag wasn't going to, they'd already turned tail. Polly told me to piss off and when I pressed her, she admitted, in a very roundabout way, that she'd managed to get an out of court settlement and didn't want to lose it. So, nobody cared, except me. Nobody was going to go after Vic boy again and I didn't have the wherewithal to blow the other nineteen wankers' stories. I knew I was finished in Fleet Street. Your lot, the toffee nosed bunch weren't going to take me in and none of the editors of the rest of the rags were going to risk screwing up their OBEs giving me a job, so I decided to make Sir Bloody Geoffrey my insurance policy. I cornered him in the car park, showed him a photocopy of the photocopy, told him I had ten people prepared to swear they'd seen him in El Vino's that evening – which I did – and that I was going to go to the police if I didn't get the first bloody editorship that came up at CIP, with full bloody perks."

"Blackmail?" Tilly's eyebrows shot up.

"Call it what you like." Roger shrugged and lit yet another cigarette. "Old Vic wasn't going to get his, Polly didn't want any more grief, the paper'd dumped me. Personally, I'd call it an insurance policy."

"And what exactly do you do here, pissed most of the time?" Tilly asked.

Roger considered her question. "Before the pubs open, I give some thought to what real information I want to try to force feed teenage girls, in the middle of all the boy band profiles and the hair tips and the diet tips and the make-up tips and the how-to-enjoy-getting-shagged-without-worrying-about-AIDS tips. Before the pubs open I assign a real bloody journalist to write one serious article a month about global warming or nuclear proliferation or child pornography or the entire female population of regions of Africa contracting AIDS without a good shag because they've been forced into prostitution by a society that doesn't give a shit about them or their children. Before the pubs open I try to make the silly cows who buy this magazine consider buying something better." He tossed back the remainder of his coffee. "After the pubs open I think about how much I'd like to eviscerate Sir Victor Bloody Ormond."

Alec was feeling enormously pleased with himself when he stepped into the lifts at C.I.P. that morning. The feeling didn't last long. He was still reeling with shock that after three pints Mandy had suggested they get an Indian take away and when pressed about the ultimate destination of same had said her flat. Then he heard Roger's gruff voice call out, "Baldwin, get in here!" His immediate obedience to the order was a result more of his surprise that Roger was there before him than any innate desire to do his supposed boss's bidding.

He drew up short when he saw the Arbuthnot woman.

"You!" he said, gaping at her.

"Me," she agreed with a smile.

"Baldwin," said Roger, "where the hell have you been all night?"

Alec started visibly. Although he had absolutely nothing to feel guilty about – he was after all over twenty-one, hellfire, he was over thirty-one – he'd always felt somehow lacking around authority figures. The fact that he'd never before considered Roger as anything other than a figure of contempt, never mind authority, didn't strike him immediately. He cleared his throat and to his utter amazement found himself saying for the third time in his life, "I say."

"Oh, for heaven's sake," the Arbuthnot woman said to Roger, "it doesn't matter where he was last night. What matters is that he's here now." She turned her attention to Alec. "I need your help."

Alec, his relief at not having to say where the hell he'd been the previous night short lived in the face of this preposterous woman making demands of him, pointed at her and said, "I know you're not a rocket scientist."

A snort of laughter escaped Tilly. "Well, congratulations, Baldwin, for being a helluva lot more alert than you were yesterday. Now look – "

"No, you look," said Alec, "I'm really rather fed up with you and whatever game it is you're playing and I don't appreciate being treated like an idiot."

"Then stop behaving like one," Roger told him.

"Listen, Baldwin," Tilly said before Alec had a chance to become further outraged, "I'm sorry for messing you about yesterday, but I had my reasons. This is very serious. The young woman you saw on the train has been kidnapped and we have to find her. We need your help."

Alec sighed and shook his head. These two dinosaurs were pulling his leg. He didn't know what the gag was supposed to be, but he was now confident that it was some horrible practical joke dreamt up by Roger to torment him. "Oh, yes?" he said. "No doubt her bag also contained the Crown jewels?"

Tilly and Roger exchanged frustrated looks. Tilly tried again. "All right, I lied to you yesterday. VACO isn't involved in a space programme."

"I know," Alec informed her smugly. "VACO Industries is a company which has made a lot of money killing things. It makes products that kill bugs and kill germs and kill pain. The fact that these things also kill people and fish and birds is of no interest to VACO whatsoever, because the link cannot be proven *scientifically*. The company has blokes in lab coats who will swear blind that not a single VACO product ever did anything but benefit the human race, same as the tobacco industry has blokes who will swear on their mother's grave that these –" he reached across the desk and held up Roger's Silk Cuts " – are actually helping your lungs. VACO has a finger in every dirty chemical pie going."

Alec smiled at the look of astonishment on Tilly's face. Kenneth Branagh he may not have been, but he'd always been exceedingly good at memorising lines.

"You have been boning up, haven't you?" Tilly said. Alec nodded. "Well, in that case you'll know that they're complete and utter bastards."

Alec gave himself a slight mental slap. He'd forgotten to mention they were bastards. "They're not very nice, no."

"No, not nice at all," Tilly agreed. "And they're about to do one of the least nice things in their lengthy history of extraordinarily not nice things. Helen, the woman you met on the train, put herself in considerable danger to provide me with evidence about this not at all nice thing they're up to."

"Yes, I know. She gave you a disk and some print outs." Both Tilly and Roger's eyebrows shot up. "Oh, come on," Alec said. "Some fantastically attractive woman comes up to you on a train, thrusts an envelope that's only closed with a metal clip into your hand, an envelope that has 'confidential' emblazoned all over it, and you don't expect the person to whom she gives the envelope to have a look inside?"

"Did it mean anything to you?" Tilly asked.

"Well, no. I suppose that's why I fell for your daft story about the space programme." He looked from one earnest face to the other. "You're serious? She really has been kidnapped?"

"Yes!" Roger and Tilly told him in unison.

"Well, wouldn't it make sense to take the material to the police? I mean, I know it's a bit dodgy being in possession of an envelope with 'VACO Industries – Confidential' stamped all over it, but if it's proof they're involved in a crime, I'm sure the police wouldn't ask too many questions about how you got hold of the evidence."

Tilly suppressed a sigh. "In the first place, we don't know if it is evidence of a crime. In the second place, I don't have it any more, because the men who kidnapped Helen rang me last night and demanded it back. Fool that I was, I handed it over, hoping they might let Helen go which they don't seem to have done. I did manage to copy the printed sheets first, but I had to give them the computer disk back, so it's lost. That's why we need your help," she seemed to hesitate before using his first name, "Alec. We need to know what happened to her after she gave you the envelope, what station you were in at the time, anything you can remember which might help us figure out where to start looking."

Alec sat down on the couch beside Tilly and thought for a moment. "There were two men. The one who grabbed her was tall and slim. He had silver, almost white hair, but his eyebrows were black. And he was a very sharp dresser." He could tell from the look Roger and Tilly exchanged that the description meant something to them. "Who is he?" he asked.

Tilly ignored his question. "What station, Bal – Alec? Where?"

"Bloody hell, I don't know. I wasn't paying that much attention."

Tilly rolled her eyes heavenwards, and took a deep breath before speaking. "You probably noticed something you didn't think about at the time. Think about it now. Is there anything you remember?"

"Look," said Alec, "I'm sorry, but the whole thing was just a bit O.T.T., if you know what I mean. Women demanding help on trains and then being accosted. I mean, I couldn't believe it was happening. I thought it was a gag, something the bloody stockbrokers on the train dreamt up. People were pouring on to the train. I didn't want to lose my seat. I hate standing on trains. I get motion sickness and I can tell you there's never a bloody toilet free when you need – "

Roger interrupted. "What do you mean people were pouring on to the train?"

"Well, it was the junction, wasn't it? People always pour on at the junction. There's never a seat afterwards." Alec paused, realising what he'd said. "Oh, I say, I did know which station, didn't I?" He smiled at Tilly, quite pleased with himself.

Tilly, who'd sensed Roger start at the mention of the junction looked at him.

"The junction," Roger said, "can't be more than a fifteen minute drive from the Ormond house in Kent."

Tilly looked back at Alec. "About this man, what did he do?"

"He grabbed her bag, looked inside it and then threw it down on the platform."

"And?"

"And nothing," said Alec. "The train pulled out and I lost sight of them." He looked back and forth between Tilly and Roger, neither of whom seemed particularly impressed by his narrative. He had to admit himself it was a bit lame. He hadn't rushed to the rescue of a damsel in distress. He hadn't tackled a villain. Altogether a singularly unimpressive performance. Hollywood Alec would have leapt from the moving train, karate chopped the bad guys and swept the heroine off to a king size bed in a five star hotel all in the blink of the eye. Lower Wipington Alec hadn't done much of anything. He shifted uncomfortably on the couch, trying to think of something, anything which might cast him in a better light. Finally it came to him. "I did copy that VACO Industries disk on to the hard drive of my computer," he said, puffing out his chest a bit.

"Really?" Again Tilly and Roger spoke in unison. After a moment, Roger asked the question they both wanted answered. "Well? Go on then. What was on it?"

Alec's chest deflated. "I don't know. You needed a password to access the file."

Tilly looked at Roger. "Are you any good with computers?"

He shook his head. "Sorry, love. I never got much past learning how to switch the thing on. It's just a typewriter with a television screen to me."

"Right." With nothing more than pure determination in her favour, Tilly stood up decisively. "Let's have a go."

CHAPTER SEVEN

Helen was comfortable, so comfortable. The pillow under her head was soft and downy. The quilt over her was warm. Soft, cosy, comfortable. Safe. Unlike the feather-light quilt, her eyelids felt as if they were weighed down by boulders. Helen struggled to open them. When she finally succeeded it was difficult to focus. Slowly she took in her surroundings.

She was in a four poster bed of carved mahogany. Across the large room was a tall chest of drawers, ornately carved of the same polished wood. Against another wall was a matching wardrobe. A huge Persian rug all but covered the parquet floor.

Despite her disorientation, Helen knew there was something familiar about the room. She turned her head and looked towards the window. Thick brocade curtains had been drawn back to allow light to pour into the room. There was a desk by the window and over the desk hung a portrait.

Helen suddenly knew exactly where she was. The desk and the portrait of Nana Ormond which hung above it were the only things clearly visible from the hallway when Victor Ormond left the door to his bedroom open.

Jesus Christ, she thought, I'm in Victor's bed. What's he done? Relieved to realise she was still dressed, she shut her eyes, pursed her lips and, breathing slowly and deeply through her nostrils, tried to concentrate on her body, on how it felt. Some minutes passed before she was satisfied. Whatever else Victor had done, he hadn't raped her.

But why bring her in here, into his bedroom? If, as she found it almost impossible to believe, he'd felt remorse for locking her up in the cellar and had decided to make her more comfortable, there were a dozen bedrooms in this house he could have used. Why his room?

She gazed around, realising with a start that her raincoat was folded neatly on the wing chair on the other side of the bed. Her shoulder bag rested against the chair, her Reeboks were on the floor. She looked across at the door which led to the hallway. Shut, yes, and surely locked? There was only one way to find out.

It was as she tossed the quilt aside and began to scramble out of the bed that she spotted the sheet of paper on top of the other pillow. She picked it up by one corner as if it might explode in her hand and read the words typed on the page: *Helen, it's time you knew where you were conceived. It's time you knew I am your father.*

Helen shook her head in disbelief. This was ridiculous. It couldn't be true. Arthur was her father. The piece of paper slid out of her hand. Horrible thoughts began to turn themselves into awful memories.

Victor, Victor, it had always been Victor: keeping her prisoner, hiring and firing tutors and governesses, refusing let her leave with her mother, using his titled QC to fight for custody. It couldn't be true. Could it?

Could her mother, whom she'd always thought despised Victor, have slept with him, here in this room, conceived a child by him, conceived *her* by him? Could Victor, not Arthur, be her father? Was that why Victor had always been so obsessed with her?

Simply allowing the idea to enter head caused the contents of her stomach to churn. The bedrooms on this floor all had their own bathrooms. Helen knew where to go, although she barely made it to the toilet in time. She heaved up all bitter-tasting remnants of her prawn dinner, shivering despite the beads of perspiration dotting her brow.

No, no, no. The word hammered in her head. No. It could not be true. Victor Ormond could not be her father. Helen gulped for breath, the air rasping painfully on her raw throat. She had to get away from this house.

In the bedroom she crammed her feet into her shoes, grabbed her coat, picked up her bag and hurried across the room. She reached for the handle and issued a silent prayer. The handle turned, the door opened. Helen fled down the corridor, down the stairs, across the oak panelled hallway to the front door. It was a moment's work to remember how the ancient lock worked and then she was outside, pounding down the gravelled drive.

A car horn honked and she heard a voice call her name. *No*, she thought, running as fast as she could, she had to escape, get away from this house, away to some place where she could think. She could hear the car engine start and the crunch of wheels on the gravel. She pushed herself and her exploding lungs even harder, sprinting the last hundred feet. The car was right behind her. She heard a door open as she reached for the heavy, wrought iron gate. At the same awful moment as she realised the gate was locked, a hand closed on her shoulder.

'No!" She turned, kicking and screaming, to face her adversary, determined Victor Ormond would never get her inside that house again.

Strong hands closed over her upper arms. "Helen, Helen. Stop it. It's me. It's Charles."

Helen stopped lashing out and looked at the man whose hands gripped her. Tall and slim, looking tanned and healthy, dressed in blue jeans and a black silk shirt, still sporting the black goatee beard she had never been able to persuade him to abandon, Charles gazed down at her, his dark brown eyes filled with concern.

Helen slumped against him. "Charles," she said, "for god's sake, get me away from here!"

"Of course, angel," he replied, quickly unlocking the gate, swinging it open and bustling her into his sports car.

Helen didn't say a word during the journey. She stared blindly through the windscreen, oblivious to the beautiful Kent countryside, which gave way to suburban sprawl, then the bustle of south London before they reached his Covent Garden flat. It was in an old warehouse – dilapidated in the days before the original Covent Garden market was swept away to make room for boutiques and bistros, now lavishly converted into flats for people who wanted to live in the very heart of London and had the ludicrous amount of money required to do so.

After miraculously succeeding in finding a parking spot, he climbed out of the car, then reached into the back to withdraw a suitcase and a duty free bag. Helen finally registered surprise at his presence. "Why aren't you in New York?" she asked.

"I just flew in," he said, which didn't tell her anything. "Come on. Let's get you inside and then we can talk."

After firmly depositing Helen on a sofa which faced the floor to ceiling window overlooking the market square, Charles took his case up to the sleeping loft. He returned a few moments later and extracted a bottle of Armagnac from his duty free bag.

"I don't know about you, but I find a shot of this helps most situations," he said. Helen nodded as Charles reached into the sideboard for two snifters. "What happened to your cheek?" he asked as he passed her a generous measure.

Helen's free hand flew up to her face. She'd forgotten Victor Ormond's ring ripping into her skin. "Oh, God. Is it bad?"

Charles leaned closer and shook his head. "I'm sure it won't scar, but you should put something on it. What happened?"

"Your bastard brother hit me."

"Vic?"

Helen nodded, then changed the subject. Right now being slapped by Victor Ormond was the least of her worries. "What time is it?" she asked.

"It's all right, Helen," Charles said raising his glass to his lips, "the sun's well over the yardarm."

"I really need to know, Charles. What time is it?"

He glanced at his watch. "Just gone three."

Helen considered this information. Just gone three. But what day? How long had she been in the cellar? How long had she been sleeping in Victor Ormond's bed? "What day is it?" she asked.

"God, you really are out of it, aren't you? It's Friday."

Just gone three on Friday. Thirty hours since Jamie had rung her on the train to say Victor was going to try to intercept her at the Junction. Thirty hours since she'd made the split second decision to entrust the VACO material to that dishevelled *Guardian* reader on the train. Thirty hours in which it seemed her entire life had been ripped to pieces.

"Do you want to tell me what's going on?" Charles asked,

interrupting her thoughts just as she was about to burst into tears.

Helen sniffed and gave him a considering look. "What *are* you doing here? I thought you weren't going to be over again until next month?"

Charles took a hefty swig of his Armagnac. "Vic called me in a panic. Big flap on." He smiled at her. "Something to do with you, I believe."

Helen sighed. There wasn't much point in pretending. "I stole some material which was proof of one of your brother's truly vile business decisions, as I'm sure he told you."

"No, actually, he didn't tell me exactly what the problem was. Why don't you?"

"You know that seed coating VACO had to withdraw?"

Charles shuddered and, leaning forward, placed his snifter on the glass and chrome coffee table. "Christ, don't remind me."

Helen gave him a dirty look. "So you did know about it?"

He shrugged, "Christ, Helen, everyone in the company knew about it. Not something we were going to broadcast, was it? At least it got caught in development. No harm done."

Maybe not at the time, thought Helen. "Well, guess what?" she told Charles. "It turns out those seeds are exactly what a certain dictator wants to help him deal with the ethnic minority in his country and your brother, Sir Bloody Victor Ormond, is planning to ship a large supply off to him."

"Jesus." Charles blew out a low whistle and sank back in his chair. "How did you find out about this?"

Helen opened her mouth to answer him, but stopped herself just in time. At the beginning Jamie had suggested they tell Charles, but Helen had vetoed the idea without hesitation. Even now, with him sitting here, his face filled with concern, she wasn't sure she could trust him with the truth. Charles, as much as she loved him, was still an Ormond, still part of the management of VACO. Of course he would try to stop the shipment, but he would also want to hush it up – and that was the last thing Helen wanted.

"I was waiting for Dad in his office," she said, giving him a version of the tale she'd told Tilly Arbuthnot. "The door was open. I heard Victor discussing it with someone in the corridor."

Charles' expression was unfathomable. "And you've got proof of this?"

Helen shook her head. "No. Unfortunately, he managed to get it back somehow."

"How?" Charles asked.

Helen spread her hands and shrugged. "How the hell should I know? First he locked me up in the cellar. Then I think he must have drugged me. Then he put me in his bed."

"In his bed?" Charles' eyebrows shot up. "Why would he do that?"

"I don't know!" Helen almost screamed.

"Okay, okay," Charles held his hands up in mock surrender. "Listen, angel, I don't know what's going on and you don't have to tell me if you don't want to, but it's pretty obvious you've been badly shaken up. Do you want me to call your mother?"

"No!" There was absolutely no way Helen could contemplate seeing her mother. She didn't know what to believe, wasn't sure she wanted to know, wanted reassurances it wasn't true. But what if it *was*? What if her mother broke down and confessed? No, she couldn't bear it.

"Okay, fine." Charles nodded without questioning her vehemence. "Your father's flying back from Singapore tonight. Do you want me to have him paged to ring me when he gets in?"

"No!" Helen said with equal force. Even if she had no doubt whatsoever about who the hell her father really was, the only place Arthur Ormond could take her would be back to that house, and Helen was determined to never set foot in it again.

"What *do* you want to do?"

"I don't know." Helen finally raised the snifter of Armagnac to her lips. The smell made her swoon. She realised how hungry she was. "I think I need to eat something."

"Well, angel, I can guarantee the cupboards here are bare. Why don't I pop out to the shops and get some supplies in while you have a bath? You look like you could use one."

Helen surprised herself by grinning. She was feeling better than she had since Jamie rang her on the train the previous morning. "Thank you so much, Charles," she said, "for being there when I got out of the house and for not browbeating me."

He returned her smile. "Helen, I know you hate Vic and I don't blame you. I can't stand the sight of him myself most of the time. But I do wish you'd come to me with this Bowinda story instead of running off to some journalist. Aside from the fact that, as you know, I'm always glad of a chance to see you, no matter what the circumstances, I might have been able to stop the shipment. I still might be able to. But I have to tell you, angel, if this story had got into a newspaper, I shudder to think what Vic might have done." Helen suppressed a shudder of her own. Charles reached over and ruffled her hair. "Go on. Run yourself a bath. By the time you've finished soaking, I'll have made some phone calls and got some food ready."

Helen grabbed his hand and gave him a beseeching look. "You won't tell Victor I'm here, will you?"

He gave her hand a reassuring squeeze. "Of course not, Helen. You know you can count on me."

CHAPTER EIGHT

"Damn it!" Tilly thumped her fist in frustration on Alec's desk.

The first hurdle she'd had to overcome was Alec's shamefaced admission that he couldn't remember what name he'd given the VACO file or where he'd saved it. After a considerable amount of frustrated searching, she'd shot Alec a scathing look. "Could it be called *Train?*"

Alec nodded and Tilly began the lengthy and ultimately futile process of trying to guess the password.

Over an hour had passed during which Tilly, consulting an old notebook she'd stuffed into her bag, had keyed in every possibility she could imagine.

Having eliminated Victor's name, date of birth, ex-directory phone number and National Insurance number, she tried his parents' and brothers' names, his mother's maiden name, and then, increasingly desperate, the location and manager's name for every VACO plant she'd ever researched.

"This is hopeless," she said, looking around to discover there was no sign of Roger or Alec. She was talking to herself. The password could be anything. Tilly stared at the computer screen in frustration, willing the file to miraculously open.

"Any luck?" asked Roger, emerging from his office. Tilly shook her head. "Sorry," said Roger. "I've hit a dead end, too. I was trying to trace the registration number for that car last night."

"You were?" Tilly couldn't hide the surprise in her voice.

"Yes, Tilly, as a matter of fact I was. I haven't completely lost my touch, you know. I do still have a few contacts on the force."

"And?"

"No go. The car was stolen last night, hours before it turned up at your place."

Tilly waited and when Roger offered no further information, asked, "From whom was it stolen, Roger?"

Roger sighed. "Sorry, Tilly, I didn't ask. I guess I have lost my bloody touch." He withdrew into his office, returning a few minutes later with a piece of paper in his hand. "Cynthia Werring," he said.

Tilly considered the name. For some reason it rang a tiny little bell. Just for the hell of it, she typed "Cynthia" and hit return.

"Christ!" she exclaimed when, instead of the now familiar *Password Incorrect* message, the file popped open and the screen filled with its contents. Roger hurried across the room and peered over her shoulder at the screen, just as Tilly said, "Damn! It's the same bloody gibberish from the computer print out."

Roger, looking at the computer screen, sighed.

Unethical Practices

```
⏣⟲⇨▽⇨  ⇨⇨⇨▲◀  ⟍◢  ⇨⇨▽◀  ▷↓▽↑⇨▽  ⇦◊◬  ◀↑
⇨  ▽▶⇨⇨▽▽⇦⟋  ⇨◊⟍▲⟲⇨◀↓◊⟷  ◊⇦  ◢◊▶△  ▲△◊⟍
⇨⇨◀⟍  ⟄⇨⇨⇨  ⇨→⇨↓⟷↥  ⟍⇨⟷◢  ◀↑⇨⟷⟌▽  ⇦◊◬  ◢◊▶
△  ↑◊▽▲↓◀⇨⟋↓◀◢⟍
```

    Alec chose that moment to return from a lengthy, Indian take-away-induced visit to the gents. Peering over Tilly's shoulder, he said, "It's not gibberish. I can see that now it's on the screen. It's been saved in a symbols font. Here." He leant across the desk, highlighted the text, moved the cursor up to the top of the screen, clicked onto fonts, chose one and a moment later words filled the screen.

```
TO:     HIS EXCELLENCY, GENERAL RADAD
FROM:   C.E.O.'S OFFICE, V.A.C.O.
RE:     DOCUMENTATION OF EFFICIENCY OF PRODUCT 17872

Your Excellency, before I go any further, may I
first reiterate my thanks for your hospitality last
night? Both the meal and the company were
delightful, as always.

Now, to business. As we discussed, I am
forwarding the final analysis completed on
V.A.C.O. 17872 by my brother Arthur Ormond, our
principal scientist.

As this analysis confirms, the unforeseen side
effects of this product, which made its
commercial release impossible, will,
fortuitously, assist you in solving your
internal problem. I am confident your people
will find everything in order.

The shipment will reach you within 36 hours of
receipt of payment in full.

Please accept my best wishes for the successful
completion of your project. Once again, many
thanks for your hospitality.
```

    "I assume," said Roger, when he'd scanned through the memo, "this would be General Radad, the Butcher of Bowinda?"

    Tilly nodded. Helen hadn't identified the country to which

a famine was to be delivered, but somewhere in the back of her mind Tilly had known.

Jolly General Radad, who had joked and charmed his way into the good books of Washington and Whitehall before overthrowing the democratically-elected government of his west African country. That was over twenty years ago and the killing hadn't stopped for a day since. Jovial General Radad, who every year held a command appearance banquet for the chief executive officers of the world's largest petrochemical and mining companies at his £25 million rococo compound. Heads of state, including British prime ministers and presidents of France and the United States, had also attended this two-day feast. All the general's guests commended him for bringing "stability" to a volatile part of the world. Of course, "stability" simply meant "open for business" and prepared to squash, by whatever means necessary, the opposition of the ethnic minority to the destruction of their land by oil wells and open pit mines. Radad had been waging war, unofficially, of course, on these people ever since he came to power. Now, thanks to VACO, Radad had found his own "final solution".

"What the hell is VACO 17872?" asked Roger.

Tilly considered for a moment. Decades of protecting her stories had stopped her telling Roger everything she knew. Now she felt the need to unburden. "It's a genetically engineered seed coating," she explained. "It'll give you a bumper crop the first year. After that, the soil is barren."

"Christ," said Roger. "Not even I can believe that fucker Ormond would dream up something like this."

"He didn't," said Tilly. "At least not intentionally. That's the 'unforeseen side effects'. They had to cancel the project, when Arthur Ormond ran a few tests nobody in the biotechnology division had bothered with. Apparently it cost VACO millions."

"And good old Sir Vic's decided to recoup some of his losses," Roger stated, rather than asked. "Bastard." Tilly nodded. Roger glanced back at the computer screen. "You notice," he said, "that he hasn't actually put his name on the memo?"

Tilly looked at the screen again. "Oh, come on, Roger. It says 'C.E.O.'S Office'. There's only one chief executive officer of that company and that's Sir Victor Ormond. And it refers to his *brother*, Arthur, doesn't it?"

Roger shrugged. "I'd still like to see his name somewhere."

"Well, we haven't seen everything yet, have we?" said Tilly.

Roger dutifully returned his attention to the computer screen as Tilly moved the cursor down. What followed was some very detailed information in impenetrable scientific jargon about the series of tests which Arthur Ormond had run on VACO 17872.

"Does this mean anything to you?" asked Tilly. Roger shrugged.

"Well, at least you got the file open," said Alec. Tilly, who'd forgotten he was there, turned and peered at him. "What was the password?"

"Cynthia," Tilly said.

"Cynthia?" Roger repeated.

Tilly nodded and grinned at him. "I assume you've got an address for this Cynthia?"

Roger grinned back. "You assume correctly."

After clicking print to get a hard copy of the 17872 specs which still made no sense despite the switch to a readable font, Tilly rummaged in her bag until she found her notebook. She scribbled the Brussels phone and fax numbers she had for Jack Conquest and handed the scrap of paper to Alec, endeavouring as she did so to arrange her features into an expression which offered encouragement, sought assistance and in no way conveyed her conviction that he was an idiot.

"Baldwin," she began, breaking off and starting again with a smile she feared was coming across as a grimace, "Alec, this is very important. I need you to phone this number in Brussels and ask for Dr Conquest in Room 702. If he's there, I want you to fax these sheets to him and tell him to ring me. If he's not there, keep trying until you get him, and then fax the material." She pulled the sheets out of the printer and held them towards him.

Alec didn't hold out his hand immediately. Instead he puffed out his somewhat concave chest and said, "Well, actually, I'm really rather busy this morning."

Before Tilly could respond, Roger had grabbed the sheets of paper out of her hand and was smacking Alec on the head with them. "This," he said, giving Alec one more whack, "is important you dozy pillock – a damned sight more important than butchering some poor bastard's copy. Just do it."

After a mere moment's hesitation, Alec, who'd suddenly realised there were points to be scored with the damsel in distress, took the papers from Roger's hand, picked up the receiver of his telephone and said, "I'm on it," in a firm tone which he hoped was more evocative of Hollywood rather than Lower Wipington Alec.

Ten minutes later Tilly, a photocopy of the VACO document folded safely in her bag, settled into the back of a black cab with Roger, who gave the driver Cynthia Werring's address. The driver did his best to avoid the worst of central London's inevitable gridlock, but it still took forty minutes to reach their destination.

Early in the journey Tilly rejected Roger's suggestion that the poor woman might genuinely have had her car stolen the previous day. "Oh, come on, Roger," she said. "Cynthia's not that common a name. It can't possibly be a coincidence. She must know Ormond. The question is how much does she know? If we can convince her that her car was used to commit some awful crime and she's in it right up to her neck, she might just tell us something helpful."

They spent the remaining thirty-five minutes working on their story until they were confident they had covered every possibility except Cynthia Werring not being at home.

"Clear?" asked Tilly as they mounted the steps to the front door of Number 17, Whitlow Square, SW3. Roger, wishing his appearance wasn't quite so unprepossessing, nodded.

Tilly pressed the bell marked Werring. A few moments later a woman's voice came through the garbled speaker system. "Yes?"

"Cynthia Werring?" asked Tilly. The woman answered in the affirmative. "My name is Arbuthnot," Tilly began.

"Tilly Arbuthnot?" the woman asked, taking both Roger and Tilly completely by surprise. This certainly hadn't been one of the possibilities they'd anticipated.

"Yes," said Tilly.

"Come in," said the woman. "It's the door on the left." With that a buzzer released the front door lock. Exchanging curious looks, Tilly and Roger made their way into the foyer of the Regency terrace which had been converted into very expensive flats.

"What now?" Roger whispered.

Tilly shrugged and mouthed, "Play it by ear."

The door to their left opened to reveal a stunningly attractive, immaculately turned out woman. Her silver blonde hair was cut in the sort of perfectly symmetrical bob which cannot be achieved for less than a hundred pounds. The two piece suit she wore was definitely not an imitation Chanel. Clearly a woman who did not care who knew she was in her fifties, she wore not a hint of make-up, nor did she need any. No amount of cunningly applied cosmetics could have improved the beauty of her luminous aquamarine eyes, the sculpted perfection of her cheekbones and jaw line, or the wide, generous mouth, smiling pleasantly now to reveal two rows of evenly shaped pearly white teeth.

"Oh, my God," said Roger and Tilly in unison, gaping at the woman who stood in front of them. Cynthia Werring's welcoming smile turned into a worried frown.

"Polly!" said Roger.

"Helen!" said Tilly.

CHAPTER NINE

Cynthia Werring, oblivious to Roger's exclamation or even his presence, fixed her gaze firmly on Tilly. "What about Helen?" she asked.

In a career which had spanned five continents and a quarter of a century, Tilly had never been so completely nonplussed. The resemblance was uncanny. She would have been prepared to wager her flat, its painstakingly acquired contents and her meagre life savings on this woman being Helen's mother. But it made no sense. Why would Helen's mother's supposedly stolen car be used by Helen's kidnappers? The concern on the woman's face was obvious for anyone to see. She couldn't possibly be a part of this, could she?

Tilly cleared her throat. "I've come about your car, Mrs Werring."

"Never mind my bloody car. I've got it back. What about Helen?"

"You've got your car back?" Tilly repeated.

"Yes, yes." Cynthia Werring waved impatiently towards the street. "I looked out the window half an hour ago and it was just sitting there. I've rung the police." She gave Tilly, who was trying to peer out the window, a hard stare. "Look, forget the bloody car. What about Helen?"

Tilly was still feeling at a complete loss. Although it seemed unnecessary, one thing had to be confirmed. "I take it Helen is your daughter?"

"Yes, of course she is. Isn't that why you're here?"

Helen, thought Tilly, Helen Werring. Well, at least now she knew Helen's last name. "I'm not quite sure how to begin, Mrs Werring."

"Ms Werring," Cynthia corrected. "It's my maiden name."

"And you're married name?"

Cynthia sighed. "Ormond, of course. If you know Helen, you must know that."

Tilly and Roger exchanged looks. Helen *Ormond*?

And then the tiny little bell that had rung earlier in Tilly's mind clanged: Arthur Ormond's rather messy divorce from his wife Cynthia had involved a custody fight over a daughter. Tilly had a report about this filed away somewhere – extraneous information compared to the sins of the company, but family details never hurt. There was something else, some quite titillating detail which was temporarily eluding her. She'd worry about that later – what mattered now was discovering the identity of her informant. The discovery brought with it a renewed suspicion that she'd been had.

She took a deep breath and looked at Cynthia Werring. "Does your daughter work at VACO?"

"VACO?" Cynthia's laugh was incredulous. "You're joking. Who on earth told you she worked at VACO?"

"She did. She approached me and told me she worked at VACO and could provide me with evidence about a very nasty deal the company was putting together."

Cynthia considered this information. "Well, she was either trying to protect her father or Jamie. If she said she could provide evidence, it was probably Jamie. I can't see Arthur going to the press."

"Jamie?"

Cynthia answered the question with one of her own. "Why can't you ask Helen that?" They were still standing in the hallway outside Cynthia's flat. Tilly asked if they might come in and they were led into an exquisitely decorated lounge. Gesturing towards the sofa, Cynthia sat down on a matching chintz upholstered chair. Her eyes never left Tilly's face.

Tilly spent a moment trying to muster her thoughts before speaking. "Yesterday morning Helen was supposed to bring me evidence about some major skulduggery at VACO. She left a message that she'd passed the information on to someone on the train and would be in touch as soon as possible. The person she gave the material to is a colleague of Roger's." Both women glanced in his direction. Tilly realised she hadn't introduced him, but she could tell by the look on Cynthia's face that his identity was of no interest to her whatsoever. "Helen never rang me."

Cynthia groaned. "Oh, God," she said, "Jamie rang last night, sounding desperate about Helen. He said he'd been trying to reach her, but she wasn't home and she wasn't answering her mobile. He thought she might be here. He didn't say what it was about and, frankly, I wasn't that worried." She saw the surprise on Tilly's face and managed a half hearted smile. "Helen has some mystery man she goes off with from time to time. I just assumed –" She broke off and looked quickly around the room as if something in it might offer a clue to Helen's whereabouts. Her eyes settled back on Tilly's face. "Do you have any idea what might have happened?" Tilly's hesitation only served to make Cynthia more frantic. "For God's sake, whatever it is, tell me."

"According to the fellow Helen gave the material, she got off the train at the junction, where she was accosted by two men, one of whom sounds like Sir Victor Ormond. Last night I had a call from someone demanding the return of the stolen material. I was worried about what might have happened to Helen, so I did as I was told. The car – "

Tilly broke off when she saw how completely the colour had drained from Cynthia's face. For several seconds the other woman sat in silence, her eyes closed. To Tilly, not normally the least bit fanciful, it almost seemed as if Cynthia Werring was fighting a demon.

Then the extraordinary aquamarine eyes which she had passed on to her daughter opened. Cynthia shot out of her chair and walked across the room to the telephone, which sat on a lovely secretary desk.

After quickly consulting her address book, she picked up the receiver and dialled a number. A moment later she said, "Victor Ormond's office." A pause, then, "This is Cynthia Werring. Put him on." Another pause. "Tell *Sir* Victor that I'm about to launch a ten million pound law suit against him and he'd better get on the phone now." After another brief pause, she slammed the receiver down and turned to face Roger and Tilly.

"I didn't really think he was there, but I had to be sure." She grabbed her bag and walked towards the door. When they didn't immediately follow, she said. "Come if you're coming, leave if you're not."

"Where are you going?" asked Tilly.

"To the Ormond house, of course. To get my daughter." After a pause she added, "And while I'm there I might just kill Victor Ormond."

Roger and Tilly followed her out into the square. Cynthia unlocked the passenger door of her car, then walked around to the driver's side. As Tilly reached for the passenger door, Roger spoke for the first time, surprising both women.

"There's something I have to ask you, Ms Werring," he said.

Cynthia, anxious to be off, looked at him impatiently. "Yes?"

"Did Victor Ormond ever assault you?"

Cynthia physically recoiled. The answer to Roger's question was written all over her face.

"I'm sorry I had to ask," Roger said. He turned to look at Tilly. "You go with her. There's something I have to do. I'll ring you later. Or you ring me if you're not going to be home." He nodded at both of them. "Good luck."

As Roger began to stride down the street, Cynthia recovered herself enough to say, "Are you coming?"

Tilly nodded, climbing into the passenger seat. She barely had time to fasten her seatbelt before Cynthia had screeched away from the kerb.

Tilly didn't attempt to talk during the drive. Truth be told, she was afraid to speak. Her earlier impression that Cynthia Werring was possessed seemed to be confirmed. The woman was driving like a maniac. Zipping in and out of lanes, hand constantly on the horn, Cynthia ignored speed limits and pretty much every other rule of the road. A journey Tilly estimated would normally take at least ninety minutes was completed in fifty.

Cynthia drove through the open gates and screeched to a stop in front of the Ormond house. Tilly climbed out of the passenger seat, relieved to no longer feel in imminent danger of a car crash. She stood for a moment surveying the exterior of the house, understanding immediately why she'd seen it described as one of the worst monstrosities of the twentieth century. The red brick, primarily mock-Victorian building looked as if it had been designed by a committee of people with completely contradictory tastes. The fake-Georgian portico was in glaring contrast to both the Gothic gables of the second floor and the Rapunzel-like turret which seemed to have been slapped on to one side of the building as an afterthought. The diamond-shaped leaded window panes, a decidedly inappropriate pseudo-Tudor touch, went with neither the Gothic nor the Georgian theme.

Cynthia rummaged in her bag, pulled out a set of keys. "God," she said, "I can't believe I still have this." She looked at Tilly and managed a smile. "Let's hope they haven't changed the lock."

The key worked and a moment later they were inside. Considering the hideousness of the outside of the house, the interior took Tilly by surprise. The entrance hall contained some very fine panelling, a gorgeous mahogany staircase and some of the loveliest friezes she had ever seen. Even after decades of wear, the Chinese carpet on the polished parquet floor made Tilly's mouth water. Not that this was the time to consider the potential for a *Country Living* spread or how good the carpet would look in the lounge of her tiny Hampstead flat. Cynthia made a move towards the mahogany staircase, placed one hand on the polished banister, then stopped, swivelling off in another direction. Tilly followed her down a corridor, through a yanked open door, down a set of stairs into a cellar. A single, dim bulb illuminated the way between racks of wine to another door. Cynthia paused outside the door long enough to take a deep breath, then grabbed the doorknob. A flick of the light switch beside the door lit another bare bulb in a storage room filled to capacity with trunks and boxes, bits of old furniture – the detritus of a home lived in for generations by one family – but no sign of a human occupant.

"Damn," said Cynthia. "I was sure this is where he'd bring her. He terrified her once when she was a child by locking her in here."

Tilly stepped into the room and surveyed it more closely. "Someone's been in here recently. The dust has been disturbed. Here," she pointed to an old side table, "and look at the floor." Numerous footprints were clearly outlined. "More than two people, I'd say."

Cynthia gave the floor only a cursory glance. "Come on. We have to keep looking."

They retraced their steps back to the hallway, where they were confronted by an officious butler.

"Mrs Ormond," the man said in surprise, "what are you doing here?"

Cynthia laughed without amusement. "Good God, Jenkins! Are you still here?"

"Mrs Ormond," although the butler's expression remained impassive, Tilly could hear the sneer in his voice, "I'll have to ask you to leave."

"Like hell you will," Cynthia said, poking him in the chest with a well manicured finger. "Where is my daughter?"

Jenkins gave Cynthia an obsequious smile. Uriah Heap had nothing on him, Tilly decided. With the slightest shake of his balding head, the butler informed them he had no idea what they could possibly be asking. He hadn't seen Helen in years. "Liar," Cynthia said, pushing past him. She glanced over her shoulder at Tilly. "Come on."

Tilly followed as Cynthia ran up the stairs. They tried the long abandoned nursery first, then returned to the first floor. Cynthia called Helen's name as she made her way down the corridor, opening doors and checking quickly in wardrobes and bathrooms. Tilly sensed rather than saw her hesitation before shoving hard against the final door. The bedroom was dominated by a huge and hideous carved mahogany four poster bed and matching Victorian wardrobe and chest of drawers.

"Check the bathroom," Cynthia said, as she reached for the wardrobe door. Tilly dutifully looked inside the bathroom. Other than an unmistakable, lingering smell of vomit the room was empty. Turning back towards the bed, Tilly spotted a piece of paper lying on the floor between the bed and the wall. Bending to retrieve it, she read the typewritten words: *Helen, it's time you knew where you were conceived. It's time you knew I am your father.*

Tilly passed the note to Cynthia, who read it, then looking

as if she'd been punched in the stomach, sank onto the bed, muttering a curse under her breath. For a moment Tilly thought Helen's mother was going to burst into tears, but she didn't. Instead, shaking her head, she cursed more audibly: "Son of a bitch, son of a fucking bitch, I am going to kill you, you son of a bitch." She looked up at Tilly. "Can you drive?" Tilly, not entirely sure her seldom used license hadn't actually expired, nodded. "Good," said Cynthia, "because I need a very large drink."

Cynthia stood up. Tilly watched as the other woman raised her chin, pushed her shoulders back and marched regally out of the room. Down the corridor, down the stairs, across the hallway, Cynthia kept her head held high. To Jenkins, holding the door open for them, Cynthia said, "If Victor Ormond has harmed one hair on my daughter's head, I will find him and kill him and then, for lying to me, I will come back here and castrate you."

Neither Jenkins nor Tilly doubted her sincerity.

CHAPTER TEN

After he left Tilly and Cynthia, Roger walked to the tube station and made his way to the police station in Covent Garden. He asked at the desk for Ted Beauchamp and was told to wait while the sergeant was summoned. A few minutes later a door opened and a wiry man of medium height emerged.

Sergeant Ted Beauchamp did not really need his uniform to convey his status as a policeman. The intense, copper coloured eyes which seemed to bore directly into the soul of anyone with whom they made contact were a bit of a giveaway. Those staring eyes set on either side of a thin, long, hooked nose – which always reminded Roger of Sherlock Holmes – managed to intimidate all but the most hardened criminals. Roger suspected, although he'd never asked, that a boot to the groin dealt with the villains the stare didn't sort out.

He nodded at Ted and held out his hand.

"God, you look rough," Ted said, reaching across the counter to shake Roger's proffered hand. It had taken Ted ten years on the force to make Inspector, a rank he'd summarily lost in the aftermath of the Ormond debacle. More than a decade later, he was still a sergeant, resigned to the fact that the blot was never going to be removed from his copybook and that he would never now attain any higher rank in the Met. Yes, he was bitter, but, as he looked at Roger Wilcox, he decided he'd definitely done the better of the two of them out of that particular fiasco. "You need another registration number checked?" he asked.

Roger shook his head. "I need to talk to you, Ted. Somewhere private."

"Right." Ted raised the desk flap, walked through and led

the way up the road to a pub. Clearly he was a regular. The barmaid greeted him with a smile and began, without having to be asked, to pour him a pint of bitter. Ted asked what Roger wanted and was astonished to hear him request a tomato juice. "Sure you don't want a vodka in this?" Ted said when the bottle and glass were on the bar. Roger shook his head, tipping the thick liquid into the glass. "Bloody hell, Roger, this must be serious."

They sat down at a table in the corner. Roger took a sip of his tomato juice, put it back down on the table and lit a cigarette. "I know why he did it, Ted," he said.

"Who?" asked Ted before tossing back half his pint of bitter.

"Ormond, of course. Well, I don't know exactly why he did it, but I know what it was about. He's got some sort of fixation on his ex-sister-in-law, Cynthia Werring."

"Isn't she the owner of that stolen car?" Ted began to evince some interest. "It turned up, you know."

"Yes, I know, Ted. I've just come from there. I'm telling you, the woman could be Polly's double."

"Let it go, Roger. You and I both know Ormond beat Polly up, but the case was thrown out. Tarts get beaten up all the time. It's an occupational hazard and nobody gives a shit." Ted shook his head. "There was one last night, hauled into University College Hospital practically dead, poor cow."

"I know it happens all the time." Roger inhaled deeply on his cigarette and rejected with some difficulty the urge to go up to the bar and add a large vodka to tomato juice. "But how many of those times have been Ormond, eh? No one ever checked that, did they? How many other poor cows have been beaten by the bastard?"

"Christ, Roger, I don't know and I don't care. I have no interest in seeing my so-called career flushed any further down the toilet. I wouldn't touch Ormond again if you brought me a cast iron case against him."

"Humour me."

"No, Roger. No bloody way. I shouldn't have even taken your call this morning, never mind checking that registration for you. Give it up."

Roger leaned back in his seat and gave Ted an appraising

look. "Are you seriously telling me you wouldn't like to nail the bastard?"

"No." Ted hesitated, then tossed back the rest of his pint. "Well, 'course I'd like to nail him. But it must be twelve or more years now, Roger. There is no fucking excuse to open up that file. The case is closed."

"What about the one last night?" Roger asked.

"What one last night?"

"The girl who was beaten up."

"Christ, Roger, I told you. Tarts get beaten up every night."

"Have you seen her?"

"Not my patch, Roger. I just heard about it from someone passing through the nick. Sounds like it was pretty fucking brutal."

"Come and see her with me, Ted."

"Why the hell should I?"

"Humour me," Roger asked again.

Ted looked at Roger, remembering him fifteen years ago, a boozer, yes, but fit and full of vitality. It would have been easy for Ted to have passed Roger in the street today without a flicker of recognition. The only thing full of vitality about the bloke at the moment was the light shining in his red veined eyes. Vengeance is mine, sayeth Roger Wilcox. And why not? thought Ted. His shift was all but over. "I must need my fucking head read." He stood up. "Come on, let's go."

Ted Beauchamp thought he'd seen it all during his twenty years with the Met, but the sight of Sally Carpenter in that hospital bed nearly did his head in. "Jesus Christ," he muttered, staring in horror at the young woman's bruised and battered face.

"You should see the rest of her," said the nurse who'd led them to Sally's bedside. "There's barely an inch of her he didn't rip open with his belt buckle."

"How do you know it was his belt?" asked Ted.

"She told me," said the nurse.

"Jesus Christ," Ted repeated, "you mean she can talk?"

The nurse shrugged. "She comes and goes. The state she's in, she's better off unconscious. I hope you catch the bastard."

Ted looked over at Roger. "Well?"

Roger seemed unable to tear his gaze away from the pathetic creature on the bed, but he shook his head. "No," he said sadly. "She's not a blonde. If I'm right, he only goes after blondes."

"She may not be a blonde now," said the nurse, reaching over to open a drawer of the bedside table. She withdrew a bloodied blonde wig and held it up for their inspection, "But she was last night."

Even hanging limply in the nurse's hand, Roger could see the cut of the wig was not dissimilar to Cynthia Werring's blonde bob.

A slight movement from the bed captured everyone's attention.

Sally Carpenter opened one puffy eye. The other eye was swollen shut completely. She tried to raise a hand to her head, winced with pain and let the hand fall back to her side. The nurse picked a glass of water off the bedside table and held the straw to Sally's cracked and swollen lips with one hand, while gently raising the girl's head off the pillow with the other.

Sally sipped at the water gratefully. She looked first at Ted, whose uniform proclaimed his identity, then at the rumpled man beside him. "Who are you?" she asked Roger. "Bleeding Columbo?"

Roger smiled at the comment on his sartorial style, but said nothing. He didn't think he could. As difficult as it was to estimate beneath the bruises, he suspected Sally was no more than his elder daughter's age.

Ted asked the nurse if Sally was up to answering some questions. When she nodded, he pulled up a chair beside the bed. "What can you tell us about the man who did this to you?" he asked Sally gently.

Sally shut her less battered eye, whether to fight back tears or concentrate on the question it was difficult to guess.

"It was that rich bastard," she said. "Everyone knows him. He only likes blondes." She opened her eye again and looked at Roger. "I thought it was me lucky day, no one else around and me in me blonde wig." She attempted a smile, then winced with pain.

Roger smiled at her encouragingly. She didn't seem to

want to make eye contact with Ted, so Roger asked the question. "What does everyone know about him?"

"He likes it rough." She tried to shrug and winced again. "Lots do. Sometimes he gets carried away. But he always pays extra for that." Her open eye suddenly looked wildly round the cubicle. "My money!" she said, trying to reach for the bedside table, crying out in pain when she failed.

Ted looked enquiringly at the nurse, who shook her head. He'd check later with the local nick, but he was sure what the answer would be. "I'm sorry, Sally," he said, "there's no money."

Although there were tears welling up in her eye, Sally stuck her chin out proudly. "Bastard," she said, fighting back the tears, "must've thought he'd killed me, so he didn't have to pay."

"Oh, he'll pay, Sally," Ted said and it was clear he meant it. "Don't you worry about that."

She looked back at Roger. "Rich bastards never pay."

He's going to pay this time, Roger promised himself silently. If it really was Ormond. "What did he look like, Sally?" he asked.

"Tall," she began, the words coming slowly. "White hair, black eyebrows, thousand pound suit, fifty thousand pound Jag."

"Would you recognise him if you saw him again?" Roger asked.

"I'm hardly likely to forget, am I?"

"Do you know any other women who would come forward?"

Sally considered. "Meg might. He roughed her up pretty bad. Mind you," she added with a painful wave of her hand, indicating her own prone form, "nothing like this. At least she got to keep the bleeding money."

Roger sensed Ted tensing beside him. Hardly surprising, really. He was close to losing it himself at the thought of Ormond beating and leaving this girl for dead. He wondered fleetingly whether he had enough money in his savings to reimburse Sally, then realised he had no savings. Time to worry about quite how much he'd been spending in the Stamford Arms later. "Anything else, Sally?" he asked. "Did he say anything?"

"Oh, yes," said Sally. "Over and over. Every time he hit me. 'Whore,' he said, 'bitch, Cynthia'."

"Cynthia?" Roger repeated.

"Yes." Sally gave up the painful attempt to nod her head. "'He always calls us Cynthia."

Roger shot a questioning look at Ted. The police sergeant, his expression hard as steel, nodded to say, yes, the case was now open again.

"Do you know who the bleeder is?" demanded Sally.

"Yeah, Sally," Roger nodded, "we do now. Thanks to you."

"Well, what the hell are you waiting for?" she asked, jerking her head painfully towards the door. "Go get him, Columbo."

Ted asked the nurse to direct him to the nearest phone. Out in the corridor he said to Roger, "I'm going to get a photographer over here. That girl's face is evidence."

"Do that," said Roger. "I'm going to Brighton."

In the fog shrouded atmosphere of the one smoking carriage on the train to Brighton, Roger sat down and lit a Silk Cut. He'd just come back from having a slash in the gents, where he'd made the mistake of looking at his reflection in the mirror, something he seldom did. The bloodshot eyes of the man who'd stared back at him were all too familiar. God knew he'd nicked himself shaving often enough staring into those eyes. He wanted a drink. A large scotch by preference, but a pissy glass of lager would do. Anything. But anything, he knew, would be one thing too much. Thank God there wasn't a bar on the train.

When they drew into the station at Brighton, Roger alighted, weaving slightly despite or perhaps, he admitted to himself, because of the lack of alcohol. He made his way to the tourist information centre, hoping he wasn't on a fool's errand.

"I'm going to open a bed and breakfast in Brighton," she'd said the last time he saw her. That was fourteen years ago. Even if that really had been her plan, there was no guarantee she was still here or using the same name. Hell, she might be married by now with half a dozen kids – and wouldn't that make her happy to see him?

In the tourist centre he demanded to see the most complete listing they had of local bed and breakfasts. It took him a while, but he found it: Magdalene Bed & Breakfast, P. Hall, proprietress. Roger smiled at the irony. Who the hell said you could lead a whore to culture but you couldn't make her think? He made his way back to the station, climbed into one of the waiting taxis and gave the address of the Magdalene B&B.

Moments after he rang the bell, the door opened. The welcoming smile on Polly's face turned into a frown as recognition dawned. "Roger," she said, "what the hell are you doing here?"

The bruises were long gone, even the scar on her left cheek had all but disappeared. Fifteen years later, the resemblance to Cynthia Werring was still striking.

"Polly," he said, "the bastard's still at it. You've got to help me."

"God, Roger, you look rough," said Polly, waving him in and leading the way to the parlour.

It was the second time in one day someone had said that to Roger, the third if he counted the time he'd said it to himself in the toilet on the train. "I know, Polly," he told her. "I haven't had a drink today." He couldn't believe it was less than twenty-four hours since Tilly had handed him that mug of coffee.

"Oh, sorry." Polly was on her feet. "Can I get you something? I've got a bottle of brandy somewhere."

"No," said Roger, a trifle more loudly than he'd intended. Polly sat down again. "Listen, Poll, I've just come from University College Hospital." He told her about Sally Carpenter, sparing no gruesome detail about the girl's appearance.

"Cynthia?" repeated Polly when he got to that part of his story.

"Does that name mean something to you?" Roger asked quickly.

"Yes," Polly said, looking down at her hands folded neatly in her lap. "He called me that that night when – " Polly paused to take a deep breath. "That night when he beat me senseless."

"Why the bloody hell didn't you tell someone back then?" Roger demanded. He knew the name Cynthia hadn't meant anything to Ted, so it obviously hadn't surfaced in the original enquiry.

"Would it have made any difference?" Polly demanded. Although there was a possibility that the name might have come up in court and Cynthia Werring might have come forward to testify about what a bastard her brother-in-law was, Roger had to admit it probably wouldn't have made any difference. "Look, Roger," Polly said, "there were a lot of things about that night I blocked out. I didn't even remember the Cynthia business until two years later when there was an old woman staying here called Cynthia. I nearly screamed when she introduced herself. It's a miracle she stayed. She must've thought I was barking. It wasn't until later I realised why the name upset me so much."

"Polly, I'm sorry to drag all this up for you again, I really am. But it's not just you. There's this girl last night and she reckons she knows at least one other woman who'll come forward. There were probably others before you. I never thought about it at the time." No, Roger acknowledged to himself, he certainly hadn't thought about it at the time. All he'd been able to think about when Polly Hall came to the paper that night was the opportunity he, Roger Wilcox, working class hero and scoop artist extraordinaire, had to stick it to a toff. That's all Polly had been to him then – until he was threatened with the dock himself – a story. "Ted Beauchamp's opening a new case against Ormond. Polly, you've got to testify against him."

"I can't, Roger," she told him.

"Oh, come on, Poll," he said, exasperated. "You must want to see him finally pay for what he did to you."

"Roger, I said I can't and I mean it. When his solicitor paid me off, I signed an agreement that I would never testify against Ormond."

"Oh, Polly, for God's sake!"

"No, Roger. I'm sorry I let you down before, but I got enough money out of Ormond to put a deposit on this place. I got out of that life for good. I'm a respectable business woman. What would I have got going to court? Five minutes on the front page and then back on the street until some other bastard killed me. As far as I'm concerned, Ormond's already paid for what he did to me."

"What about the others, eh, Poll? He didn't pay Sally Carpenter. He left her for dead and took his money with him." Polly winced. Roger wished he'd waited to get a photo of Sally from Ted. "Come on, Poll. Come back to London with me and talk to Ted."

"How old is she, this girl?" Polly asked.

"I don't know. It's hard to recognise her as a human being. If I had to guess, I'd say nineteen."

Polly shook her head sadly. Roger leaned forward to press his advantage, but she held up a silencing hand. "No, Roger, I'm not coming up to London with you. I'm not talking to Ted Beauchamp and if you send him here, I'll deny ever hearing the name Cynthia before. I've worked hard to put all that behind me and I'm damned if I'm going to put myself through it again. You've got the girl. Put her black and blue face on the front page this time. I'm out of it."

Roger opened his mouth to speak, but there was no point. Polly was already holding the parlour door open for him.

On the train back to London, the smoking carriage was mercifully empty, although it still reeked of stale tobacco smoke. Roger realised with annoyance that he only had one cigarette left in his pack. He lit it and considered what to do next. He wished Tilly all the luck in the world trying to prevent VACO shipping its catastrophic seeds to Bowinda, but frankly African famines were the last thing on his mind. Victor Ormond had ruined Roger's life and Roger wanted to nail him, not for unethical business practices, but for the crime which had lost Roger his job, his wife and his home. Victor Ormond beat up women for kicks and if it was the last thing Roger did, he was going to see to it that Victor Ormond went to gaol for it.

Roger became aware of a pungent odour overpowering even the stale smoke. It took him a moment to identify the smell and when he did he sighed. Christ, he thought, when was the last time I had a bath?

CHAPTER ELEVEN

Twenty minutes after leaving the Ormond estate, Tilly and Cynthia were seated at a table, the only customers in one of those newly refurbished, Identikit, supposedly rustic pubs which seemed to have replaced all the honest to God country pubs Tilly remembered from her youth in Suffolk. The drive had been excruciating for Tilly who hadn't been behind the wheel of a car in years. Luckily Cynthia had been far too distracted to notice the regular crashing of gears.

Tilly purchased an orange juice for herself and a large gin and tonic for Helen's mother. After they'd taken seats at a table by the window which offered a scenic view of the car park, Cynthia looked at her and said, "Do you smoke?"

Tilly shook her head. "No. I gave it up years ago."

"Yes," Cynthia nodded, "so did I." She glanced around the pub, excused herself and stood up. Crossing to the cigarette machine on the wall to the left of the bar, she inserted several coins, and returned to the table with a packet of Benson and Hedges, which she began to unwrap.

Tilly waited patiently until the other woman had her cigarette going before prompting her. "Do you have any idea what this is about?"

"Oh, yes," Cynthia replied, "I know what this is about." She flicked her cigarette in the ashtray, looked up towards the ceiling as if seeking inspiration, lips pressed tightly together, then glanced back at Tilly, shaking her beautifully coifed head. "I just don't know where to begin."

Tilly smiled encouragingly. "The beginning is usually a good place to start," she said.

Cynthia considered for a moment, then nodded. She sucked in some more smoke, then began. "I was hired by Amelia Ormond to redecorate part of the house after her husband died. I went to the house for the weekend. I knew as soon as Amelia introduced them to me before dinner that both Victor and Charles fancied me," Cynthia made this last statement in the dismissive tone of a woman used to being instantly fancied by men. She was still a beautiful woman. Tilly, who simply couldn't imagine herself ever having to worry about tripping over inert suitors, didn't doubt for a moment that in her younger years Cynthia Werring had done a lot of tiptoeing around the men who'd fallen, smitten, at her feet. "I wasn't the least bit interested. Victor might have been quite handsome in those days, but he was creepy as hell." She shuddered as she said it, then leaned forward to stub out her cigarette. "Charles was just another rich pretty boy, full of himself and how irresistible he was."

It was Arthur, the quiet, nondescript one, to whom she felt drawn. No one was more surprised by this than Cynthia. Despite all her efforts over the weekend to make it clear to Arthur that she liked him and to Victor that she didn't, it was Victor Ormond who turned up, uninvited, at her flat the following week with a diamond ring in his pocket and the notion clearly fixed in his head that she would be amenable to a marriage proposal.

"I should have known then that he was insane," she said, reaching for her gin and tonic and taking a sip. "He seemed so astonished when I told him I couldn't possibly be less interested. He wasn't hurt, more angry, as if I'd been leading him on." She glanced at Tilly. "I assure you I hadn't been."

Tilly nodded. She believed Cynthia, although frankly she didn't care. She was more interested in the certainty with which the other woman claimed that Victor Ormond was insane. Ever since the beating of the prostitute which had cost Roger his job, she'd thought of Victor Ormond as a very nasty piece of work, and certainly any man who beat up women had some seriously unacceptable behavioural problems, but she'd never quite made the jump to thinking the head of VACO was actually insane. As she watched Cynthia pull another cigarette from the pack in front of her, she found herself thinking of Nancy Astor and lengthy, undisclosed illnesses.

"What did Robert Ormond die of?" she asked.

Cynthia paused in the act of lighting up, the match flame hovering half an inch from the end of the cigarette. "I wish I knew," she said, dropping the match in the ashtray when the flame had almost reached her fingers. "All I can tell you is that Arthur, back in the days when we were happily married, used to have nightmares sometimes about his father's illness. After one particularly awful nightmare, he told me his father was basically a ranting, slobbering, occasionally violent gibbering idiot for the last two years of his life. Apparently their grandfather had been more than a little gaga towards the end, too. Arthur used to have the odd bouts of doubts about the long term prospects for his own sanity." She picked up the book of matches and finished the job of lighting her cigarette. "Arthur's fine. If Robert Ormond had any mental disorders to pass on to either of his sons, they all went straight to Victor."

There it was again, thought Tilly, the terms of Robert Ormond's will fresh in her mind from going through her VACO files the other night. Either of his sons, Cynthia had said, not any of his sons. Of course it might just be a grammatical error. God knows there were an astonishing number of seemingly bright people whose grasp of grammar was far from perfect.

"What about Charles?" she asked.

Cynthia smiled. "Other than being far too full of himself for his own good, Charles is free from the curse of Robert."

Ah, thought Tilly, so she'd been right to wonder about the wording. Still, from what she'd read about him, it was odd that Robert Ormond would have accepted and given an equal share in his estate to another man's son. Before she could ask the question, Cynthia was supplying the answer.

"About three months after Arthur's Uncle James died, a young woman turned up with a one-month-old baby who was the right blood type and the image of James in his baby pictures. Amelia took one look and fell in love with the baby. The young woman was paid off, a birth certificate secured and an announcement placed in the *Times*."

No wonder Charles Ormond's arrival in the world had been described as unexpected. "Does he know?" Tilly asked.

"Oh, yes," said Cynthia. "Victor never tired of calling him

'the bastard' when Amelia wasn't around. Charles couldn't stand him, which was hardly surprising."

Cynthia's early relations with Charles had been quite jovial. She'd been furious when she found out that it was Charles who'd put Victor up to proposing to her, particularly when he announced that he'd only got Victor going so that he'd be doubly upset when he, Charles, stepped in and succeeded with Cynthia. Still, unlike Victor, he'd taken it in his stride when she firmly rejected his advances, and wished her joy when his shy and painfully slow moving brother Arthur finally got around to proposing.

Cynthia had accepted his proposal without qualm and set about divesting herself of her thriving business. "My London friends thought I was mad," she told Tilly, after describing the "darling little cottage" she and Arthur had bought for their home. Tilly, who'd never been married nor particularly close to ever becoming married, had never been able to fathom women who just blithely gave up their lives after the ring went on the third finger of their left hand. Well, of course, there was one possible exception.

"Were you pregnant?" she asked.

Cynthia glanced at her sharply and Tilly could tell she'd hit a nerve, although she wasn't sure why. It wasn't as if it was the most extraordinarily tactless question Tilly had ever asked. It had, after all, been the seventies. Why should the question trigger quite such an intense reaction?

"No," Cynthia said finally, her tone stiff, "I wasn't." She seemed to give herself a mental shake, reached for the cigarettes, tossed the pack back on the table, then looked up at Tilly, whose puzzlement must have still been clear on her face. "I'm sorry," she said, deciding to light up yet another cigarette after all. "You just cut straight to the chase there."

Tilly lifted her glass and took a sip of her orange juice, knowing the other woman would continue without prompting, which she did.

"It took me four years to get pregnant," Cynthia told her, "and even then it was a bit of a miracle. After two years I went for some tests. After three years I finally convinced Arthur to do the same. It turned out his sperm count was practically in the minus range."

Tilly couldn't help wondering if Arthur's sperm count might not have been affected by all the chemicals he'd been exposed to as a child in his father's lab, but decided a conversational detour down Endocrine Disruption Road probably wasn't useful at the moment. Besides, she doubted Cynthia would have any idea what the endocrine system was. Instead, she simply said, "You must have both been thrilled."

There was another hesitation before Cynthia said, "I think I need to set the scene for you a little."

Three and a half years after Cynthia and Arthur's marriage, Amelia Ormond had suffered a stroke which left her virtually paralysed on her left side. Although she would never have dreamt of making the request, it had been clear to both Arthur and Cynthia that what Amelia wanted was to have her family together under one roof. Against her better judgement and on what Arthur had promised would only be a temporary basis, Cynthia had agreed to move to the Ormond estate.

Despite her best efforts over the years to establish a cordial in-law relationship with Victor, she still found contact with him a strain. Yes, he could maintain a veneer of civility when she and Arthur visited the house, but there would invariably be a point when Cynthia would turn to find Victor's icy grey eyes boring into her, an expression of absolute loathing on his face. Charles, who seemed to be the only other member of the family who was aware of the tension, had suggested, his serious tone belying the smile on his face, that she might want to avoid being alone with Victor. Cynthia had hardly needed the advice.

By the time of Amelia's stroke, Charles had set himself up in New York as the VACO presence in North America. He visited frequently immediately after the stroke, but the relief his presence provided Cynthia was only in fits and starts.

The days spent working with Amelia and the physiotherapist had been fine. Cynthia had a deep and abiding love for Amelia, who had in so many ways become a mother to the orphaned Cynthia. Her desire to help the indomitable Amelia regain her physical strength and pride had helped her spur her mother-in-law far past the limited bounds of the physiotherapist, who would have otherwise been forcibly ejected from Amelia's presence in short order. Although she cursed both her daughter-in-law and the physiotherapist, Amelia's gratitude to Cynthia had been heart-warmingly obvious.

After three months, Amelia's progress had been astonishing. Although she would walk with a cane for the rest of her life, she had regained most of the strength in her left hand and all of her impaired speech. She had insisted then that Cynthia, who'd worked herself into a state of exhaustion, must have a vacation.

What Cynthia had really wanted was her own home, but she had settled for a month in Spain with Arthur. One night, after a fairy tale-like day touring the Alhambra, the stunningly beautiful Moorish palace in Granada, Arthur and Cynthia had retired to bed early and to sleep late. Cynthia had known the moment she woke up the next morning that she was pregnant. Recalling old biology lessons, she'd reminded herself that it wasn't the moment of ejaculation that counted, that fertilisation could be hours later. Perhaps it hadn't happened yet, but she'd been as sure as anything she'd ever been sure of in her life that at that moment, one of Arthur's sperm was successfully battling the odds and swimming like a fiend.

She hadn't dared say anything to Arthur, because he was a bloody scientist and if he'd tried to challenge her woman's intuition she would have had to thump him. Instead, she'd hugged the knowledge to herself, looking forward eagerly to returning to England, making an appointment with the doctor and presenting Arthur with irrefutable proof.

Unfortunately, no sooner had they returned to Kent than Arthur discovered some catastrophe had erupted in their absence, requiring his immediate presence in Asia. Oh, well, Cynthia had thought, it's only been a week, the doctor might not even be able to tell yet. She had been alternately thrilled to learn that Amelia was feeling sufficiently recovered to accept an invitation from an old friend for a weekend of bridge and gossip, appalled at the prospect of spending a weekend alone in the house with Victor and relieved to hear that Charles was planning a short visit en route to a conference in Amsterdam.

Charles arrived from New York the next morning just as Arthur was departing for Bangkok. It was a blisteringly hot day and it hadn't been difficult for Charles to persuade her to go for a swim. Cynthia had been dying to tell someone her news, so when Charles made some crack about her stunning figure, she'd grinned and told him she doubted he'd say the same in eight months. When the penny failed to drop, she'd announced her happy state.

Charles had appeared suitably impressed, especially as Arthur had led him to believe that children were going to be unlikely. He'd asked if she was sure. Cynthia hadn't hesitated a moment before assuring him she was indeed pregnant. Charles had simply grimaced and said rather her than him.

Cynthia, who'd assumed Charles would be around for dinner that evening, was dismayed to discover she was dining alone with Victor. Squashing the urge to plead a sudden headache, she'd seated herself opposite her brother-in-law, hoping for the best. Her hopes had been almost immediately dashed.

When Victor looked up from his plate, his icy eyes had been filled with hatred. This was, she'd realised, the first time she had been alone with him since the night she'd so unceremoniously rejected his proposal of marriage. The realisation had been quite nerve racking.

After several attempts to start an innocuous conversation were met with nothing but Victor's intense stare, Cynthia had finally done what she should have when she walked into the room and found herself alone with her brother-in-law. She excused herself with the announcement of the sudden onset of a blinding headache. It had not been far from the truth. Victor had thrown a pall over her high spirits.

A long soak in the tub had helped considerably – that and the large gin and tonic she'd taken in with her. She'd surrendered herself to thoughts of the daughter she was convinced she was going to have. I am, she'd decided as she towelled herself dry, going to be the best mother any child ever had.

After wrapping a dry towel around herself, she'd walked

through the door which joined their bathroom to their bedroom. It had taken her a moment to spot Victor sitting in a chair, staring at her. He was between her and the door where her robe was hanging on a hook. She'd tightened the folds of the towel under her arm and demanded to know what the hell he was doing there, although it was a rhetorical question at best.

The way he was leering at her had needed no explanation. Somehow managing to sound considerably more calm than she felt, she'd told him to get the hell out.

He hadn't budged for several seconds, and when he did it was to stand up and take a step towards her. In a tone, belied by the madness in his eyes, as falsely calm as her own had been, he had informed her that she had humiliated him, first with Charles, then with Arthur. He was the eldest. By rights she should have been his.

When she'd threatened to scream for help, he'd simply laughed and told her he'd given the servants all an unexpected night off. There was no one to hear her if she screamed. Besides, he'd said with a sickening smile, he knew this was what she really wanted.

Cynthia, fighting to keep the rising hysteria from her voice, had assured him it was certainly not what she wanted and tried to remind him that she was his brother's wife.

The sickening smile disappeared, but the scowl which replaced it had been no improvement. Arthur, he told her, couldn't have everything. First he'd stolen their father's attention from Victor, then he'd stolen Cynthia. It wasn't right.

Cynthia's heartbeat had been so frenzied she could hear the blood rushing around in her head. No amount of heaving gulps seemed to be able to get any air into her lungs. She could see there was to be no reasoning with him. Even if she could somehow get past him, get to the door, where would she go? There were cars in the garage, but were there keys in the cars? The servants had been sent off. If she screamed, no one would come. Even if someone had still been in the house and heard her scream, would they come? Would they be in time? Over her fear and over her revulsion at the thought of Victor Ormond touching her, over everything, all Cynthia had been able to think about was the need to protect the precious life within her.

It was too soon. Victor's attack could dislodge the baby from her womb. There might never be another child. Somehow she had to placate him. Somehow she had to prevent this awful thing happening to her. Fighting back tears, she had pleaded with him to go away, promising never to tell anyone, if he would just go away.

The sickening smile had returned. He took another step towards her. Cynthia had recoiled instinctively. The smile vanished from his face. Suddenly he was across the room, his hand wrenching the towel from her grasp. Cynthia had screamed then, although she knew it would do her no good. She raised her hands and, with every ounce of strength she possessed, had shoved against Victor's chest. Surprised and knocked off balance, Victor had fallen to the floor. Cynthia had tried to run, but he grabbed her ankle.

The next thing she knew, she was on her back on the carpet and Victor was on top of her, clawing and slobbering over her body, groaning and cursing. As he tried to prise her legs apart, Cynthia had fought him with all her might, punching at his head and chest. But, desperate as she was, she was no match for the strength of mad Victor. At the very moment she'd thought it was over, as, tears streaming down her cheeks, she'd braced herself for the horror of Victor thrusting inside her, an awful sound, like no sound she'd ever heard a human make, had escaped from him. And then he'd collapsed on the floor beside her.

There was a sticky, warm puddle on her belly. She'd grabbed the towel and used it to frantically rub at the awful liquid, but no matter how hard she rubbed, it had still felt as if her skin was on fire. Victor had turned away from her and was curled up in the foetal position, his body racked with sobs. Cynthia had crawled on her hands and knees across the room. Using the doorknob, she'd pulled herself upright and removed her robe from the back to the door.

Standing in the corridor shivering and clutching the robe tightly around herself, she had looked up and down the hallway, knowing she must find somewhere to hide before Victor regained what limited sense he possessed. But she couldn't move. She took one tentative step, then collapsed on the floor. Giving in completely to her sense of desolation, she had leaned against the wall, knees up to her chin, tears flowing down her cheeks.

That was how Charles had found her when he came up the stairs a few minutes later.

CHAPTER TWELVE

Tilly stared at Cynthia in horror. She had on more than one occasion in more than one war torn hellhole been attacked. She could certainly empathise with the woman sitting opposite her. Except Tilly, of course, had never been fighting for the survival of a foetus.

"Bloody hell," she said, not quite sure what else to say or do. She was not, had never been the sort of person to throw her arms around almost complete strangers to give them reassuring hugs. Besides, Cynthia did not seem the sort of person who would welcome a reassuring hug from an almost complete stranger. A pat on the hand would be wholly inadequate. "You rang the police?"

Cynthia shook her head as she reached into her bag for a lacy white handkerchief. "Charles wanted me to, but all I could think of was what it would do to Amelia – and Arthur." She sniffed as she dabbed at her eyes with the handkerchief. "God, I wish I had. In the end it would saved a lot of misery." With that pronouncement, she blew her nose, a robust and surprisingly loud blow for such an elegant woman.

Tilly glanced surreptitiously at her watch. It was three o'clock. As appalling as this insight into Victor Ormond's psyche had been and as certain as she was that there was a great deal more to Cynthia's story, she wasn't any closer to finding Helen or fitting the pieces together for her article. "I think we should get back to London," she said, fervently hoping Cynthia would agree. Tilly sure as hell needed to get back as soon as she could and unfortunately the car was not hers.

Cynthia stuffed the now sodden handkerchief back in her bag. "Yes," she said decisively. "I have to get on to the police. I should have done that straight away, but I was so sure I knew

Unethical Practices

where she'd be." She rolled her eyes as she stood up and managed a tight lipped smile. "I can tell you the rest of the sordid story on the way back."

Tilly nodded with relief and stood up. As she was shrugging into her Mac, Cynthia rooted round in her bag and pulled out a mobile phone. "Damn," she said, tossing it back in her bag. "Battery's flat." Cynthia looked around the pub, spotted a phone on the wall. Making towards it, she said over her shoulder, "Just let me try Helen's flat. I'll feel such a fool going to the police if she's sitting at home. And, if she's not at her flat, I'll try Jamie. Perhaps he's heard from her."

As they walked towards the phone, Cynthia began to fish through her purse for change. Tilly, recalling Jamie's name being mentioned earlier, asked again who he was.

"He's Helen's oldest friend. They seem to have had a falling out when Helen found out he'd taken a job with VACO. He's a chemist. He works with my husband."

Ah, ha, thought Tilly, finally. "If you don't find Helen, could you ask Jamie to meet us at your flat?"

Cynthia nodded, although it was obvious she could see no purpose in the request, then deposited a pound coin and punched in a number. After several rings, Tilly could hear the beeps of an answering machine kicking in. Cynthia cleared her throat, then spoke into the phone.

"Helen? Darling, it's Mummy. If you're there, please pick up." She listened for a moment then said, "Darling, ring me the second you get in. I know Victor's tried to hurt you. We must talk. It's a lie." Cynthia glanced up at the nicotine-stained pub ceiling, clearly fighting back tears. "Helen, it's not true. Ring me."

She severed the connection, then punched in another number, asking for Jamie Mortimer. Their conversation was brief. When it was finished, Cynthia looked at Tilly. "Jamie sounds worried," she said, sounding far from sanguine herself. "He says he'll call round later."

"Some other friend?" suggested Tilly.

Cynthia shrugged. "Not that she's ever mentioned." Her gaze, when her astonishing aquamarine eyes met Tilly's, was sad. "My daughter and I get on very well, Ms Arbuthnot, but she can be quite secretive. The only reason I know she's got

115

some fella is the unmistakable glow when she comes back from one of their trips."

Tilly decided she'd better check her own machine. She fished in her pocket for some change. "Arthur?" she asked, reaching for the receiver. It seemed a long shot, but you never knew.

Cynthia shook her head. "No. Helen told me he's in Singapore."

Tilly paused in the middle of punching in numbers, glanced over her shoulder. "Charles?"

"Charles?" repeated Cynthia, her tone incredulous. "She hasn't seen Charles since she was six."

There were ten messages on Tilly's machine. The first two were from Baldwin, mumbling something about not getting through to Dr Conquest. The third was from Gus MacPherson, the news editor, asking somewhat sarcastically when she planned to deign to tell him whether or not she had a story for the next morning's paper. The fourth message was from Baldwin, informing her he'd contacted Dr Conquest and sent the fax. The fifth was Gus again, sarcasm replaced by urgency.

The sixth message was from Jack Conquest: "Holy shit, Tilly. Call me when you get this message. I've borrowed someone's brain fryer. Here's the number." Tilly scribbled the number down as Jack's voice reeled it off, noticing after he'd rung off that he hadn't given her any idea what bloody country the phone was registered in, let alone any dialling code. The seventh message was Jack ringing back to correct that oversight. The eighth message was from Roger, informing her that he was on to something – no mention of what – and would try to contact her later. The ninth and tenth messages were from an increasingly apoplectic Gus demanding an instant reply which Tilly decided there was little point in making until she knew whether or not she actually had a story.

With an apologetic smile to Cynthia, she quickly punched in Jack's mobile number. He answered after the first ring and wasted no time on pleasantries. "Listen, Tilly, I'd have to verify this, but if Arthur Ormond's dotted his i's and crossed his t's, this is one scary fuck up. Have you rung the police?"

"And told them what?" she answered his question with a question.

There was a silence while Jack considered. It was, of course, true that no law had been broken. VACO had withdrawn the product. "Okay, listen," Jack repeated, "I don't know whether that blithering idiot who rang me was supposed to fax the memo from Ormond to Radad as well, but he did."

"Shit," was all Tilly could think to say. Bloody Baldwin. It wasn't that she minded Jack knowing. She'd maintained enough confidences for him over the years to know she could trust him with hers. The expletive was more a response to the urgency of the situation. While she'd been accompanying Cynthia Werring on this wild goose chase to Kent, Victor Ormond, wherever he was, was organising the shipment of a freeze dried famine to Bowinda. Even if she rang the police, there was nothing they could do except cite her for wasting their time. If, God forbid, she couldn't find Helen in time, the shipment would be gone and even a front page story in the British press might not deter Radad from magnanimously handing out the seeds to the Kisga. "Shit," she said again. There must be something she could do. "Listen," she threw back at Jack, "how's your green credibility at the moment?"

Jack chuckled. "A few people owe me favours, if that's what you mean."

"Could you call them in?" Better eco warriors than no warriors. "That shipment's due to leave VACO HQ this evening. Any chance of organising a rent a mob?"

There was a crackling noise at the other end of the line. Tilly thought the mobile had packed in, but a moment later Jack was back. "Leave it with me. No promises, but I'll see what I can do. I'm in a taxi on the way to the station. I couldn't change my flight, so I'm getting the train. I'll be back in London tonight. Keep me posted."

Holy shit, thought Tilly, echoing Jack's first phone message. Jack Conquest giving up an opportunity to lecture Eurocrats? That research must be scary.

Cynthia, who'd given up and gone to the Ladies, returned just as Tilly and Jack said their goodbyes. Before she could recommence her foot tapping, Tilly shot her another apologetic smile and walked away from the phone. As they passed their table, Cynthia paused to pick up the packet of Benson and Hedges. She stared at it for a moment, then tossed it back down.

Outside the pub, Cynthia claimed, despite her emotionally wrought state – not to mention two large gin and tonics – to be quite capable of driving. Tilly wasn't sure which was more harrowing, Cynthia's driving or her own. The other woman would certainly get them back to London much faster. She handed back the car keys.

"Arthur really is Helen's father?" Tilly asked when they were both settled in the car and Cynthia had switched on the ignition. She attempted to make her tone as diplomatic as possible. If Cynthia had actually been impregnated by Victor during a rape, Tilly could certainly understand her not wanting to admit it to anyone, including herself.

"Oh, yes," Cynthia answered flatly as she accelerated and, gravel flying, they shot out of the pub car park and onto the B road. "I insisted we have blood tests done after Arthur got it into his head that Charles was Helen's father."

"Charles?" Tilly repeated. Bloody hell, where did that leap get made?

Cynthia sighed, keeping her eyes on the road, which was just as well, the speed she was going. "It was, if you'll pardon my French, a fucking nightmare."

Charles had, Cynthia told Tilly, dealt with Victor by packing him off the morning after the attack to the conference in Amsterdam which Charles himself had been planning to attend. He had then gone to work on Amelia, convincing his mother it was her idea Cynthia and Arthur should get back to their own home. By the time Victor had returned from Amsterdam, Cynthia and Arthur were safely back in their cottage, basking in the doctor's confirmation that Cynthia was indeed pregnant.

When Helen was born with a full head of jet black hair, the colour Victor's hair had been before it turned silver, it had given Cynthia a bit of a turn. But she knew there'd been no penetration, no chance that Victor could have impregnated her during his attack. She'd felt much better after the jolly Jamaican nurse informed her that babies born with full heads of hair never kept it, that the black hair would soon fall out and be replaced, in all probability with Cynthia's own white blonde hair. Arthur and Amelia had both been thrilled with Helen's birth, but neither could have been as happy as Cynthia herself.

"He came to the hospital that night," Cynthia said, as she shot the car on to the motorway right in front of a lorry, the driver of which let her know what he thought with a long blast of his horn.

"Victor?" Tilly asked for confirmation, as Cynthia rolled down her window to give the lorry driver the finger.

"Yes," Cynthia said, cutting across another two lanes and earning another two horn blasts. "I woke up and there he was, bending over the bassinet. I nearly had a heart attack."

Tilly, whose own heart was beating rather rapidly thanks to Cynthia's driving, gripped the edge of her seat and said she could well understand.

Victor had wasted no time informing Cynthia that Helen was his daughter. Cynthia, unable to convince him it was biologically impossible to impregnate a woman by ejaculating on to her stomach, had rung for a nurse, who took one look at her patient's distraught expression before frog marching Victor out of the room with surprising ease.

Still hysterical, Cynthia had rung Charles in New York. He'd managed to get himself on to a flight that night and was at the nursing home by mid-morning. Once again he'd tried to persuade Cynthia to report the attempted rape to the police, or, at the very least tell Arthur about it. Once again she'd refused, unable to bear the thought of what the revelation might do to Amelia.

"Stupid decision," said Cynthia, shaking her head at the memory and flashing her headlights at the driver of a Granada who was stubbornly refusing to exceed the speed limit or to pull over into the other lane. Cynthia kept her foot down on the accelerator and moved to within what seemed to Tilly an inch away from the Granada's rear bumper. Just as Tilly was shutting her eyes and bracing for the crash, the Granada driver veered into the other lane, sounding his horn as Cynthia sped past.

Bloody hell, Tilly thought, this was worse than the drive

down, which had been bad enough. Cynthia Werring was not the worst driver Tilly had ever encountered, but she was certainly the worst driver she'd come across who actually – presumably – had a licence. Nor was this the most alarming experience she'd ever had as a passenger, although it was certainly the worst she'd had outside a war zone. She cleared her throat. As much as she was interested in hearing the rest of the story, she was loath to ask any questions, lest the distraction of answering should cause the fatal car crash which was beginning to seem inevitable. "Do you think you could slow down a bit? I'd really like to get back to London in one piece."

Cynthia shot Tilly a somewhat exasperated look, then glanced at the speedometer which was pushing past 110 miles per hour. "Crikey," she muttered, gripping the wheel in a much more reassuringly firm manner and slowing down to a mere 90 miles per hour. "Sorry about that," she said, shoulder checking and pulling into the centre lane where she slowed down ever further to a modest 80. "I hardly ever drive on the motorway these days and I forget how powerful this car is."

Tilly's heart rate quickly returned to normal or at least what she took to be normal, in the absence of a medical check up in the past ten years. "Did Victor say anything to Arthur?" she asked, unable to believe Victor Ormond would keep it to himself, if he, however misguided, believed himself to be the father or Cynthia's child.

"No," Cynthia answered. "Even though I refused to go to the police, Charles told Victor I would report him if he ever repeated his foul lie about being Helen's father. For good measure, Charles said he would have no qualms about lying to the police and telling them he'd actually witnessed and interrupted the attack."

The threat seemed to do the trick. Cynthia and Arthur had taken Helen home to their cottage and Victor had steered well clear of them. The only times Cynthia saw her detested brother-in-law had been family occasions when there were plenty of other people around and Victor kept his distance.

Four and a half blissful years had passed. Then, late one Saturday night, Amelia Ormond had a second stroke. Of course, Arthur and Cynthia had packed Helen into the car and driven straight to the estate and, of course, they'd said they would stay for a while.

Helen had slept in a cot in the dressing room the first night. The following night she'd been quite happy to be put to bed in the nursery she knew so well from visits to her grandmother's home. Cynthia had tossed and turned a great deal that second night, before getting up to check on Helen. When she got to the nursery, she found Victor there, bending over Helen's bed, stroking her cheek and cooing nonsense. Cynthia had scooped her sleeping child into her arms and made to leave, but Victor had blocked the way. Unlike that other, horrible night years before, she hadn't been afraid. The house was full of people. She'd scream if she must.

Victor had smiled at her, the self satisfied smile of the victor. He'd spoken quietly, but even in a whisper, she'd been able to hear the insanity in his voice and suddenly she was afraid. He told her he would never let her leave with his daughter again. She'd tried once more to reason with the man whose reason was so entirely gone, tried once again to explain that Arthur was Helen's father, that there was no possibility that Victor could have impregnated her, but he hadn't been listening. He just kept smiling. When she'd told him she would go to the police and report his attack, that Charles would back her up, he'd laughed out loud. He said it was too late, that no one would believe her, certainly not Arthur, if Charles was her only witness. Before she could respond, he'd reached out, trying to grab Helen from her arms. Cynthia, without thinking and with precious little satisfaction later, had kneed him in the groin, before fleeing to the room she shared with Arthur. It wasn't until they were outside the door that Helen awoke, her eyes filled with panic. It was, Cynthia had told first Helen, then Arthur, just a nightmare. No lie there – it certainly was a nightmare. She'd kept Helen with them again that night and the next morning had moved her from the nursery back to their dressing room. If anyone thought she was being over protective, no one had said so. Even if they had, Cynthia would not have cared.

"I just thought," Cynthia said, risking a quick glance at Tilly as she signalled left and made for the motorway exit, "oh, God, I don't know what the hell I thought. I thought if I could just get Amelia fixed up again, Arthur and I could go back to the cottage and life could get back to normal."

Once again the physiotherapist had been summoned and once again Cynthia had gone to work with her mother-in-law. After four months, Amelia Ormond had made another extraordinary recovery. Cynthia hadn't realised quite how much it had taken out of her until Barbara, her oldest and dearest friend had descended on them unexpectedly one weekend, straight off a flight from Los Angeles which signalled the end of her marriage to a Hollywood producer.

"Barbara told me I looked like death warmed up and when I actually looked in a mirror, I realised she was right."

Barbara's prescription had been a weekend in London during which Cynthia could help her figure out how to make the Fulham flat she'd got in the divorce settlement habitable. Cynthia, having ascertained that the invitation included Helen – whom she would not have dreamt of leaving alone in the same house as Victor – had accepted.

She had arrived at Barbara's flat to find a surprise party in full swing. All the old Chelsea Bright Lights were there, including Nigel, stylist to the stars, who had taken one look at Cynthia's hair, shrieked in horror and turned the kitchen into an instant salon.

She had arrived back in Kent with a new hair style and a new outlook. The next day she had advertised for and, with the assistance of a visiting Charles, hired a nanny, a cheerful young woman named Jenny, who, with clear infatuation in her hazel eyes, made an unquestioning promise to Charles that she would never, under any circumstances, allow his brother Victor to be alone with Helen. With Jenny on the scene, Cynthia had felt safe popping up to London once a month to lunch with Barbara, see old friends, shop, take in a matinee or the pictures. The brief, monthly escapes had helped, but they weren't enough.

"Amelia was so much better. I just wanted to get back to the cottage," Cynthia said to Tilly, turning sharply down a side street, then slamming on the brakes when confronted with the stationary traffic. Before she could reverse back on to the main road, another car had pulled up behind her. "Damn!"

She pushed the cigarette lighter in, then reached down

beside Tilly's feet to grab her handbag. After peering inside it, she sighed and yanked the lighter back out. "Damn. I knew I shouldn't have left those cigarettes in the pub." She then gave the horn several sharp blasts.

Tilly had never been able to figure out why so many drivers felt the need to sound their horns when they were so far back in the traffic jam they could not possibly surmise the cause, let alone affect the speed at which the problem might – or might not be – resolved. "Do you find that speeds things up in any way?" she asked when the other woman hit the horn again.

Cynthia lifted her hand from the wheel and managed a somewhat rueful smile. "No, obviously it doesn't. It just relieves a bit of the aggravation I suppose."

Just adds noise pollution to the car pollution, Tilly thought but didn't say. Instead she asked, "What prevented you from moving back?"

Cynthia leaned back against the head rest and ran her fingers through her silver blonde hair. "Arthur mostly. He just didn't seem keen. Couldn't see why I wanted to go back to a poky little cottage when I had a huge house filled with servants to take care of my every need." She glanced quickly over her shoulder to see if the traffic behind had magically disappeared, then looked at Tilly, her fingers tapping impatiently on the steering wheel. "I finally put my foot down when Helen was due to start school. I wanted her to have friends, go to the village school, be normal. Arthur eventually agreed, although he did ask that Amelia be given the summer to enjoy her granddaughter." She sighed. When she spoke again, Tilly could hear the bitterness in her voice. "It seemed like such an innocent request."

Tilly waited while Cynthia put the car in gear to move the two and a half feet which had opened up between them and the car in front. "What happened?"

Cynthia thumped her hand on the horn again, although clearly the traffic jam was not the cause of her fury. She turned and looked at Tilly, the look more a glare. "My bastard husband sold the cottage without even telling me."

"Did he say why?"

"Oh, yes." She shook her head at the memory. "He'd been

odd for months. We'd stopped having sex completely. Whenever I asked him what was wrong, he just said he was exhausted from working all the hours God sent at the lab, which he was. I should have known better, but I believed him." Pause while the car leapt forward another eighteen inches. "When the estate agent rang about the cottage and I confronted Arthur about it, he looked so pleased with himself. He said I'd only wanted to move back to the cottage so I'd have more time for my London lovers. Lovers! Jesus. I told him he must be mad. All I ever did in London was have my hair cut by Nigel, who didn't fancy women, and have lunch with Barbara, who, to the best of my knowledge, didn't fancy women either. I said, 'Arthur, unless you imagine I'm shagging someone in the toilets on the train, I don't see how you think I have time for lovers.' He just stared at me, as if he didn't believe a word I was saying. I felt as if I was with an alien. Then I realised I was. Arthur had been contaminated by Victor, filling up his head with God knows what. Arthur as much as admitted it."

Tilly waited for Cynthia to say she'd then told Arthur to get stuffed and stormed out of the house, but Cynthia didn't say any such thing. Tilly told herself not to be so hard on the other woman. An astonishing number of people – both men and women – stayed in relationships long after the curtain should have been brought down on the final act. Something of what she was thinking must have shown in her face, because Cynthia turned in her seat to look directly at her.

"Listen," she said, "I know this must all sound unspeakably lame or as if I'm some sort of nutter, putting up with all that." Tilly said nothing, although she knew her expression probably confirmed the suggestion. Cynthia sighed. "Have you ever read Nancy Mitford's novels about her family?"

Tilly nodded. As improbable as it might seem to many of her acquaintance, she had indeed devoured Nancy Mitford's novels, along with a pile of other delightfully light reading her friend Stella had supplied in the hospital when Tilly was laid up with a bullet wound from Angola. She'd thoroughly enjoyed them all. What she hadn't enjoyed had been the sympathy Stella lavished upon her – bit over the top, given that the other four passengers travelling in the jeep with her were all dead.

Unethical Practices

"Remember the Bolter?" Cynthia asked.

Tilly smiled to acknowledge that she did – the Bolter was the children's mother who was partial to adventures with adventurers.

"Well," said Cynthia, "that was my mother. It was awful when I was a child. Her final fling was when I was in Florence studying art. She ended up in Mexico, abandoned, as usual, and eventually reclaimed by my father. They were on their way to the airport when their car crashed and they both died." She closed her eyes for a moment and took a deep breath, then looked at Tilly again. "I sowed a lot of wild oats in the Swinging Sixties, but when I married, I took my vows very seriously. I didn't want to be a Bolter. It was – or so I thought – for keeps."

A horn blaring behind them drew Cynthia's attention to the fact that the traffic jam had suddenly disappeared and, like so many of these jams in London, did so for absolutely no visible reason. Cynthia shifted gears with her left hand, rolled the window down with her right and, as she accelerated away into the Fulham traffic, gave yet another finger to yet another driver.

In the ten minutes it took them to cover the remaining distance to the South Kensington flat, Cynthia filled in the details of her last weeks at the Ormond estate.

"I went up to London the next morning, something I never did on the weekends. I didn't care what Arthur thought. I just needed to talk to someone sane." Tilly, looking at Cynthia's profile, saw her grimace, then smile slightly. "Not that my friend Barbara is completely sane. I certainly didn't really need to hear what she had to say." She shook her head at the memory, but didn't elaborate until Tilly prompted her.

"Which was?"

Cynthia glanced at her, hesitating a moment, rolling her eyes. "God, it sounds awful to repeat it after all these years, but she said that beautiful women like me should only marry very handsome men who are far too vain to ever suspect their wives of looking at another man." Tilly, who couldn't imagine herself ever being given such advice, said nothing. Cynthia nodded. "Told you it sounded terrible. But Barbara was right. Once the rot set in, there'd never be any going back, at least not while we were still in that house."

They pulled up at a red light and Cynthia turned to face her, holding up an immaculately manicured hand.

"Barbara told me I had three choices. One," she began counting off on her fingers, "I could spend the rest of my life doing everything in my power to convince Arthur I was as pure as the driven snow. He wouldn't believe me, even if he said he did, and I'd be miserable. Two, I could leave him. I'd be miserable, but not forever. Or three, I could have the affair he thought I was having. With a bit of luck I'd actually have some fun before I was miserable, but, again, I'd only be miserable for a while."

"Or," said Tilly, reasonably confident Cynthia had ignored her friend's advice, "none of the above."

Cynthia nodded as she put the car into first gear and moved into the intersection. "Precisely."

"And what was Victor doing all this time?" Tilly asked.

"Lurking," Cynthia replied with a vicious tone and a crash of misjudged gear changing. "Biding his time. Waiting."

"He didn't bother you again?" Tilly found that difficult to believe.

"No." Cynthia shook her head, signalling to turn right to the bottom of her road. "He kept his distance. Except for one time when he cornered me in the hallway after Amelia's birthday luncheon." She shot a quick smile at Tilly before executing the turn. "I'd barely had time to feel afraid of him, when Helen came out of the drawing room, saw him and ran over to kick him in the shin. He howled, rather as I've always imagined a banshee would. It was quite the performance."

Although they were practically at Cynthia's door by that point, it took an almost complete circuit of the square to find a parking spot, and then it took several goes for Cynthia to coax her car into the limited space. While the search and manoeuvre were being conducted Tilly asked what it had finally taken to get her out of the Ormond house.

"Amelia died," Cynthia said simply. "It was another stroke. It killed her," she snapped her fingers, "like that. The night after she died, Arthur came to our room. He'd been sleeping in another room for weeks. I thought he wanted me to comfort him. Instead he came in, fucked me as if I were some sort of whore and went back to his room." As Tilly watched, Cynthia pressed her lips together and it was obvious she was struggling not to cry at the twenty year old memory. She took two unsuccessful shots at squeezing the car into the first parking space they found before continuing. "Two days after the funeral, Barbara rang, desperate to find someone to cat and flat sit for a week. I didn't even think about it. Told her I'd be up that afternoon and would use the week to find a flat or house in town. 'Lovely,' she said, 'and not a decade too soon'. Nor was it."

"Arthur agreed?" Tilly asked as Cynthia finally decided the only gauge of the amount of space available was to keep going until she'd made contact with first the front bumper of the car behind, then the rear bumper of the car in front, repeating the bumps until they were no more than a foot and a half from the kerb.

"I didn't give him any bloody choice, did I?" Cynthia said, shoving her door open and climbing out into the road, oblivious to the oncoming Mini which had to swerve to miss her. "Told him I'd had enough, that I was going to find a house for the three of us, but if it had to be just Helen and me, so be it."

Tilly voiced her surprise that Arthur, and more particularly Victor, had agreed to let Cynthia take Helen away for a week.

"I didn't try," Cynthia told her. "I thought it would be too tiring for her, traipsing all over London looking at houses and flats. I figured she'd be safe with Jenny. Charles was over for the funeral and was staying for a few days. I thought it would be all right. He offered me a lift up to London and the whole time we were driving up I kept making him promise to keep an eye on Helen." She turned and strode purposefully across the square, moving surprisingly quickly for someone in such high heels.

Tilly, with her long legs and sensible cowboy boots, had no difficulty keeping up. She was almost certain she'd guessed the result of Cynthia's last trip to London, but she had to ask. "What happened that week?"

Cynthia stopped so abruptly, Tilly nearly crashed into her. Even in high heels, face to face Cynthia had to look upwards to meet Tilly's gaze. Her look and stance, fists wedged firmly into hips, were quite belligerent. "I finally gave Arthur what he wanted. I had a bloody affair and in the process lost my daughter for six bloody years." Her shoulders sagged. Her fists fell to her sides. And then Cynthia Werring burst into tears.

This time Tilly didn't hesitate about slipping her arm around the other woman's shoulders, leading her over to a bench. Tilly pulled a red and white spotted hankie out of her shoulder bag and handed it to Cynthia, who once again managed an astonishingly hearty blow for such an elegantly turned out woman.

Tilly waited until Cynthia was somewhat recovered before saying, "The affair was with Charles?"

"Oh, yes," Cynthia nodded, her expression showing no surprise that Tilly had guessed. "That's what Arthur couldn't forgive. I don't know what came over me. Charles drove me to Barbara's flat. I invited him in for a coffee." She gazed at Tilly and shook her head, after all these years still unable to believe what happened next. "He just touched the back of my neck. The next thing I knew we were ripping one another's clothes off and screwing in the middle of the lounge. We didn't leave the flat for two days. On the third day I made Charles go back to New York and I did what I originally came for. I found a flat. Then I went back to Kent."

"You told Arthur about the affair?"

"I didn't have to tell him. When I got back to the house, he and Victor were waiting for me. They had pictures of Charles and me, along with a dossier this big," she held her thumb and middle finger as far apart as she could, "about every man I'd bedded before I met Arthur, every party I'd ever attended, every joint I'd ever smoked. Arthur wouldn't listen to a word I said. I was in a state of total shock. I just packed a bag and fled. I wanted to get Helen out of the house, but I knew they wouldn't let me. I thought, you see, that I could simply find a solicitor and get her back."

"You did get her back, didn't you?" asked Tilly.

Cynthia blew her nose again. "Only because Arthur finally believed me about Victor being a threat to her." Thinking back to that time, Cynthia sighed and again shook her head at the memory. "It's funny, you know. Charles really thought

I would go straight to him in New York. He couldn't believe it when I said no. It was like a game of pass the parcel for him." She held the now sodden handkerchief towards Tilly, then, thinking better of it, shoved it into her own bag. "Thanks," she said, standing up and flashing Tilly a smile so radiant it was possible in that moment to understand how all three Ormond brothers could have become immediately and simultaneously smitten with this woman.

Five minutes later they were entering Cynthia's lounge. The light on the answering machine was blinking. Cynthia pounced on it and pushed the play button.

It was a deep voice, the speech slightly slurred. Although Tilly had only heard it once, years before, in a solicitor's office, she recognised the speaker immediately. When Cynthia heard the speaker, she flinched.

"Cynthia," said Sir Victor Ormond, "I'm sorry. I didn't mean to do it. I didn't mean to kill her. It was you. It's always been you." There was a sob, then, "I'm so sorry, Cynthia. I didn't want to hurt her, but she was you." Another sob, then a click.

Cynthia began tearing at her immaculately cut hair. "Oh, sweet Jesus, my baby, he's killed my baby." She began to sob hysterically. Tilly, feeling completely and utterly useless, tried to wrap her arms around the distraught woman in the hope of calming her, but Cynthia pushed her away. "I've got to ring the police. Oh, my God, I never should have gone to Kent. I should have rung them straight away."

Cynthia reached for the telephone receiver, but Tilly grabbed her arm before she could dial. "We need to find out where he was calling from."

Cynthia nodded, understanding immediately. She punched in 1471 and listened. After scribbling a number on the pad by the phone, she groaned.

"Christ, where the hell is that?" Cynthia asked, before depressing the receiver cradle briefly, then dialling the number she'd written down. Fighting back tears, her foot tapping involuntarily on the floor, Cynthia listened to the phone at the other end ring and ring, fifteen, twenty, thirty times, before finally slamming the receiver down. After a moment, she grabbed the receiver again and dialled 999.

CHAPTER THIRTEEN

Helen lay soaking in the huge, sunken marble tub in the Covent Garden flat. So much had happened since the phone call three days ago.

One phone call, a phone call offering her the revenge she'd wanted for so long. One phone call bringing her full circle, changing completely the life she'd lived for the past four years.

"Helen, it's Jamie," he'd said when she picked up the phone. "I need to talk to you." She could tell he was in a pub from the background sounds of numerous conversations, snooker balls clinking, some stupid Spice Girls song playing on a jukebox. "I'm in the pub around the corner," he said, confirming the location. "Can I come round?"

"Of course," she said.

As soon as she saw him, she knew something was dreadfully wrong.

"You look as if you could use a drink," she said. He shook his head, told her he'd already had far too many, sitting in the pub working up the courage to call her. Helen smiled. "Jamie, you don't need courage to ring me."

He followed her into the lounge and lowered his tall frame onto the sofa before answering. "I did this time, Helen."

She sat down beside him, looking at him with concern. "What's up, Doc?" she said, a joke she'd used ever since he'd acquired his doctorate. There wasn't the slightest hint of a smile from him in response.

"You were right," Jamie said, groaning, bending forward to rest his elbows on his knees and cover his face with his hands.

Helen waited several moments, then placed a hand gently on his arm. "What was I right about?"

"About Victor," he said as if the words were being torn out

of his body. "About VACO. About everything." He lowered his right arm, turned to face her. "Satisfied?"

"No." Helen shook her head. "No, I'm not, Jamie. I have no idea what you're talking about."

Jamie groaned again, then flung himself back against the sofa. "Get me that drink and I'll tell you."

Helen uncurled her legs from underneath her, went out into the kitchen and poured generous measures of cognac into two snifters.

Jamie tossed back half of his without flinching, then looked at her. "You know that seed coating the biotech people came up with?" Helen shook her head. Jamie seemed surprised. "Your dad didn't tell you about it?"

"No, Jamie. Dad really doesn't talk to me much about VACO."

"He should have told you about this. If it wasn't for him there would've been a catastrophe."

"Well, he didn't tell me, Jamie, so why don't you?"

And so Jamie told her about the pesticide-resistant seed coating developed by VACO's genetic engineering department, about the phenomenal results and the plans to begin shipping the product to customers all over the world, about Arthur's eleventh hour tests which revealed the appalling long term consequences and resulted in the cancellation of the project.

"Bloody hell, that's awful," said Helen when Jamie paused. "But that was three years ago. Why are you telling me now?"

Jamie's hesitation was only momentary. "One of the blokes from shipping waylaid me in the car park this evening. He was around three years ago when the original shipments were suddenly cancelled. He didn't know why, but he figured there must be something wrong. He wanted to know if we'd solved the problem, because they'd been told to prepare a shipment. It didn't say on the order that it was the coated seeds, but he recognised the containers."

"Have they fixed the problem?"

"No, but that doesn't matter if it's just what the dictator ordered." When Helen simply frowned, he continued, "I didn't tell you where the shipment's going – Bowinda."

Bowinda. Helen sank back against the sofa, shutting her eyes as if this could block out the implication of Jamie's words. While she may no longer have been as engrossed in world affairs as she was in her university days, anyone who ever read a paper or glanced at the television news knew about the semi-genocidal war being waged by the military dictator of Bowinda against the Kisga ethnic minority.

General Radad had obviously decided to take the semi out of semi-genocidal.

When she opened her eyes, the horror in them told Jamie she understood what he was saying. "Radad's decided to get rid of the Kisga," she said.

Jamie nodded. "That's my guess."

Helen grabbed his arm. "Who, Jamie? Who gave the order?"

"I don't know, Helen, but I'm telling you, there are only two people high enough up at HQ to authorise this — Victor or your father." As her mouth opened to protest, he raised a silencing hand. "It's all right, Helen, I know it wasn't your dad. I know how much he loathes biotech. I've heard him often enough myself calling it Pandora's Box. I just had to tell you it could be."

"Have you told him about this?"

"No." Jamie shook his head. "I could probably get hold of him in Singapore and get the shipment stopped."

"Then why haven't you?"

Jamie rubbed the back of his hand against his forehead. It was a gesture Helen remembered from their teens, something Jamie always did when he was frustrated.

"Dammit, Helen, just stopping the shipment isn't enough. That bastard uncle of yours has got to be exposed and I know your dad won't do that." He looked at Helen. "That's why I needed several drinks before I came to talk to you. I was working up the courage to kiss my career goodbye." He smiled. "I'm going to get my hands on some proof and take it to the media. Maybe someone else will hire me after VACO sacks me, but I'm not going to hold my breath."

"Can you really get proof?"

"I'm pretty sure I can, yes."

"Okay," Helen said, making her mind up in an instant, "get it and give it to me. I'll go to the press. I'll have the great satisfaction of nailing Victor and you'll save your job." She pointed a finger at him. "But you have to promise me you'll leave VACO asap."

Jamie shook his head. "I don't know, Helen."

"Oh, come on, Jamie. You of all people know how much I want to do this." And she had wanted to be the one who blew the whistle. Three days ago, before this awful thought that Victor might be her father, her fear and detestation of him had made the idea of exposing this scandal, of quite possibly being the one who sent Sir Victor Ormond to prison, had seemed to her the most magnificent revenge imaginable.

Despite her enthusiasm, Jamie shook his head, not at all persuaded. "I don't know. Perhaps we should ring Charles in New York?"

"No." Helen's tone was far more vehement than she'd intended. This was the big one. With any luck Victor would actually go to gaol. The last thing she wanted was Charles attempting to talk her out of it – especially as there was an awful possibility that he might succeed. "If you think Dad wouldn't expose Victor, there's even less chance Charles would," she offered by way of explanation.

Jamie nodded. "You're probably right. I like Charles, but I'm not sure I trust him."

"Right." Helen stood up and headed out to the kitchen for the cognac bottle, calling over her shoulder, "We need a plan."

At points during the ensuing discussion, when Jamie got excited about something and began frantically waving his arms around the way he used to, he reminded her so much of the gangling youth with the wild red hair she'd first met so many years before. He'd filled out a fair bit and had, since she'd last seen him, grown a beard, deep red speckled with gold. The extra weight suited him. So did the beard, which toned down the effect of his reddish brown freckles.

Three hours of arguing the pros and cons of various scenarios later, they had a plan.

"Do you want to stay?" Helen asked when she realised it was nearly midnight.

Jamie turned to look at her, an extraordinary play of emotions sweeping across his freckled face – surprise, delight, confusion, doubt, decision. And, in the brief moment it took for all these feelings to be reflected in his eyes, Helen realised why it was that Jamie Mortimer had never asked a single girl out in the entire time he attended Chelsea Grammar. How could she have been so obtuse? Her own eyes widened in surprise – surprise and something else she could not define. Before she could speak, Jamie stood up

"No," he said, reaching for his jacket. "I better go. I'm going to need to get into the lab early."

Helen nodded, wishing he wouldn't go, unable to ask him to stay. She walked him to the door, and, unable to resist the impulse, threw her arms around his neck. "It's so good to see you again, Doc." His arms closed around her tightly and he murmured something in her hair. She looked up at him, smiling. "What?"

Jamie smiled back, shook his head. "Nothing," he said, letting go of her and opening the door.

Nothing, eh? thought Helen. Although she didn't say so, she'd heard him quite distinctly. She smiled after the door closed behind him and whispered, "I love you, too, Jamie." Then she'd leaned forward, gently but firmly banged her forehead on the door. Christ, she thought, this isn't going to be easy.

Three days later, stretched out in the marble tub, Helen thought about that realisation and sighed. Charles chose that moment to push open the bathroom door. He placed a tray containing croissants, freshly squeezed orange juice and steaming mugs of fragrant coffee on the side of the tub. Much to Helen's dismay, he then began to unbutton his shirt.

"No, Charles," she said.

His eyebrows shot up. "'No, Charles?'" he repeated. "I don't seem to recall ever hearing you say that before."

For the first time in four years, Helen found herself cursing Jamie for having chosen that particular day to fly off to California.

CHAPTER FOURTEEN

It was September 2000. She'd just seen Jamie off and was walking across the concourse of the departure terminal, feeling glum after waving goodbye to her best, her only friend.

Her mother was in Australia, helping with the wedding plans of her old friend Sheila who'd moved to Sydney and, against all odds, had met and fallen in love with an Australian named Bruce. The flat would be empty of her mother's presence for a month, during which Helen was going to have to tackle her own postgraduate tasks of finding a job and a place to live.

As Helen made her way towards the exit, her attention was suddenly riveted by a tall, elegant, raven haired man striding purposefully towards the Air France ticket desk. She hadn't seen him in more than fifteen years, but she would have recognised him anywhere.

"Charles!" she called out.

He paused mid-stride and turned, his eyes searching the crowd. When they alighted on Helen, he took a step backwards, looking as if he'd seen a ghost. "It's me," she said, walking towards him and adding, when his astonished expression failed to change, "Helen."

Charles dropped his case, reached out both hands, holding her at arms' length.

"Helen?" A smile spread across his face, crinkling up the corners of his eyes. "My God, look at you!"

Helen found herself smiling back, happier than she could believe at seeing him. "You didn't recognise me," she accused.

Charles dropped his arms to his sides and laughed. "Hardly surprising, cherub. You were," he held one hand out just above his knee, "about this tall the last time I saw you." His hands came up to grasp her shoulders again.

"My God, I can't believe it. Where are you off to? How much time have you got?"

"Nowhere," she told him, still grinning inanely. "I was just seeing a friend off. What about you? Are you jetting in or jetting out?"

"Both," he said. He let go of one of her shoulders and jerked his thumb towards the Air France desk, "I'm just on my way to Paris for a conference."

"Lucky you."

"Have you ever been to Paris?"

"Not since school."

His grin widened even further. "Come with me. It would be marvellous to catch up with you."

Yes, thought Helen, it would. She couldn't think of anything more likely to lift her out of the doldrums of Jamie's departure than a couple of days spent with her so long missing, wildly witty uncle. "I don't have any clothes," she pointed out.

"Oh, lord." Charles glanced at his watch. "Look, there's another flight in a couple of hours." He pulled his wallet out and stuffed twenty pound notes into Helen's hand. "Grab a cab, go home, make him wait, throw some things in a case and meet me back here." He bent his head to look directly into her eyes. "Yes?"

Helen nodded. "Yes."

As she was hurrying towards the exit, she heard him shout, "Bring some glad rags. I want to show you off!"

Helen looked over her shoulder, grinned and gave him a thumb's up.

Seven hours later they were in a luxuriously appointed hotel suite in Saint Germain, Helen's weekend bag deposited in the smaller of the two bedrooms.

"Put those glad rags on," instructed Charles. "I'm going to take you to one of my favourite restaurants."

Helen returned to her room and shook out a black cotton knit dress, run through with shimmering aquamarine threads which exactly matched the colour of her eyes. She had purchased the dress during a shopping expedition with her mother. Although she'd balked at the price, her mother had insisted the dress was a miracle – not only did it fit Helen perfectly and set off her eyes, but the fabric was such that the dress could be screwed up in a ball at the bottom of a case and all it would take was a quick shake for it to be ready to wear. Take it, her mother had urged. Helen took it and, standing in front of the hotel bathroom mirror, was very glad she had. The dress really was incredibly flattering.

She extracted a jet-encrusted comb from her toiletries bag and used it deftly to pull up her hair, then slipped into a sequinned bolero jacket – like the jet comb, found by chance at the market in Portobello Road.

When she entered the lounge, Charles whistled. "Somehow," he said, "I don't think cherub's quite right any more." He tilted his head to one side, appraising her. "How about angel?"

Helen smiled. Although she clearly remembered Charles calling her cherub when she was a child, she wasn't at all taken with it now. "Angel's fine."

They left the hotel and Charles led the way down the busy Boulevard Saint Germain to a small side street at the end of which was the Café Michel. "*Et voila*," said Charles, holding the door open for her.

A waiter whose nose was so far up in the air it looked as if the world's worst odour had been permanently imbedded in his bristling moustache was pushed aside by Michel, the rotund proprietor, who greeted Charles effusively. Helen's rusty schoolgirl French allowed her to follow little of what was being said. She was impressed by the ease with which Charles spoke seemingly flawless French. Michel, talking non-stop, led them to a table. As the proprietor held Helen's chair for her, Charles said something which caused the other man to throw back his head and laugh uproariously.

"*Oui, Michel, c'est vrai*," Charles insisted. "*C'est vrai*."

Michel simply continued to laugh and walked off to fetch menus.

"What's true?" Helen asked, her French up to that simple statement.

Charles grinned. "Michel refuses to believe you are my niece. Apparently that's what all middle aged men say of the beautiful young women they escort."

"Oh," said Helen, the realisation that she was blushing

serving only to make her blush all the more furiously. "You're not middle aged," she protested.

"Darling Helen," he said, "I'm more than double your age and almost certainly more than half way to my grave, so I think you could safely say my age is in the middle."

Michel returned at that moment with two menus, which Charles waved away. More rapid fire French followed. "*Bien sûr, M'sieur Ormond*," said a beaming Michel before walking away in the direction of the kitchen.

"What did you order?" asked Helen.

"No idea," Charles informed her. "I just told him to provide us with the best dinner his chef could produce."

Another waiter appeared with a bottle of champagne, an ice bucket and two glasses. When their glasses had been filled, Charles raised his to Helen and said, "To the swan."

It took Helen a moment to understand the reference and when she did her face fell. "Oh, God," she said, "was I really an ugly duckling?"

"No, angel. From the moment you were born you've always been completely adorable, but, you must admit the last time I saw you, you were a bit rolly polly." Charles smiled. "A description which could no longer be further from the truth. You look wonderful"

Helen sipped her champagne, blushing at the compliment. She'd been told she was beautiful many times by many men, each meaningless compliment a prelude to some crude and unwanted seduction attempt. Compliments did not flatter Helen; they made her cringe. Until, she realised with some surprise, now. For some reason a compliment from Charles did not make her cringe, but instead made her quite ridiculously happy.

Whilst still pondering this, she remembered the last time she'd had dinner with her father. His most interesting item of news had been the fact that Charles' second marriage had just ended in an extremely acrimonious divorce. How rude of her to have not even mentioned it yet.

"I was sorry to hear about you and Mary Ann," she said, as a waiter placed two bowls of what turned out to be a delicious cold apple soup in front of them. Charles responded to this sudden change of topic with a grin which showed a distinct lack of concern about the fate of his marriage or of his now ex-wife. "What happened?"

He shrugged. "Same thing that happened the first time. I thought an actress would take fidelity a little less seriously than a lawyer, but I was wrong. Mary Ann turned out to be every bit as incapable as Karen was of accepting my inability to resist a pretty face." He tasted the soup and rolled his eyes appreciatively, then added, "I'm just not cut out to be a husband."

"Oh."

Her surprise at his candour must have been obvious. Charles reached across the table and squeezed her hand. "Don't worry, angel," he said. "Although you are exceedingly pretty, you're perfectly safe. I'm not quite that bad."

Helen, confused by the realisation that she wasn't entirely sure whether she was relieved to learn she was safe from Charles or quite the reverse, decided to focus her attention on her soup. She glanced around the restaurant filled with well heeled, elegantly turned out diners. There was no doubt about it. The charming, urbane man with the long, thin face and patrician features sitting opposite her was the most attractive man in the room. The thought alarmed her.

"Penny for 'em," Charles said.

"Oh," Helen replied vaguely, "I was just thinking I must be getting used to that beard of yours. It doesn't look as stupid as it used to."

Charles feigned astonishment. "I'll have you know some women find my beard devilishly attractive."

I'll bet they do, thought Helen. "Oh, really?" she said.

The soup was followed by a salad, followed by Tournedos Roquefort with a wonderful bottle of red wine. Charles kept her so entertained throughout that she was able to relax and think of him once again as her wildly witty uncle and, she said firmly to herself, *nothing else.*

When she'd finished the third course, Helen pushed her plate to one side and groaned. "I hope we don't have any dessert coming," she said. "That was delicious, but I couldn't eat another thing."

Charles puffed out his cheeks and nodded in agreement. "You're right," he said, signalling for the bill. When that had been dealt with, he grinned at her. "I think we should go somewhere and burn off a few calories, don't you?"

Helen blinked. He couldn't mean what she thought he meant, could he? "What do you mean?"

Charles leaned back in his seat, eyes filled with delight, a wolfish grin on his face. "What do you think I mean?"

To hide her confusion, Helen picked up her linen napkin and found a bread crumb to brush off the table cloth. "I don't know," she said, still staring at the table, "that's why I asked."

"You do dance, don't you?" Charles asked. "It's not against some religion you picked up at university?"

Helen looked up, surprised. "Yes," she said, smiling and hoping Charles would put her flushed complexion down to the rosy lighting inside the restaurant, "I dance. I just didn't know middle aged men danced."

Charles threw back his head and roared with laughter. "Okay," he said, pointing a finger at her, "I'll give you that one. I walked right into it." He tossed his napkin on the table and stood up. "Come on, young Helen. Let's see what these decrepit old bones of mine can do on a dance floor."

Those decrepit old bones of his did very well indeed. In Helen's experience, most Englishmen's idea of dancing was to shift their weight awkwardly from one foot to another whilst flapping their hands in an out-of-beat imitation of seals. By comparison, Charles might well have been a professional dancer, so graceful and rhythmic were his movements on the nightclub floor.

Helen was feeling quite outperformed when they first began dancing. Then Charles impatiently grabbed her hand and began to lead her with remarkable ease through a complicated, hip swinging cross between a tango and a jive. As Charles pulled her in towards him at one point, he yelled, "Let your hair down." Helen reached up with her free hand and yanked the jet comb out of her hair, which tumbled down around her shoulders. "Better," he mouthed after he'd flung her practically to the floor then yanked her momentarily back into his arms before flinging her away again at arm's length.

One song led quickly into another until Helen lost track of how long Charles had been swinging and twirling her around the floor. Out of the corner of her eye she glimpsed a couple on the other side of the room executing a dramatic move, then realised with amazement that the tall, raven haired man and the woman with white gold hair who seemed to be flying across the floor were herself and Charles reflected in a mirrored wall. God, she thought, is that really *me*? She became aware of other dancers watching them, shifting to the sides of the dance floor to give them more room.

Then, just as she'd decided, like Eliza Doolittle, that she could have danced all night, she got an excruciating stitch in her side. She soldiered on, not wanting to stop, but when the song ended she grabbed Charles and begged for a break.

As they left the floor, Charles acknowledged the applause of the other dancers with a smile and wave over his shoulder. Helen collapsed into her chair, grasping her side and gasping for breath. She looked up accusingly at Charles, who was showing absolutely no sign of exertion. "You," she informed him, "are far too energetic to be anybody's uncle."

"And you," he said, leaning across the table and planting a gentle kiss on her cheek, "are far too beautiful for anyone's good." He straightened up, grinning. "Now, if you'll excuse me, young Helen, I need to find the gents. See if you can rustle us up a couple of champagne cocktails, will you?"

Too beautiful for anyone's good. Helen repeated the words to herself. What the hell was that supposed to mean? And why was it sending anticipatory tingles down her spine? What exactly was she anticipating?

Charles came back. They danced, they laughed, they drank, they danced. When a slow song came on after a particularly lively performance by Charles, he pulled her close and folded her into his arms. Her right hand and his left pressed between their chests, her left hand wrapped around his shoulder, her head resting against him, his chin leaning on her head, Helen couldn't help thinking how ironic it was that no man had ever made her feel as comfortable, relaxed or happy as this man, her bloody uncle. She pulled her head back to look up at him.

His gaze seemed far away, then he glanced down at her and smiled. "Penny for 'em," she said.

Charles sighed and pulled her even closer. "I was just wishing I'd managed to do this twenty years ago."

"Twenty years ago I was two years old," she pointed out.

"So you were, angel," he agreed dreamily. "So you were."

The song ended and he stepped away from her, holding up his hand to pirouette her one last time, before leading the way back to their table.

"I've had enough ear shattering music for one night," he said, grabbing his jacket off the back of his chair. "Come on, let's get out of here."

"Where to?" Helen asked when they got outside.

Charles swivelled his head to look at her. His eyes narrowed. His expression was unfathomable. "Do you like jazz?" he asked eventually.

Helen shrugged. "I don't know."

Spotting a taxi, Charles raised his hand to flag it. He held the door open for her and said, "Time you found out."

The jazz club, in a basement somewhere on the Left Bank, was hot, the air fogged with tobacco smoke. The trio on stage – a pianist, bass violin player and drummer – were starting a new number as the waitress led them to a booth at the back. As Charles ordered another bottle of champagne, Helen listened to the music, enraptured. How, she wondered, could she have never paid any attention to jazz before? When the tune ended, she applauded more enthusiastically than anyone else.

"That was gorgeous," she said to Charles.

"It sounds better when Thelonius Monk does it. But," he agreed with an approving nod, "not bad."

Halfway through the third number, a sax player wandered in from the wings and joined in. Helen thought the sounds he produced from his instrument were the sexiest music she'd ever heard. At the end of that number, the other musicians leaned away from their instruments, reached for cigarettes and drinks and simply waited for the sax player to start. Everyone in the club seemed to be holding their breath. Charles took a swig of champagne, then sat back, stretching his arms out along the banquette.

The moment the sax player began his solo, she knew she'd been wrong. *This* was the sexiest music she'd ever heard. As the music swept over her, she kicked off her shoes, pulled her feet up onto the seat of the booth and, as if it was the most natural thing in the world, leaned back into Charles. And, as if it was the most natural thing in the world, he immediately bent his elbow to wrap his arm around her and rest his hand on her shoulder. And, as if it was the most natural thing in the world, he began to run his fingers gently up and down her arm, across her shoulder, up her neck.

Helen shut her eyes, surrendering herself to the music and, for a short while at least, the delicious havoc the feather light feeling of Charles' fingers on her neck was having on the pit of her stomach.

When she decided the feelings she was experiencing were driving her quite mad and that the only solution was to turn around and kiss Charles, right now, this instant, she sat bolt upright instead, grabbing the near empty champagne bottle to explain her sudden movement.

Jesus Christ, she thought, I want to fuck my uncle. This is crazy. She guzzled some champagne. *I'm* crazy. She kept her eyes fixed firmly on the sax player, not daring to risk a glance at Charles. Even after the song had ended and she'd joined automatically in the ensuing applause, she continued to stare straight ahead.

Charles leaned forward, resting his chin on her shoulder. "Are you okay?"

She managed to shrug her shoulder away without, she hoped, him noticing the way she'd almost jumped at his touch. "It's very hot in here," she said, still not looking at him. "I'm feeling a bit funny." Well, that was certainly true.

"Okay." Charles stood up, held out his hand to her. "Nothing's going to top that rendition of *Harlem Nocturne*. Let's go."

Helen ignored his proffered hand and slid around the other side of the booth. "Is that what that song's called?"

"Yes." Charles grinned. "It's incredibly sexy, isn't it?"

Helen, unable to think of any reply which wouldn't choke her, merely nodded and led the way out to the blessed relief of the cool night air.

It was nearly four by the time they got back to their hotel.

"Excellent," said Charles, when his eyes alit on the bottle of champagne sitting in a silver ice bucket on the coffee table.

"Did you order that?" Helen asked.

"No, darling," Charles said, "but the prices this place charges, they can afford to throw in the odd bottle of Bolly."

Darling, thought Helen, appalled by how much she liked being called "darling" by Charles.

He popped the cork on the champagne, filled two glasses and motioned for her to join him on the sofa. "I want to thank you, young Helen," he said, raising his glass to her. "I can't remember the last time I had so much fun."

Helen frowned. "Stop calling me *young* Helen. It's incredibly patronising."

He smiled apologetically. "Sorry, angel. I just need to jog my memory occasionally."

And what the hell was *that* supposed to mean, Helen wondered as she sipped her champagne and observed him over the rim of her glass.

She had to admit, she couldn't think of any time in her life when she'd had so much fun. And, while there was absolutely no law against having fun with one's uncle, she'd hardly been thinking of him in that role in the jazz club when she'd nearly kissed him or for most of the rest of the evening for that matter. It was proving even harder, sitting here drinking champagne, to resist the temptation to kiss him now.

I should go to bed, she thought, I've had too much to drink. I should put my glass down this second, thank Charles for a lovely evening and scarper to my room.

"Am I really safe?" The words and all they implied were out of her mouth before she could stop them.

Charles raised his eyebrows. "Do you want to be?"

Oh my God, thought Helen, it's now or never. "No, not really," she said.

Charles considered her reply. "I hope this isn't some sort of test of my moral fibre, angel, because I have to warn you, I simply don't have any."

"No, Charles, this isn't a test."

For what seemed to Helen an eternity, Charles said and did nothing except stare into her eyes. Then he raised his hand and ran a finger down her cheek. A shudder ran through her entire body at his touch. "Are you sure?"

Helen nodded, never more sure of anything in her life.

Charles groaned. "Oh, Christ," he said, spreading his arms to embrace her. "Come here, you."

Helen went.

The only word to describe the way Helen felt the next morning was bliss. Every inch of her flesh, every nerve ending in her body tingled. Nothing in the frantic fumblings of Sheldon had prepared her for the way Charles had managed to make her feel.

Sunlight filtered into the room through the shuttered window. Helen was lying on her back. Charles was asleep on his stomach, his face, the face she had failed until yesterday to realise was so incredibly handsome, pressed into the pillows. His arm was draped across her. Helen sighed with contentment.

Charles' hand squeezed her waist. "Thank God," he muttered, "I thought it might have been a dream."

"No dream." Helen snuggled up beside him.

Charles opened one eye and grinned at her. "More?" he asked, pressing against her just enough to make her aware of his ability to turn word into deed.

Helen began to smile, readied herself to say yes, please, but before the words were formed, the smile froze, half formed, on her lips.

What in God's name was she doing in a Paris hotel room with her *uncle*? It was bad enough they'd spent half the night devouring one another at *her* instigation. But that at least she could pretend to blame on the drink. Between dinner and the nightclub and the jazz club, God knows how much booze they'd consumed before opening the bottle of Bollinger when they got back to the hotel. But this was morning and, as sexually inebriated as she may have been feeling, she was actually stone cold sober. They were both sober. She had no business wanting him to make love to her again. He certainly had no business suggesting it.

She managed to sit up, but before she could swing her legs over the side of the bed and scramble out, Charles had wrapped his arm around her, holding her back. "Where do you think you're going?" he asked.

"Charles," she said, "let's not make this any worse, okay?"

"Helen, look at me." It wasn't a request, it was a command.

Helen obeyed without thinking, glancing over her shoulder and meeting his warm brown gaze. "Aren't you forgetting something?" Her eyebrows puckered together. Charles smiled. "I'm a bastard."

Helen turned her head away, struggling, albeit half heartedly, to pull his arm away. "Please, Charles, let me go. It's nice of you to try to take the blame, but I remember enough to know I started this. This is awful enough already. It's – " She broke off, unable to say the word. Incest. Was it? Was sex with your uncle incest? Oh, God. Helen groaned.

Charles laughed a deep, throaty laugh and circled his other arm around her. In one lithe movement he was sitting up behind her, his long legs encircling her, holding her in place. His beard tickled her shoulder as he whispered in her ear, "Do you want me to make love to you again?"

More than anything Helen wanted to lean back against him and say yes. Lie, she told herself. Say no. Lie, lie, *lie*. "Yes," she barely whispered as she leaned back against him,

"Right." Charles slid his hands up to her shoulders, turning her to face him. "I wasn't trying to take the blame for anything, angel. I was reminding you that, despite the fact that I inherited a third of the Ormond lolly, I am, in fact, your father's uncle's bastard son, as Victor can be so partial to pointing out. So," he raised her chin and leaned forward until barely an inch separated their mouths, "while you are so luscious I cannot guarantee I would not screw you even if you really were my niece, I thought you could do with a reminder that I'm not actually your uncle. You are not committing incest by even the wildest stretch of the imagination. You are in bed with an extremely randy middle aged man who wants to ravish you, if you'll let him."

Helen stared at him for a moment, then burst out laughing and threw her arms around his neck. "Yes, please," she said.

"I have a feeling you're going to turn out to be insatiable," he said, dragging her back under the covers.

"Oh, I think so," Helen agreed, astonished by just how insatiable she felt.

In the midst of everything she couldn't help but be struck by the irony. The fear of sex instilled in her by one uncle, the loathing of her own beauty and the effect it had on men, both were magically gone, banished by her other – sort of – uncle. She grinned at him. "What about your conference?"

"To hell with my conference."

They didn't leave the hotel suite for three days. When they arrived at Heathrow, Helen clung to Charles all the way to his departure gate. At the entrance, he turned to her and said, "Come to New York."

"When?" she asked, unable to keep the excitement out of her voice.

"Next week. Give me a chance to clear everything off my desk, then come for a month. Come for two months. Christ. Just come."

"Charles, I can't come for two months. I can't come for a month. I've got to find a job. I've got to find a flat. I can't stay with Mum forever."

"A fortnight," he countered.

Helen nodded. The idea of waiting more than a week to see Charles again was unbearable. "All right," she said.

Charles reached for her hand, raised it to his lips, his expression suddenly serious. "Promise me something, angel. Promise me you will never say anything to your mum or dad about this."

Helen hesitated. Somehow she couldn't imagine telling her father. It wouldn't kill him, although he might just have a stroke. But her mother? They were so close, and, while her mother might not approve whole heartedly, might in fact object quite strenuously, Helen was in love. She didn't feel ready to say the words to Charles yet, but she felt that if she didn't say them to someone, she was going to burst. Jamie was gone. There was no one but her mother.

"Charles," she said, "I know there's a huge difference in our ages, but as you said yourself –"

He placed a silencing finger on her lips. "Angel, you and I might be able to see things that way, but, trust me, your parents won't. One word to either of them, and it will be over," he snapped his fingers under her nose, "like that." He bent over and kissed her. "Promise me."

Helen nodded. He was right. Both her parents would go totally ballistic. "I promise." Then, because all other options were effectively blocked, she threw her arms around him and rushed the words out before she could stop herself, "I love you, Charles."

Instead of making the matching declaration she'd hoped for, Charles reached up and disengaged her arms from around his neck. Holding both her hands in his and staring at her, his eyes devoid of humour, he said, "Darling Helen, as flattered as I am, I have to tell you falling in love with me would be the worst possible thing you could do."

She opened her mouth to protest, but before any words were out, he was kissing her and taking his time about it. When he finally let her go, he winked and said, "I'll send you a ticket."

And then he turned and walked away, one wave over his shoulder before he disappeared into passport control. The excitement which had been welling up within Helen every waking moment of the past few days began to deflate. It was too bloody late to tell her not to fall in love. She already had. And what about Charles? After the time they'd just spent together – and the way they'd spent that time – he must be at least a little bit in love with her, too? Surely?

Of course, infatuated as she was, Helen knew the relationship was impossible. It may not have been exactly what Alfred Douglas had in mind, but this was definitely a love that dared not speak its name. And that, she realised was what he'd been trying to say: they had no future together as a couple, this could not be a happily ever after story. Well, that was fine, as far as Helen was concerned. She didn't know how it would end, but she was determined to enjoy every minute she could until she got to the finish.

A week later, sitting at the table in the dining room of Charles' New York apartment, wearing his silk robe and eating the wonderful meal he'd managed to prepare in what seemed like seconds, Helen smiled at him and said, "Teach me things, Charles."

He smiled back at her. "What sort of things?"

"Everything." She pointed at her plate, "Food," then lifted her glass, "wine," her smile widened, "bed. Everything."

Charles laughed out loud, another deep throaty laugh. "Helen, you're not going to need a lot of lessons about bed.

You're a natural. As for the rest, yes. Everything and more. It'll be fun."

Charles was true to his word. During those two weeks and the many rendezvous which followed, he taught Helen to cook, to appreciate fine wine and cognacs. He took her to operas, to jazz clubs, to symphony concerts. He taught her about books and plays and, most lovingly, about art, leading her around galleries in New York, London, Florence and Paris. He worked on her French until she could converse, then made her do all the talking in restaurants and shops during a five day trip to Alsace. And, despite his protests that no lessons were required, her did indeed teach her about bed.

After a year together, Helen found it difficult to believe there was a position – or costume or gadget – she hadn't tried. She was wrong. Charles continued to surprise and delight. Helen left each rendezvous more sated, more bemused and more addicted to him than she'd been before.

Not long after returning from her first trip to New York, Helen had found a small flat in Camden and a job as a freelance editor for a small publishing house which specialised in history text books. It wasn't a terribly challenging or exciting job, certainly not what she'd had in mind when she was at university, but then Helen had excitement enough in her life. Freelancing gave her something no other form of employment could – the freedom to go anywhere, anytime with Charles.

"I suppose," her mother said one day when they were lunching together at Harvey Nichols, "he's married, this mystery man of yours?"

"Yes," Helen told her, because it was a lot easier than telling the absolute truth and her mother knew her too well to ever believe an outright lie.

Cynthia sighed. "Darling, it's a mug's game. They always promise you the moon and swear they'll leave their wives and they never, ever do."

"What if I don't want him to leave his wife?" asked Helen. "What if I'm only involved with him because the sex is unbelievable?"

If she'd hoped to shock her mother, she failed completely.

Cynthia simply raised her exquisitely plucked eyebrows and said, "Lucky you, darling. Be careful, that's all."

On the second anniversary of their first weekend in Paris, Charles arrived on her doorstep with a dozen red roses in one hand. From the index finger of his other hand dangled a key.

"What's this?" she asked taking the key from his finger.

"It's for the flat I just bought in Covent Garden."

Helen's eyes lit up at the intoxicating thought of Charles being around on a much more permanent basis. "You're moving back to London?"

"Sorry, angel," he said, leaning forward to present her with the roses and a toe curling kiss. "I have to stay in New York. But I wanted to have somewhere in London. Somewhere for us."

"For us?" she repeated, gesturing vaguely behind her. "I've got a flat."

"I know, Helen," he said. "And you should keep it for when you're not with me. But I want there to be a place that's just for us." He held out his hand. "Wanna see it?"

The Covent Garden flat in a renovated warehouse was beautiful – exposed brickwork and parquet floors, a gleaming, chromium, state-of-the-art kitchen, a bathroom with a massive marble tub, big enough for four people, let alone two. Almost the entire wall at one end of the open-plan flat was filled with a window overlooking the market. At the other end, a narrow wrought iron staircase ran up the wall to a large sleeping loft, built halfway down from the eighteen foot ceilings.

"That's handy," Helen said, pointing at the loft and grinning. "I'll need somewhere to hide if Dad ever stops by unexpectedly."

Charles assured her no one would ever know about the existence of the flat except the two of them. Then he asked her a favour. "You may have noticed the lack of furniture. I don't have time to buy it. Will you? You can get whatever you want, do whatever you want."

Helen's grin widened. The idea of creating an oasis for the two of them from the blank canvas the flat represented was enormously appealing. "All right," she said, "but we're going to have to figure out some way of paying for everything. I don't make a huge amount of money."

"I already thought of that," Charles said, reaching for his wallet. He extracted a gold American Express card which he handed to her.

Helen glanced at the card and realised with a shock that it was made out in her name.

She scoured auction rooms, galleries and quality furnishing shops.

In the end, she created an eclectic mix of old and new – intended, she informed Charles with a grin, to represent the difference in their ages – antique furniture mixed with space age lamps, the high-tech kitchen contrasted with the Victorian cherry wood table, chairs and sideboard.

Charles pronounced himself delighted with her work – despite the age differential crack. "You should talk to your mother about going into business with her," he said.

"According to you, I shouldn't talk to my mother about anything connected with this flat," Helen replied.

Charles nodded. "And don't you forget it," he said as he led her up the loft stairs to bed.

Four years after their affair began, Helen could not believe the thrill of excitement she still experienced every time she heard his voice on the phone, the electric shocks his slightest touch could still send coursing through her body.

And then one night Jamie Mortimer whispered "I love you" into her hair. And suddenly the whole thing, the relationship which had been her life for four years, seemed so wrong.

"No?" Charles repeated, his fingers still on the buttons of his silk shirt. He gave her an appraising look. "What's up?"

Helen lowered her eyes, unable to meet his gaze. "I'm sorry," she mumbled, reaching for one of the mugs of coffee on the side of the tub. "I'm too upset. There's too much going on."

Charles squatted down, reaching over to lift her chin. She flinched from his touch and knew he felt it. "Is there something you want to tell me, angel?" he asked when he'd forced her to look at him.

"Charles," she said, willing him to understand, "we shouldn't be doing this."

"Ah." He leaned back on his heels, his eyes never leaving

her face. "Do you mean right at this particular moment or ever again?"

Underneath the surface of the bath water, Helen dug her nails into the palm of her hand. It had been so easy the other night to decide to end things, so easy when Charles wasn't there, but it was quite another thing to contemplate it now.

Part of her, an alarmingly large part, wanted nothing more than to make love with Charles in this bathtub, as they had so many times before. Part of her wanted to reach out to him and forget everything. But she fought the urge, knowing that if she succumbed to it, she would never break free.

"Ever again," she said reluctantly.

"I see." Charles stood up. "What's brought this on?"

"We can't ever be together, Charles, not properly. You've said so yourself, over and over again. I need more. I deserve more. Maybe, just maybe, I'd like to settle down, have children, do the whole boring, normal thing."

"I see." A smile twitched at the corners of his mouth but did not form. "Do you have someone in mind?"

Helen looked down at the mug of coffee and took a tentative sip. "No," she said, shaking her head. She was lying and she knew Charles knew it.

He surprised her by saying, "All right, Helen. I can assure you marriage is never the answer to anything, but I can understand you thinking it might be. However, I do need you to level with me about something."

Helen looked up. "What?"

"I've made a couple of phone calls while you've been soaking. No one at HQ knows anything about this shipment. I don't know what proof you've got or who helped you get it, but if you want me to try to stop it, you're going to have to tell me."

Helen wanted to believe him. The shipment had to be stopped somehow and Charles could stop it. She'd like to think she hadn't been bedding a man for years whom she did not trust, but the fact was she wasn't sure.

Charles sighed. "Angel, please. Let me help."

She had no other choice. Victor had somehow retrieved the proof she and Jamie had conspired to get. Tilly Arbuthnot would never be able to write a story without it. She nodded.

"Let me dry off. I'll ring my friend, get him to come around here. I didn't even have a chance to look at his evidence before Victor got to me. I don't know what he had. He can tell you."

Charles smiled. He reached down and ruffled her hair. "Good girl."

CHAPTER FIFTEEN

When Roger disembarked at Victoria station, he hesitated, wondering what to do next. He should, he supposed, go back to his office, maintain some pretence of actually working there. He should probably ring Ted or try to find Tilly again and see what she was up to. Or he could simply go into the station bar and get shit faced, a scenario with much to recommend it. To hell with it, he thought. Pausing to buy twenty Silk Cut from the kiosk, Roger exited the station and climbed into one of the many waiting taxis.

His flat, when he entered it, was a depressing sight. Even if it hadn't been littered with dirty glasses, overflowing ashtrays and take away food containers, the furniture and fittings in the rented flat would have been enough to lay anyone low. No expense had been spent by the skinflint landlord, who had provided end-of-the-roll, almost psychedelically patterned carpet, which by no stretch of the imagination could be said to go with the hideous brown, gold and orange floral curtains or the purple, plastic-upholstered sofa or the plaid, tweed covered chairs. The wall paper was peeling away in several places and the size of the damp patch in the ceiling suggested most of it was likely to fall on top of him sooner rather than later.

Roger sighed. He went into the bathroom and started the water trickling from the taps into the tub. However long it was since he'd been in the bathtub, it was clearly much longer since he'd cleaned it. In fact, he had no recollection of ever having done such a thing. Well, today was not the day to start. Knowing there was plenty of time before there would be anywhere near enough water in the tub to cover half his legs, he went through to the galley kitchen and made a cup of instant coffee. Studiously ignoring the welcoming cry of the whiskey bottle, he carried his coffee back to the bathroom and

Unethical Practices

placed it on the edge of the tub. Stripping off his rumpled clothes, he let them fall to the floor, then climbed into the tub. In another ten minutes there was enough water for a proper soak. Leaning back, he decided that having a bath was a very pleasant thing which he should definitely start doing more often.

What the hell had happened to him?

At one time he'd been one hell of a journalist – fearless at sniffing out scandals, exposing corruption, bringing down politicians. The paper he worked for was a sensationalist rag, but it was a rag read by millions every day. While Tilly had been writing thoughtful exposés for thoughtful left wing readers, Roger's pithy prose had, he hoped, made a few working class gits who'd fallen for Maggie's bull shit think again. One minute he'd had everything he'd ever wanted, the next he was living alone in this god awful flat, job gone, home gone, wife and daughters gone. Why the hell hadn't he fought harder?

Roger was more than a little irritated when the ringing of the phone broke into his contemplation of life's cruel tricks. Sod it, he thought, let the bloody machine get it. He'd had the thing for five years and not once had the little red light been flashing when he lurched into the flat. The only people who ever rang him were his daughters, once a month from Australia, the calls timed to ensure he would no longer be sleeping off Saturday night's excesses, but had not yet really started to work on Sunday's. Although he'd known for years exactly how they timed their calls, today was the first time the thought made him want to weep.

Just as he began to think the damned machine would never cut in, he heard some clicks and then Ted's voice saying, "Roger, you wanker, ring me as soon as you get in. I need your help with Sally's mate." As Ted began to reel off various numbers where he might be reached, Roger hauled himself out of the tub, covering the bathroom floor with water, and squelched as rapidly as his body weight and the slipperiness of the lino would allow into the lounge.

He managed to yank the receiver out of the cradle just as Ted was about to ring off.

"Oh, you're there, are you?" asked Ted.

"Apparently," said Roger. "What's up?"

"I'm at the hospital. Sally has convinced her friend to talk, but she wants to see Columbo. I've tried to explain you're not with the police, but she's being very bloody minded. Get your arse over here."

Roger padded back to the bathroom and dried himself off with a towel which reeked of mildew. After making a mental promise to discover the location of the nearest laundrette, he padded through to the bedroom, opened the door of the minuscule wardrobe and peered into it pessimistically. As he suspected, there was little from which to choose. By the process of eliminating the most wrinkled, stained and smelly clothes he managed to assemble an ill assorted outfit.

At the hospital, Roger found Ted waiting outside Sally's ward.

"Where the hell have you been?" Ted demanded.

"I went to Brighton to track down Polly. I thought she'd want to come forward again, but she doesn't want to know."

"Never mind Polly," Ted said. "Sally's mate's ready to talk and I've been through the files. I've got at least twenty possibles – tarts who ended up in the hospital but wouldn't talk to the police about who beat them. I've got a couple of constables trying to round them up, although I'm not holding out a lot of hope of finding them. It's a bit like trying to herd cats. Still, just one would help."

"Are you going to arrest Ormond?" asked Roger.

"Oh, yes. As soon as I find the bastard, he's nicked. I've already been to his office and sent someone to his house. No one's seen him since last night. I've put out an alert on his car." Ted turned towards the door of the ward. "Come on, Columbo."

Roger placed a restraining hand on Ted's arm. "Level with me, mate. I'm practically wetting myself at the prospect of finally nailing this son of a bitch, but he got away with it before. Are Sally and her pal going to be enough?"

"Oh, come on, Roger. He's been at this for years. As soon as his face gets in the papers with a request from the police for assistance with the prosecution, don't you think it's going to turn into Tart Central down at the nick?"

Roger nodded, although he was far from convinced. Perhaps Polly really had been the first. Perhaps that was why no other women came forward then. Perhaps not. Time would tell. "Okay, let's go."

Inside the ward, the curtain was still drawn around Sally Carpenter's bed. Roger pulled the curtain back slowly, flinching when he saw her face. He'd thought at the time that what Ormond had done to Polly was bad, but it was nothing compared to this.

Sitting in the cubicle's solitary chair was a hard faced little madam with dyed blonde hair. Too much make-up and too little skirt made the nature of her livelihood blatantly obvious. Although, Roger admitted with an inward shudder, she didn't look any worse than most of the models in the ads in *Sweetie*.

He forced himself to smile at the girl in the bed. "Hello, Sally."

"Hallo, Columbo," she said, remembering just in time not to smile. "Where the hell have you been? Have you caught the bleeder yet?"

Ted answered before Roger could. "No, Sally, but I told you there's a warrant out."

Sally shrugged then winced with pain. "Well, sergeant, like I said, I want to hear it from Columbo."

Roger smiled. "Sally, I'm flattered, but it's Sergeant Beauchamp here, who's going to arrest the bastard."

"Maybe, but I can tell it's personal with you. I dunno why and I don't care, but I know you're not going to stop 'til you get him."

"It's personal with me, too, Sally," Ted assured her in a hard, convincing voice. "We all want this swine."

Roger gestured towards the bed. "May I?" Sally's minute nod gave him permission. He perched on the side of the bed and turned to face the young madam. "You must be Meg."

"Who wants to know?"

"Oh, for God's sake," said Ted. "Here we go again."

Roger waved a silencing hand towards the sergeant. "Look, Meg, I realise you're probably frightened, but you have to –"

"Too bloody right I'm frightened," said Meg, her hard little mouth beginning to tremble. "He's rich. What if he's got friends who decide to help him out by shutting up witnesses? What if he decides to have me killed? Him going to gaol wouldn't be much bleeding use to me then, would it? Or Sally." She shot Ted a mistrustful look. "I said I didn't want to talk to you."

Roger could sense Ted's rising anger. He also knew yelling at or trying to browbeat Meg wasn't going to do any good. "Meg," he said, keeping his voice friendly and reasonable, "whatever you tell me, I have to tell the sergeant, if it's evidence."

"I don't give a damn who you tell. I just don't want to talk to him."

Roger looked over his shoulder at Ted and raised his eyebrows.

"Oh, for Christ's sake." Ted turned and walked out of the cubicle. "Ten minutes," he said as he made his way out of the ward.

"Right." Roger looked back at Meg. "What've you got?"

"No offence, Columbo," said Sally, drawing his attention back to her, "but what's in this for us? I mean, Meg's right, isn't she? He could come after us."

Roger considered for a moment. He wasn't shocked or surprised that the satisfaction of sending Ormond to prison might not be enough for them. Ormond behind bars wouldn't feed or clothe them or protect them from a life of violence. "What would you do if there was some money in this?"

"Go for a holiday," said Meg instantly.

"How much money?" asked Sally with a bit more thought.

"I don't know. Say several thousand."

"Go for a fucking good holiday," said Meg just as quickly.

"Get the hell out of London," said Sally. "Go to college somewhere, finish me A levels, study art."

Roger smiled at Sally. She really did remind him of Polly, the determination to better herself. Her mate Meg would have a holiday in bloody Benidorm, dance all night in the discos, lay on the beach all day working on skin cancer, and two months later she'd be back on the street. But Sally wanted out and he could help her.

"All right," he said, "a lot of the rags are going to want to talk to you after the trial's over and if you play your cards

Unethical Practices

right and sell an exclusive, they'll pay well. I can probably help you sell the story. But they're not going to want a nice story, they're going to want a dirty, nasty story, not the sort of thing you might want your mum and dad reading."

Meg snorted with derision. "My mum and dad? One's a drunk, the other's a pervert and you don't get any marks for guessing which one's which. I couldn't care less what they think."

He looked at Sally.

She shrugged painfully. "Me mum doesn't know who me dad was and, no, I don't really care what she reads about me if it's going to get me out of this life."

"Right," said Roger. "I'm not promising you anything, but I'll do my best for you." He turned his attention back to Meg. "So, what did you want to tell me?"

Meg shifted uncomfortably in the chair and refused to meet Roger's gaze when she began to speak. "The first time I went with him, it wasn't so bad, a bit rough, but no worse than a lot of them. And he paid a damn sight better than most. The second time was worse. He started off telling me how bad I'd been and how I knew he was going to have to punish me. I really thought twice about getting the hell out of there, but he offered double the money and my rent was due. He slapped me around a bit, then did his usual."

"His 'usual'?" Roger interrupted.

"Oh, yeah." Meg finally looked at him, her eyes filled with contempt. "He gets so excited slapping you and trying to bite your bloody nipple off, he comes in his trousers most of the time. Sometimes he manages to get his trousers off, but he never actually does the business. Then he cries for a while, asks you why you never loved him and then he goes."

Roger glanced at Sally, who nodded minutely in confirmation.

Meg continued. "Anyway, the second time I realised afterwards, he'd left this gold tie clip with initials carved on it. I thought about hawking it, then I thought maybe I could make more money selling it back to him. I mean, posh geezer like that wouldn't want his family knowing what he got up to, would he? So, next time he came looking for me, I memorised the registration number of his Jag. There's this copper I do free sometimes for a bit of insurance." She paused to smile at Roger. "He's married, but his wife isn't very experimental, know what I mean?" Roger simply nodded. "I thought he might get a name and address for me. I figured I'd get more money from old silver top for the tie clip at his house than I would in my room, know what I mean?" Although she required no answer, Roger nodded again. "So, we get to my room and then he goes completely mental on me. Starts screaming and shouting how he's going to make me pay for what I've done to him. I thought he was going to kill me. If someone hadn't pounded on my door to find out what the hell was going on, I think he would have." Meg, remembering that night, smiled and shook her head. "Never thought I'd be grateful for having that nosy old cow living opposite me."

"Did you go to the police?" asked Roger.

"Not officially. Didn't see the point. My word against his and he's a rich bastard. Nah. I didn't do nothing except live off the bastard's money 'til me bruises healed enough to go back to work." She looked over at Sally and Roger was touched by the depth of affection he saw in that look. "I wouldn't be talking now if I hadn't seen what that fucker did to Sal." Roger could see tears welling up in her eyes when she looked back at him. "Are you going to get him for this?"

"Yes." There was no doubt in Roger's mind, not this time. "Will you testify against him?"

"Too right."

"Do you still have the tie clip?"

Meg nodded and reached into her bag, extracting a gold tie clip and a piece of paper which she handed to Roger. "And the bleeder's registration number."

Roger looked at the tie clip and couldn't prevent a smile spreading across his face. Carved in gold were the initials VO. This time they *were* going to get the swine. He positively beamed at Meg, his mood so infectious, both women smiled back at him. "Your neighbour," he asked, "the one who knocked on the door, did she see him?"

"Oh, yeah," said Meg, "just before he sent her flying."

"Would she be willing to try to identify him?"

Meg considered for a moment. "Yeah," she said, "I think she would. She hates what I do. Hates me, but she was shocked by what he did to me and she was mad as hell about being knocked over."

Roger could barely contain his glee. Ted was going to love this. Ormond's tie clip and registration number *and* a sweet little old lady to support the evidence. "When was this?" he asked, hoping the incident would still be fresh in the old girl's mind.

Meg didn't hesitate. "Last September, the twenty-seventh, the day after me mate Stef's birthday."

Less than six months, thought Roger, good. Just as he was thinking he couldn't wait to tell Ted, the ward door opened and he turned to see Ted advancing towards them. When he was still five feet away, Roger heard an insistent beeping noise. Ted reached down to remove a pager from his belt and glanced at it.

Before turning on his heel and returning to the corridor to use the telephone, Ted pointed an accusing finger at Meg. "Don't you start thinking about trying to scarper. I'll be able to see those doors from where the phone is."

"Yes, sir, Sergeant Beauchamp, sir." Meg's voice was heavy with sarcasm. She poked her tongue out at his retreating back.

"Why didn't you want to talk to Sergeant Beauchamp?" Roger asked.

Meg rolled her eyes. "Who the hell do you think the fucking copper is I've been fucking for nothing?"

"Did you tell him when you got beaten up?"

"Yes."

"What did he say?"

"He said tarts get beaten up all the time and rich bastards never go to gaol."

"Did you show him the tie clip? The registration number?"

"What for? He made it quite clear he didn't give a toss."

"Oh, God," said Roger. He couldn't even look at Sally's battered face. Of course Meg could not have known she should have pressed Ted, should have given him the tie clip, described the man who'd beaten her. If she had, Ted would have worked it out. He might be a cynical bugger, but he was a damned good copper whose career prospects had been scuppered by Victor Ormond. He would have twigged. He would have gone after Ormond and if he had, Sally Carpenter wouldn't be laying in this hospital bed. Roger couldn't tell Meg any of this. She'd be mad as hell at Ted, but she'd also feel guilty as hell herself and that would not be fair. There was no way for her to have known about Ted's history with Ormond, not if Ted hadn't told her himself, and Roger was sure Ted didn't share his professional humiliations with prostitutes.

When the sergeant returned minutes later, he walked straight up to Meg. "Have you told him what you know?"

Meg batted her eyelashes at him. "Yes, sir, Sergeant Beauchamp."

"Right." Ted turned to Roger. "Come on, let's go. The Werring woman's just rung to say she thinks Ormond killed her daughter."

Roger stood up and followed Ted. As they reached the door, he heard Meg call out, "Give my love to your wife, sergeant."

"Slag," muttered Ted.

Roger looked at him. "Bit like the pot calling the kettle black, Ted," he said.

Ted stopped abruptly in the corridor, turned to face Roger. His face was almost purple with rage.

"Don't start on me, Roger. Don't you think it's been doing my head in ever since I found out who Sally's mate was, knowing that if I'd listened to Meg months ago I might have been able to prevent that? Don't you think Sally Carpenter's face is going to haunt me for the rest of my life? Because it fucking well is. The only thing I can do for her now is catch Ormond and expose him for the sadistic bastard he is. And I'm going to do it. All right?"

Roger nodded. "All right."

When the lift doors opened at the ground floor, Ted collided with a woman carrying a huge bouquet of flowers. Offering a brusque apology, he quickly stepped around her, heading for the exit. Roger, who'd recognised the woman, reached out and grabbed at Ted's jacket.

"Polly," said Roger, "what are you doing here?"

Polly looked at him and smiled a quite radiant smile. "After you left I worked out the bank interest rate on the money Ormond gave me and I realised I could afford to pay him back." She turned her head to look at Ted. "We need to talk."

Ted nodded. "Good for you, Poll. Ring the station and tell them where I can contact you. I'll be in touch in the morning."

Polly looked back at Roger, then raised her eyes in the direction of the wards above. "Do you think she'll mind me coming to see her?"

Roger thought about the determination he'd sensed in Sally Carpenter to get herself off the streets, the same determination Polly'd had. All right, Polly'd made good with a pay off from Ormond, but she'd made good. It would have taken her longer without Ormond's money, but he knew she would have got there in the end.

"Polly," he said, "I think you are probably the very best person she could see right now."

"Thanks, Roger." She stepped into the lift and reached for the button. "I'm glad you came to see me today," she said as the lift doors closed.

"So am I, Poll," Roger told the doors.

"Will you come on?" said Ted, hurrying off without checking to see if Roger was following.

They drove in silence for several minutes, before Roger, unable to conceal his disgust, said, "Christ, Ted, how old is that girl?"

"Meg? I don't know. Nineteen, twenty, twenty-one?"

"And how old are you?"

The traffic light ahead of them was turning red. Ted waited until the car had come to a stop, before turning to face Roger. "I'm a forty-six year old man whose wife hasn't wanted to have sex with him for twenty years since their first and only child died. I don't want to force myself on her. So, if some tart wants to occasionally satisfy my needs in return for helping her out if she gets in trouble, that's fine with me. I don't think it's disgusting and I don't give a fuck if you do. So drop it and tell me what Meg told you."

The light changed and Ted started driving again. Roger relayed the information he'd been given by Meg and handed over the tie clip and registration number. While he was speaking, he realised he was in no position to criticise Ted. In his own day, he'd shagged everything that moved without ever giving a thought to his wife and children. It was all very well blaming Victor Ormond for the break up of his family, but by the time that court case came up he'd thoughtlessly forfeited any right to expect his long suffering wife to stand by him. Compared to him, Ted deserved a bloody medal.

As they approached their destination, a thought struck Roger. "You seem to be in charge of this investigation," he said.

"So?" Ted snapped.

"So, given who Ormond is, I would have thought they'd have put a DCI in charge."

"Yes, well," said Ted, his face grim, "seeing as I'd be a bloody DCI if my career hadn't been flushed down the crapper by the Ormond cock up and seeing as how I now seem to be vindicated, I guess they decided they owed me one. Are we nearly there?"

CHAPTER SIXTEEN

When Cynthia's doorbell rang, Tilly jumped up to answer it. She was getting decidedly antsy. Fascinating as it had been to see Sir Victor Ormond's bedroom and to hear about the beautiful Cynthia's screwed up relations with the Ormond brothers, none of this was getting her any closer to Helen, Jamie Mortimer or whoever Helen's source at VACO was, or to the proof she needed to get her story written. She should have rung Gus hours ago. He'd be apoplectic by now and, for all she knew, had probably given away her space in tomorrow's paper. She should have been chasing leads, not wild geese. Still, as eager as she was to be on her way, she couldn't abandon Helen's distraught mother. And, as desperate as she was to get on a phone, she couldn't tie up Cynthia's line in case the police – or Helen – were trying to get through. A bit late in the day to regret being one of the few people in the entire country who didn't have a bloody mobile.

She crossed the black and white tiled floor of the common hallway and opened the street door, planning to make the arrival of the police her cue to scarper. Her jaw dropped when she spotted Roger standing behind the uniformed sergeant. Before she could ask what the hell he was doing there, the sergeant was demanding to know if she was Cynthia Werring.

Tilly shook her head. "She's just inside," she said, waving vaguely towards the flat door and shooting Roger a quizzical look over the sergeant's shoulder.

"And you are?" the sergeant asked.

Roger performed the introductions, identifying Tilly simply as a colleague. None the wiser, Tilly led the way into Cynthia's picture perfect lounge. The blonde woman, standing by the mantel, took a step towards the new arrivals, her hand extended, an introduction forming on her lips which remained unspoken.

"Bloody hell," said Ted, glancing over his shoulder at Roger. Having seen the former prostitute so recently, he couldn't miss the resemblance. "She *does* look like Polly."

Cynthia, who'd evinced no interest in the reappearance of Roger, looked at him then. "You said 'Polly' when you arrived earlier. Who is she?"

Ted answered for him. "Polly Hall is a prostitute your brother-in-law Victor got away with savagely beating years ago. She bears a striking resemblance to you, Mrs Werring."

"To me?" Cynthia's aquamarine eyes widened in shock. She shook her head, as if to free herself of this unwelcome news. "All I remember about that case is seeing an awful picture of the poor woman on the front page of one of the papers, but, well, I mean, it was impossible to tell from that picture what she looked like. I had no idea. How ghastly."

"Did you read about the case at the time?" asked Ted.

"Well, yes, of course I did. I assumed he was guilty and I was hoping he would go to prison. It was just after – " Cynthia broke off. Her mind seemed to be grappling with the implications of the thought which had just occurred to her.

Ted prompted her. "Just after what?"

"Just after I'd tried to get him locked up for trying to abduct my daughter Helen. The police refused to arrest him, but they made it clear they would if he ever went near her again. In fact, it must have been a day or two later, because, when I heard he'd been charged with something, I thought at first they'd decided to take the business with Helen more seriously."

Ted turned to look at Roger, shaking his head in amazement. "I don't believe this. Victor Ormond was in trouble with the police the day before he beat up Polly and there was no record of it when we arrested him? The prosecution might not have folded so easily if they'd known about that."

"Look," Cynthia interrupted, taking three paces towards Ted until she was standing right in front of him, "please don't think I'm not sympathetic about what happened to that woman, but all this has nothing to do with why I called."

Everyone in the room could hear the hysteria rising in her voice. "Victor Ormond left a message on my answering machine telling me he'd killed my daughter. Why the hell are we talking about anything else?"

"I'm sorry," said Ted, brought abruptly back to the present. "Could we hear the message?"

They were all still standing. Tilly, the closest to the desk, pressed the replay button. Victor Ormond's voice filled the room.

Ted listened to the message, his brows furrowed in concentration. After a moment he asked to hear it again. When the message had finished the second time, he shook his head, looked at Cynthia and said, "Why are you so sure he's talking about your daughter?"

Cynthia could not disguise the exasperation in her tone. "Because he kidnapped her yesterday and no one has seen her since."

Ted shot Roger a fierce, questioning look. Roger, who, the moment he spotted the resemblance between Victor Ormond's ex-sister-in-law and Polly, had forgotten all about Helen Ormond and Bowinda and coated seeds, shrugged an apology.

"Right," said Ted, "I think we'd better begin at the beginning." He turned to Cynthia. "But before we do, Ms Werring, I want you to know I don't think that message was about your daughter. Last night your brother-in-law left a young woman for dead in an hotel room. While he was beating her, he called her a number of names, including yours. I'm sure that's the murder he's talking about. There's a warrant out. We just need to find him."

Tilly watched the colour drain from Cynthia's face. Bit bloody brutal, she thought, just tossing that nasty titbit at the poor woman. Clearing her throat to draw Ted's attention, she picked up and handed him the piece of paper on which they'd written Victor's number. "We did a 1471. This is the number he was ringing from We've tried it. There's no reply."

Ted grabbed the paper from her hand, swearing a moment later when he realised he'd left his mobile at the station. Had Till not stepped aside, he would have shoved her out of his way to get to Cynthia's phone. Snatching the receiver out of its cradle, he punched in a number, then spoke with urgency to someone at the other end, providing them with the number Tilly had given him and instructions to ring him back immediately at Cynthia's number.

When he'd finished his call, he looked first at Cynthia, then at Tilly. "Who wants to start?"

"I will," said Tilly, pulling out the desk the chair, sitting down and crossing her long legs. Cynthia perched on the edge of a chintz covered arm chair. Ted just dropped his wiry frame onto the matching sofa, where Roger, after a moment during which he wondered if anything on his clothes might stain the upholstery, sat down beside the sergeant.

Quickly and succinctly, Tilly described being approached by Helen with an offer to provide proof of an unethical deal VACO was concocting, of the message from Helen she'd found waiting on her answering machine and the one from Alec, of Alec's description of Helen's apparent abduction by a man who looked like Victor Ormond, of the phone call she'd received demanding the return of the proof Helen had provided.

"So you have no idea what was on this disk?" asked Ted.

Tilly knew she didn't dare look at Roger. Willing him not to contradict her – she was after all still working on a story and Roger should understand – she shrugged. "I couldn't open it on my computer. The print out seemed to be in some kind of code."

At that moment the telephone rang. Cynthia began to stand. Ted, ignoring her, leapt to his feet, leaned over Tilly, snatched the receiver and barked his name into it. He listened for a moment, then said, "Well, get someone the hell over there. Wait a minute, just a sec." He placed his hand over the receiver and glanced over his shoulder at Cynthia. "That number is for a house Victor Ormond owns in Gloucestershire. Anything you can tell me about it?"

Cynthia shook her head. "I didn't know he owned anything other than the house in Kent." She thought for a moment, then added, "He used to enjoy shooting."

Ted frowned. "So, there could be guns?"

"I don't know. I vaguely remember him talking years ago about wanting a shooting estate in Scotland. Maybe he decided Scotland was too far away." She shook her head apologetically. "Sorry, I simply have no idea why he has a house there."

Ted spoke back into the phone. "Okay, listen, there's a chance he's got guns there, so make sure people are tooled up and tell them not to be stupid. Put Walker on." A moment later he said, "Okay, tell me what you've got." He pulled a notebook out of his pocket and began scribbling. "Good work. I'm going to call you back in a bit with some more possible dates. Send someone back to the Ormond house in Kent and get them to put the frighteners on the staff. Tell them they'll all be held as accessories to a kidnapping which has a twenty year sentence. Tell them they're all going straight to fucking gaol if they don't tell you where the hell Ormond and his niece Helen are. There's a house full of bloody servants. One of them knows something... What..? I didn't ask them this afternoon because I wasn't looking for her then, was I? I was looking for him. I didn't know," Ted gave Roger a disgusted look, "she was missing then, did I? So, just do it."

He replaced the receiver and turned to Cynthia. "Right, Mrs Werring, as you've heard, I'm getting someone to check on your daughter, but my gut feeling is she isn't with Ormond. I suspect she got away from him and she's lying low somewhere. I'll tell you why I suspect this in a moment, because I'm going to need you to help me put some of the pieces together. All right?"

Cynthia nodded and Ted crossed the room, squatting down in front of her. "First," he said, "I need to understand why you think Ormond is such a threat to your daughter. Is it just because of this stolen information or is there something else I should know?"

Cynthia gaped at him, as if unable to believe his obtuseness. She reached behind her and picked up a silver framed photograph, which she turned towards him. From across the room, Tilly could see that it was a photograph of Helen, taken in a garden somewhere, sunshine turning her long, white gold hair almost platinum. "That's my daughter, Sergeant," Cynthia said. "She looks just like me when I was her age. You've just finished telling me that Victor Ormond makes a practice of beating up women who look like me."

Ted glanced briefly at the photograph, then raised his gaze

to Cynthia's and said, "Forgive me, Ms Werring, but you didn't know about the other women when you rang, so you must be concerned about something else. I'd also like to know why you think he wants to beat up women who look like you."

"Isn't it obvious?" asked Cynthia. "He's completely insane."

"It may be obvious to you, Ms Werring, but I need some help understanding."

Cynthia looked down for several moments at the immaculately manicured hands she was squeezing together in her lap. Finally, without looking up, she said, "Is this really necessary?"

"Yes, I'm afraid it is."

Cynthia sat, head bowed, for another moment or two, then stood up abruptly, nearly unbalancing Ted, still hunkered down in front of her. "I understand that you need to know this, Sergeant. Forgive me if I really do not want to tell you myself." She glanced over at Tilly. "I told Ms Arbuthnot the whole sorry story this afternoon and I freely give her my permission to tell you whatever you want to know. While she does, I'm going to the kitchen to make some tea."

Ted, struggling to his feet, looked as if he was going to give her an argument. Tilly, who didn't see why Cynthia Werring should have to go through the whole thing twice in one day, stood up quickly and smiled at Ted. She locked her cobalt blue eyes unto his, in the same unwavering and, she'd been told, mesmerising stare she had over the years used successfully on cabinet ministers and industry captains who were attempting, unsuccessfully, to steer her off course. "Yes, Sergeant Beauchamp," she said, slipping her arm through his and guiding him towards the sofa Roger had just abandoned.

Roger was moving towards the doorway, offering to help Cynthia. It was clear both to Roger and to Tilly, observing from the sofa, that Cynthia was torn between the desire for company of any sort and the desire to be two days in the past when none of this had happened. "Yes," she said, "as long as you don't mind if I burst into tears."

Roger smiled. "You'll never believe this looking at me, but I actually have a very clean hankie in my pocket."

Cynthia returned his smile. "Follow me, then."

As she led Roger towards the kitchen, Tilly began to tell

the story of Victor Ormond's far from magnificent obsession. She left out the brief affair with Charles, because she didn't think it was any of Ted's business, but included the younger Ormond brother's efforts to force Victor to stay away from Cynthia. She also, of course, left out all details about Bowinda, General Radad and VACO 17872, although these were the details preying most heavily on her mind. When, she wondered, could she decently make her escape?

She still didn't have any proof, nothing, as Roger had been quick to point out, with Victor Ormond's name connecting him to General Radad. If she went to Gus with nothing but hearsay and suspicions, he'd never print it.

Even with Jack Conquest swearing blind on his scientific bible that VACO 17872 could have been an ecological disaster of the worst magnitude, it didn't mean anything. Corporations were constantly working on new products. Some, like this one, didn't pan out. Never mind that its withdrawal had been a bit of eleventh hour good luck. The fact was there hadn't been a disaster. Good news was not news.

She had no proof that a shipment was being prepared, God forbid might have already left for Bowinda. Gus wouldn't run the story. Neither would she, if she was in charge. All Victor Ormond had to do if a story ran was cancel the shipment and ring his solicitor.

When she'd gone after VACO before, she'd had her ducks all lined up nicely. It had galled her then that she hadn't been able to prove that Victor Ormond was personally responsible for steaming the labels off those canisters of nerve gas before they were shipped to India, but she'd had the proof that someone at VACO had. Thinking back to that afternoon in Ormond's solicitor's office, she remembered the look of absolute astonishment on Ormond's face when the paper's solicitor presented Tilly's evidence. At the time she'd assumed he was simply amazed that she had managed to lay hands on the proof to back up her allegations. Ormond had come into the room confident and sneering. He'd left stunned and defeated. Tilly hadn't given it a second thought. Someone at VACO had authorised the alteration of that product. Victor Ormond was the chairman of the board. Who else could have been responsible?

Tilly glanced at Ted, who was nodding, as if everything she'd told him fitted in with his theory — which was what, exactly? Although part of her wanted to bolt, curiosity won. What was this copper so cocky about? She decided it was her turn to extract some information. "Why are you so sure Helen's all right?" she asked.

In the state of the art kitchen, much the same conversation was unfolding between Roger and Cynthia. After switching on the kettle, she'd turned to him and said, "Forgive me, I've forgotten your name and I haven't the faintest idea how you're involved in all this. Are you with the police?"

Roger, uncomfortably aware of how shabby he must look to this sleek, chic, elegant woman, shook his head. "No, I'm not with the police. My name's Roger Wilcox. I was the journalist who broke the story about your brother-in-law beating Polly. I'm the one who was fired and bankrupted when the case against him was thrown out."

"I'm sorry," she said with genuine sympathy.

"So am I." Roger spoke with rather more venom than he'd intended.

Cynthia leaned back against the tile counter and crossed her arms in front of herself protectively. Her expression was thoughtful, the sad shake of her head almost imperceptible. "God, I wish I'd known that poor woman looked like me. If I'd known that was why he beat her, I'd like to think I would have come forward. I don't know if it would have helped. It might have."

"I shouldn't worry about it," Roger said. "I doubt it would have made that much difference. Polly herself blocked out a lot of that night. She didn't remember until a couple of years later that he kept calling her Cynthia when he beat her." As soon as the words were out of his mouth he regretted them.

Cynthia bit her lip and blinked back tears which suddenly filled her eyes. "He really did that? He really called her by my name?"

"I'm sorry. I shouldn't have – "

"No. I want to know. Tell me, please."

The kettle began to boil. Roger looked around unsuccessfully for a teapot. Cynthia crossed the room and opened a cupboard door. After warming the pot, she began to spoon tea leaves in to it. As she filled the pot, she shot Roger a pleading look

"All right," said Roger. "I think I know where Ted's going with this. Polly was beaten up just after you had the law on him all those years ago. The girl last night, it's pretty easy to work out that had something to do with you and your daughter. There's at least one other girl we know about who he beat pretty badly last September."

Cynthia stared at Roger, her eyes wide with dismay. "When in September?"

Roger thought for a moment. "The twenty-seventh."

"Oh, God." Cynthia reached for a chair to support herself, then sank into it.

"The twenty-seventh of September is my birthday," she said. "I went out for a meal with some friends. Victor turned up at the restaurant. I don't know whether it was by accident or design. I suspect the latter, because I suspect everything about him. He tried to talk to me. I told him if he didn't leave I'd ring the police. We'd all had rather a lot of champagne by then. Two of my friends took it upon themselves to frog march him put of the restaurant. He was furious." She paused and shook her head. "I never thought, I mean, it never occurred to me he'd vent his anger by going out and beating someone. I feel awful."

"Well, you shouldn't," Roger spoke firmly. "Why should it have occurred to you? No sane person would behave that way."

"But that's the point. I've known for years that Victor is completely mad. I just didn't think he might be a danger to anyone except Helen and me." Tears welled up in her eyes and began to trickle down her cheeks. Cynthia ignored them. "Christ. I should have gone to the police when he tried to rape me." She looked up at Roger, an appeal in her brimming eyes. "I didn't want to hurt my mother-in-law. I didn't want my husband to know. Oh, God. If I'd gone to the police then, none of this would have happened."

Roger rummaged in his pocket and withdrew a handkerchief which he was relieved to find was unused. He handed it to Cynthia, who used it to try to stem the flow of tears, then wiped her nose. "Unless there's something you're not telling me," he said, "like you killed his puppy when he was a boy, you really can't blame yourself. Victor Ormond's an evil swine and I'm not a man who throws the word evil around lightly. After seeing what he did to that girl last night, frankly, it's my opinion he wants putting down. It's not your fault he beats up women. It's his."

Cynthia tried, without a great deal of success, to smile. "Thank you."

"Don't mention it." Roger looked vaguely around the kitchen. "Where are the cups?"

"Oh, here, let me do that." Cynthia quickly set up a tray. "Could you bring the pot?" she asked, leading the way back into the lounge.

Tilly was only half listening to Ted as he outlined his theory that Victor Ormond went off his head and sought out blonde prostitutes to beat whenever he was annoyed with his sister-in-law or niece.

If true, it certainly gave her an entirely new reason to detest the chairman of VACO. Although, seeing him in prison for assault would not be sufficient consolation if she failed to stop the shipment to Bowinda.

Roger and Cynthia returned with the tea and the news that there was a match for the night of Meg's beating. Ted produced the list of similar attacks he'd been given on the phone and began to check these with Cynthia.

The first three matched dates she could remember when acrimonious incidents between herself and Victor had occurred. The fourth and fifth meant nothing to her. As Ted reeled off another date, Cynthia held up a protesting hand to silence him.

"Sergeant," she said, "I am perfectly willing to help you with this exercise, but you must understand, this isn't helping me find my daughter."

Ted hesitated. It was clear to Tilly that he was far more interested in matching dates than missing daughters, but it was also obvious he realised he was being unfair. Tilly watched as he struggled to tear himself away from his mission. She was surprised when he turned to face her.

"You said you recognised Victor Ormond's voice on the

answering machine as soon as you heard it this afternoon," Ted said. "Was it the same person who rang you last night?"

Tilly couldn't believe she hadn't thought of this herself. "No," she said, "definitely not. It was cultured voice, not terribly deep, but not high pitched, just, I don't know how to describe it, very relaxed, but very firm. Definitely not Victor Ormond."

"What about this other fellow at the junction, the one with Ormond?"

"Oh," said Cynthia, who'd been in the room when Tilly offered Alec's description of the two men on the platform, "that's Johnson, Victor's henchman. He's been with him for years. He has a strong Cockney accent and, for a man his size, a surprisingly high pitched voice."

She looked at Tilly, who shook her head emphatically. "The man on the phone last night didn't have a hint of a Cockney accent." Something niggled in the back of her mind. There was something else about the voice, something she couldn't quite pull back from the conversation the previous evening.

"Right," said Ted, "so there's a third man involved. Someone from VACO, I should think."

"What about the car?" asked Roger. His gaze shifted from Ted to Cynthia. "It can't be a coincidence someone stole your car of all the cars in London to make this pick up."

Ted nodded his agreement. "Does anyone else have the keys to your car, Mrs Werring?"

Cynthia shook her head. "Helen used to have a set. But she lost them after she'd borrowed the car last year for a trip to Alsace. I've been meaning to get her another set cut, but I never have."

Tilly stood up. She didn't really care how the hell Victor Ormond or whoever it was had got hold of Cynthia's car keys. She had to ring Gus and tell him she was coming in to write her copy. Even if she didn't have everything she needed, she had to make sure she still had some space in the morning's paper. She reached towards the telephone receiver, but before she could pick it up, the phone rang. Cynthia almost jumped off her chair at the sound of the bell. All eyes turned towards Tilly. She picked up the receiver and handed it to Ted, who was already reaching for it.

He listened for a moment, then said, "Right, what's the date on that one? *How* long ago? Jesus Christ. Okay, keep me posted." He handed the receiver back to Tilly and looked at Cynthia. "Nineteenth August nineteen eighty-one?"

Cynthia sank back against her chair. "That's two days after Helen was born."

Ted glanced at Roger. "Looks like Polly wasn't the first. Just the first to come forward."

Cynthia put her face in her hands and shuddered. "This is a nightmare," she said, more to herself than anyone else in the room.

Ted placed a hand gently on her arm. "Mrs Werring, I realise how difficult this must be for you, but if you could try to remember any other dates when you and Victor Ormond clashed in some way?"

With an effort, Cynthia lowered her hands back into her lap and straightened. "All right, Sergeant Beauchamp," she said. "Let me think."

Clearly there were two stories now, thought Tilly, watching Ted and Roger scribble down everything Cynthia said, but the second story, the story of Victor Ormond's vicious assaults on young women, that story belonged to Roger. Tilly didn't know if this vindication would bring him peace, but she was certain his name would appear at the top of at least one more national press story. And he deserved to savour every moment of it.

She was just reaching for the receiver again to ring Gus when she remembered Jamie, Helen's friend, the mysterious VACO scientist, who was supposed to be calling round. Tilly glanced at her watch. Surely, he should be here by now? She absolutely had to talk to that young man.

"I'm sorry to interrupt," she said. Three heads turned to face her. "Helen's friend, Jamie. You said he was going to call. Shall I ring him and see if he's heard anything?"

Cynthia flashed her a smile radiant with gratitude. "Yes, please. How wonderful of you to remember. His number is in my book by the phone. It's under M for Mortimer."

Ted spoke while Tilly was looking up the number. "Keep it short. I'm expecting calls."

"Of course," said Tilly, although she needn't have bothered.

Unethical Practices

Before the words were out of her mouth, Ted had already reclaimed Cynthia's attention.

Tilly, her back to the others, pulled a pen and small notebook from her jacket pocket. Pressing the receiver against her ear with her shoulder, she quickly wrote down Jamie's address and telephone number with her right hand as she punched the number in with her left. At the other end of the line the call was answered almost immediately.

"Helen?" asked a deep, eager voice.

"No," said Tilly. "I'm ringing on behalf of her mother to see if you've heard from her."

"Who is this?"

"Tilly Arbuthnot."

"Ah, Ms Arbuthnot. I'm glad you're there. We need to talk."

In her head the Hallelujah Chorus began. Yes, she thought, I'm going to get the evidence I need. "Have you heard from Helen?" she asked.

"Is Cynthia with you?"

"Yes."

"Can she see you?"

Although she had no idea why he wanted to know, she could sense that it was important. "Not really, no."

"All right," said Jamie. "I'm not supposed to tell anyone this. I promised Helen I wouldn't. She's just rung me, but she doesn't want her mother to know where she is. I don't know why, but she doesn't want to see her. Helen's fine. I'm going to meet her now. Where can we meet you later?"

"When?"

"I'm not sure. An hour? Two at the most."

Tilly thought furiously. She knew enough to get the story started. Even if she didn't have hard evidence in her hand, if Jamie really worked at VACO and was willing to be quoted, she could go ahead. She lowered her voice. "Are you willing to talk to me?" She didn't explain what she meant and prayed Jamie understood.

"Yes," he said. "I want this exposed."

Hallelujah, hallelujah, hallelujah. "Meet me at the paper," she said, quickly giving him the address. "I'll be in the news editor's office."

"We'll be there," he promised. "Tell Cynthia I'm sorry, I

can't tell her more. I promised. But tell her Helen is safe and she's fine. All right?"

"Absolutely."

Tilly could sense a movement. She turned to find Cynthia standing beside her, reaching for the receiver. "Has he heard from her?" Cynthia asked. Tilly nodded. Cynthia snatched the receiver from her hand. "Jamie? Jamie it's Cynthia. What have you heard? Where is she? Is she all right?... What?... What do you mean you can't tell me?... Jamie, for God's sake, I'm at my wit's end... All right, just tell me this: is she with Victor?... You're sure?... All right. Please, just make sure you get her to ring me as soon as you can... Bless you, Jamie. You're an angel."

Cynthia replaced the receiver, then looked at Tilly. "She doesn't want to see me because she believed that ludicrous note. That's it, isn't it?"

Tilly shrugged. "From everything you told me this afternoon, yes, I'd say you were right."

"God." Cynthia pounded her fist on the desk so hard, the phone rattled in its cradle, pens jumped about and the shade on the lamp rocked gently. "I am going to kill Victor Ormond. I swear I am."

Behind them, Ted Beauchamp cleared his throat. "Mrs Werring, I know you don't really mean that, but it's not the sort of remark you should make in front of the police."

Despite himself and the seriousness of the situation, Roger guffawed. "Oh, come on, Ted. It would make more sense to tell her to get in the bloody queue." He looked at Cynthia. "If you really want to get Victor Ormond, the best thing you can do is help Ted locate the women the bastard's assaulted."

Cynthia smiled. "Yes, of course. Now that I know Helen's all right, I'll tell you whatever I can." To Tilly she said, "She will get in touch with me, won't she? There are so many things I should have told her years ago, but I couldn't make myself talk about it. She'll understand why I couldn't face telling her about Victor, won't she?"

Tilly, who had no idea how she was supposed to know the answer to any of these questions, nonetheless squeezed Cynthia's hand. "I'm sure she will," she said. "I must go. I'll ring you later."

"Thank you," said Cynthia. "Thank you for listening. For everything."

Tilly was reaching for the street door when Roger caught up with her.

"Where the bloody hell are you going?" he demanded.

Tilly pulled the door open and looked at Roger over her shoulder. "I've got to get to the paper. There were three messages from Gus on my machine three hours ago. If I don't get there soon, he's going to drop the story."

"But you don't have your story."

Tilly smiled and tapped the side of her nose, mocking Roger's knowing gesture earlier that day. God, she thought, was it really just this morning? "I will if Jamie Mortimer, Helen's source at VACO, keeps his promise to meet me there."

Roger grinned back at her. "Jammy."

"You won't tell Ted?"

"'Course not. What do you take me for? But it'll cost you."

Tilly sighed. "What?"

"Ask Gus to save me some space. After the way I got dumped on by the red tops, I'm buggered if I'm going to give any of them first shot at this."

CHAPTER SEVENTEEN

Tilly flagged a taxi near South Ken station, gave the driver the address in Farringdon Road and climbed into the back. As the cab chugged its way through London, she found herself again wishing that she'd given up earlier and bought a mobile phone. It had been more bloody mindedness than concern about fried brains. The way people looked at you as if you were some sort of dinosaur when you confessed you didn't have a mobile got right up her nose. She had absolutely no desire to be available, as the current phrase had it, 24/7. Humanity had survived quite nicely without mobiles for a very long time, and Tilly had intended to prove that she could survive without one indefinitely. But she had to admit it would have been useful this evening. She should have rung Gus to let him know she was on her way, but she knew Ted Beauchamp would have grabbed the phone out of her hand if she'd tried to use it at Cynthia's. She should have also tried to check in with Jack, find out where he was.

Of course, there were a lot of things she should have done in the past two days which she'd abysmally failed to do. She could spend the journey chastising herself or she could start mentally composing her story.

Forty-five minutes after flagging the cab, she entered the newspaper building and, appalled by the lax security in the early evening hours, walked past the empty reception desk to board a lift to the fourth floor newsroom. The news editor, Angus MacPherson – 'Gus' to his friends amongst whom he clearly did not number Tilly at that moment – was standing in the middle of the big, open plan room. He began to holler as soon as he spotted her.

"Where the hell have you been?" he demanded. "I gave up on you an hour ago, you stupid cow. This isn't some old film,

Tilly. I can't just hold the front page. What the fuck's the matter with you?"

Despite the curses and name calling, Tilly simply smiled at Gus. She'd known him for twenty years. They'd first met in an hotel bar in Beirut and for a decade afterwards they'd been reunited in trouble spots all over the world, until Gus decided his marriage and his mortgage required a desk job in London. She knew his nose for news wouldn't let either of them down.

"Just listen for a minute, before you have a stroke," she said. "Not only will I have a VACO scientist in here very soon, who is prepared to swear on a stack of bibles that VACO is planning to ship an ecological disaster to Bowinda, but Sir Victor Ormond is about to be arrested for assault and attempted murder."

Gus held up his hands to silence her. "No, you listen to me, Tilly Arbuthnot. I will give you," he looked at his watch, "ninety minutes to produce the Bowinda story, but after what happened to Roger Wilcox, I am not touching an assault charge against Victor Ormond until the bastard's in gaol."

Tilly shook her head and perched on the side of a desk. "Gus, this time they've got him bang to rights. I've just been with the police. They're on their way to arrest Ormond as we speak and Roger was the one who got them to reopen the investigation. It sounds as if they have women crawling out of the woodwork to testify against him. And," she added triumphantly, "Roger is prepared to offer you an exclusive on this for tomorrow's paper."

"No chance, Tilly. Roger Wilcox hasn't drawn a sober breath in years. I'm not risking a lawsuit for him."

Tilly rolled here eyes. "I'm telling you, Gus, there won't be a lawsuit. This time they've got Ormond and Roger's been in on it from the start. You know I don't normally go for sensationalism, but Sir Victor Ormond gets his thrills beating up women, he's going to be arrested for it and he deserves to have it splashed all over the front page, especially after he got away with it before. The other papers will all run with it tomorrow, you know they will, but they won't know what Roger knows, and he, I promise you, is stone cold sober today."

Gus considered Tilly for a long time before saying, "All

right, but if this backfires and I end up sacked, I swear to God, I will hound you until the day you die and, if it turns out there is an afterlife, I will hound you throughout eternity. Understood?"

"Absolutely, Gus."

"Right. Where's your bloody story?"

Tilly pointed at her head. "Just lead me to a computer and tell me how to get in touch with whoever does your who's in town beat."

"Such as?" asked Gus, indicating the desk Tilly should use.

"World leaders. I need to know when Radad was last in England." Five minutes later she was on the phone with a woman named Allison, who assured her General Radad hadn't been in the UK in the past two years. This left Tilly needing to know when Sir Victor Ormond had been to Bowinda to meet with the General. Allison suggested Tilly contact Lynn, the business reporter who covered the energy and chemical industries. Lynn, it turned out, was still in the newsroom, working on an equally tight deadline to finish a story about an oil spill off the coast of Brittany.

"Never," said Lynn, after Gus had introduced them and Tilly had asked her question. She didn't even glance in Tilly's direction, her eyes remaining glued to her computer screen.

"How do you know he's never been to Bowinda?" Tilly asked.

Lynn sighed, tore her eyes away from her screen, leaned back in her chair and looked at Tilly. "Little known and not for publication fact: Sir Victor Ormond is terrified of flying. He's never been off the European continent. That's why he put his brother Charles, whom he detests, in charge of the US end and overseeing operations on all the other continents."

Well, wondered Tilly, after thanking Lynn and allowing her to get back to her story, how the hell did I, in all my research into Victor Ormond, never manage to unearth that particular titbit? Unless Sir Victor's greed had somehow overcome his aerophobia, he and General Radad must have had some sort of unofficial meeting in the UK and that was going to be difficult to prove. Still, it wasn't essential to the story. She had the print out of Arthur Ormond's report on VACO 17872 to prove her allegations about the product and

Jamie Mortimer would be here soon to confirm the plan to ship the seeds to Bowinda. There was plenty to work on until the VACO scientist arrived.

Taking a deep breath, she began to type: *In 1998, chemical giant VACO Industries patented a new product from their biotechnology laboratories. Until today, few people will have heard of VACO product 17872 which was successfully designed to...*

She typed furiously, unaware that Gus had left his office and was standing behind her, reading over her shoulder until some time later when she heard him say, "Jesus Christ! Can you prove this?"

Tilly nodded. "As soon as my scientist gets here." She did not turn to look at Gus. They'd known one another too long and been in too many tight corners together. She knew he would pounce on any uncertainty in her eyes and she had to admit she was beginning to feel a twinge of anxiety. The fact was, she didn't have an original of Arthur Ormond's report and had no way of proving where she got the information. It was over an hour since Jamie Mortimer had told her he and Helen would be here in an hour. Or two, she reminded herself, and hour or *two*. Tilly wasn't breaking into a sweat yet, but her whole story depended on their verification. Without it, Gus would never take a chance. Gus trusted her as no other editor in the country did. If he didn't run the story, no one would.

The thought of VACO Bloody Industries successfully conspiring with that bastard Radad in the genocide of the Kisga people because she couldn't persuade the press or the authorities to stop them filled her with dread – and fury.

Tilly slumped back in her seat, closed her eyes. Bowinda. How many years was it since she'd been to Bowinda? Eight? Ten? And yet she could shut her eyes and hear the voice of Jeremy, the gentle Kisga giant, talking to her as they stood watching the gas flares lighting up the night sky over once fertile farm land. She had seen with her own eyes the pipeline spills which had destroyed that farmland and poisoned water holes, had seen the people sharing out the poisoned crops they grew in what little arable land was left to them. And still the Kisga would not be subdued. Their leaders, people like

Jeremy, spoke out against Radad, against the moral and environmental crimes perpetrated in their land.

'Radad would kill us all if he thought he could get away with it, but he can't,' Jeremy had said to her that night. 'Not even his greedy corporate friends could tolerate that.' And now one of those greedy corporate friends was planning to help Radad do just that.

Too late to warn Jeremy about the threat. He'd been assassinated by Radad two years earlier, following the verdict of a kangaroo court convened to find Jeremy guilty of some bogus charge. Until now this had been Radad's favourite form of problem solving. Not long ago four other activists had suffered a similar fate. And, just to underscore the way the world was run, a fortnight later jolly General Radad and his brutal regime were being hailed as bastions of stability at a U.N. conference on Africa.

But, Tilly realised, her eyes snapping open, even if she could not stop the shipment or lay the villainy behind it at Victor Ormond's feet, it was not too late to get a warning to the Kisga people to reject the generous general's gift of seeds. She might not get Ormond, but she could and she would foil Radad's plan.

Tilly, who'd completely forgotten Gus was standing behind her, was startled when she heard him speak. "I assume this is why a herd of greenies have locked themselves to the gates at VACO?"

Jack! With everything else going on she'd completely forgotten asking him if he could exert any influence with the rainbow warriors. He'd done it, God love him. "How long have they been there?" she asked. Oh, lord, was it possible? Had they stopped the shipment?

Gus leaned against her desk and shook his head. "God knows. I just heard it on the radio. Normally they send out a press release as long as your arm with a dozen bloody footnotes referencing all their science." He gestured with his head towards the other side of the office. "I checked the news desk e-mail and the fax machine. Not a dicky bird. Just rang their press officer on call and she didn't seem to know what the hell they were doing or why. Gave me a load of cobblers about VACO being evil incarnate, but no bloody facts."

Unethical Practices

"That's wonderful," Tilly said.

Gus clearly could not see why. He stood up, frowning. "Let me know when your scientist gets here," he said, tapping his watch. "Half a fucking hour, Tilly, and I'm going to have to decide whether or not to pull the plug on you."

She gave him a radiant smile, filled with a confidence she did not feel. "Don't worry, Gus," she said, reaching for the phone to ring Jack. "Go take your blood pressure medication. Everything'll be fine."

Gus pointed an accusing finger at her. "Eternity, Tilly. I'm not fucking joking."

CHAPTER EIGHTEEN

It was several hours since Victor Ormond had arrived at the house in Gloucestershire and left his message on Cynthia's answering machine. He'd spent the time drinking first claret, then cognac. When the phone started to ring, he'd unplugged it. He couldn't talk to anyone. He had to think.

All day long anger and disgust had been warring within him. Anger at all the love, rightfully his, which had been withheld from him – first his mother, then his father, then Cynthia, then Helen. All of them refusing to give him the love he deserved. It was so unfair.

That Cynthia refused to acknowledge the strength of their feelings for one another was the cruellest of all. They could have been so happy together, but, no, she'd chosen Arthur, just as his father had. But he had been so sure he was the one she really wanted. That's why he'd had to make her admit it, but even after they'd been together, still she pretended she hated him.

It hadn't been easy to act as if there was nothing between them, but when he found out Cynthia was carrying his child he knew he had to maintain the pretence. Of course, she was obliged, for Arthur's and Amelia's sake, to say the child was Arthur's, but Victor knew the truth. He also knew how cruel Cynthia could be.

He couldn't understand it. Why did she act as if there was nothing between them? Why did she taunt him so? In his dreams, she was an angel of submission, allowing him to do whatever he wished with her. But in his waking hours she treated him at best with fear, at worst with contempt. How could she prefer Charles to him? How could she have married Arthur when he'd asked her first? Why, oh why had she tormented him so?

And then he'd found her in that hotel bar, just after Helen's birth, tarted up with her hair slicked back, sitting on a stool, wearing an obscenely short, tight skirt that displayed sheer black tights up to her ass, sitting there, smoking a cigarette, letting men, any man but him, ogle her, smiling at them in a way she never smiled at him. He'd been furious, sitting in a booth, watching her at the bar. Eventually she'd become aware of his eyes on her, had turned and smiled that seductive smile at him. When he made no move to join her, barely able to contain his rage, she'd slid off her bar stool and slithered across the room, leaning her palms on the table, her breasts almost touching his face, the smell of her perfume assaulting his nose.

"Buy me a drink?" she'd asked, touching her hip against his arm to suggest he move over and let her sit down. Finally, Victor had thought. Finally she's admitting she wants me. He shifted along the booth and she pushed in beside him. He could hear the sound her tights made, pressing one leg against the other as she moved closer until her thigh was touching his. He signalled to the waiter to bring two more drinks and turned to look at Cynthia. He didn't like her hair that way, didn't like her dressed that way. It made him even more furious with her than he was when she pretended to treat him with contempt.

As the waiter placed another scotch in front of him and something frothy in front of her, she reached under the table to place her hand between his legs. He slapped her hand away. She looked at him and, after a moment's consideration, asked him what was wrong.

"You know what's wrong," he'd told her. "You've been very bad."

Instead of looking ashamed, she'd smiled at him, dimples he'd never noticed before appearing in her cheek. "I know," she'd said. "What are you going to do about it?"

Victor had hardly been able to believe his ears. For the first time in his waking hours she was admitting how wrong she'd been, how badly she'd behaved towards him. He grabbed the wrist of her hand which was once again inching across his leg and squeezed until he saw her wince. "What I want, Cynthia," he'd hissed, "is to give you what you deserve."

Her eyes widened and he realised for the first time that she must be wearing coloured contact lenses, as her aquamarine irises were brown. The hair, the clothes, the contact lenses. What was she doing here? Why was she behaving like this? It made no sense, but before he could think it through, he realised she was smiling at him, assessing him through now almost closed eyes. "I have been bad and I should be punished," she'd said, "but it'll cost you." With her free hand, she picked up the frothy pink drink, tipped it back against her lips and downed it in one go. Then she'd looked at him, her smile broadening, that dimple reappearing. "Got a room here?"

He hadn't, but he soon acquired one. The satisfaction he'd felt at being able, in his waking, feeling hours, to do whatever he wanted to her was well worth the price she'd charged. He'd certainly wiped that knowing smile off her face.

And finally he'd understood the rules of her game. If he wanted her, he could find her. He just had to go out looking and he just had to be willing to pay.

She'd got even with him for that first beating, forcing Arthur to take Helen, his, Victor's child, back to that cottage. If his mother hadn't had that second stroke, he might never have got Helen back, but once they were in the house, Victor was determined of one thing: his daughter would be raised under his roof. Cynthia could deny him herself, but he would never allow her to deny him his child.

Part of him hated her game. Part of him wanted to take her in the house, right under Arthur's nose. But there was his mother to consider. And, besides, part of him liked the game, liked the hunt, liked knowing he'd earned the right to do whatever he wanted to her. If she hadn't done anything really dreadful to him, hadn't angered him beyond endurance, then he could just take her after making her degrade herself. But, if she pushed him beyond endurance, like the time she'd sent the police after him when all he'd done was try to get his daughter back, she had to be taught a lesson.

He understood the game. It was all about money. If he needed to make her pay for humiliating him, then he had to pay for hurting her. Once or twice he'd got it wrong, misjudged the amount or the extent of his own rage. There was the time she'd had him arrested. He was furious, but he realised he was going to have to make good the insult. His solicitor had dealt with that, and the times she'd merely threatened court. Everything had been fine for years.

Until last night.

Disgust overtook his anger. Simply thinking about how much he'd wanted to take Helen last night was causing him to have an erection. The desire to have her had been overwhelming. If he'd gone back into that room, he would never have been able to control himself.

He remembered how enraged he'd been when Arthur gave her back to Cynthia, undoing in one day all the work he'd put into keeping her. He remembered the look of contempt on his brother's face as he said, "She's not safe with you, Vic. I don't want you anywhere near her."

Victor reached for the cognac bottle and began to weep. In his mind, Cynthia and Helen had become one. Never mind that she'd driven him to it. That was no excuse. He'd killed her and he knew this time money wouldn't save him.

A wave of remorse and despair engulfed him. It was almost dark, but there was enough light left in the room to make out the outline of the gun cabinet to which his eyes were irresistibly drawn. There was only one way to pay this debt. He knew it and yet he was paralysed.

As he sat and stared at the cabinet, he heard a distracting noise in the distance. He looked out the window. The house was perched on top of a hill with a commanding view of the surrounding countryside. That was one of the reasons he'd bought it. Although it was still some miles away, he could see the flashing lights of a police car. When the car turned off the A road onto the B road which led to the village just down the road and then to this house, the siren and flashing lights were turned off.

Not for a moment did he doubt the police car was coming for him. There was no alibi, no salvation this time. They knew.

It would still be several minutes before they got to the house. He had time to act, to do something, but he couldn't think. He tossed back the remainder of his cognac, then plugged the telephone back in and dialled a number.

As soon as he heard the voice at the other end, he said, "The police are coming. What should I do?"

"Do you want to go to gaol?"

"No!" The thought horrified him even more than the sins he'd committed.

"Then you know what you have to do."

"Yes." He'd known since he arrived hours ago, probably since he'd left that horrible hotel the night before, what he had to do. The knowing didn't make the doing any easier.

He replaced the receiver and reached for the door of the cabinet. Removing his favourite shotgun from the rack, he opened the drawer which contained the bullets. When the gun was loaded, he placed the barrel in his mouth, his finger on the trigger. The siren had been switched off, but even without it, he could hear the car approaching. He willed himself to do what he had to, but he could not make his finger press the trigger.

He could hear the sound of tyres crunching to a stop on the gravel drive. All the lights were out in the house, but the Jag was parked right outside the door. If they didn't guess he was inside, they'd wait, knowing he couldn't have gone far.

He tried to focus all his attention on the gun, on his finger, on the trigger, but no matter how hard he tried, he could not make his finger move.

Someone pounded on the door. Victor removed the gun from his mouth, pointed it at the wall opposite the door and squeezed the trigger. He was acutely aware of the ensuing noises: the blast of the shotgun, the shattering of glass as the bullet hit a print on the wall, the sound of the frame hitting the stone floor, and outside the curses of the police officers, footsteps on the gravel, car doors opening and closing.

"Victor Ormond," a voice garbled through a loudspeaker, "this is the police. We want to talk to you. We are armed and will use weapons if forced to do so, but nobody wants anyone to get hurt here. Toss your weapon through the front door and follow with your hands up. No one will shoot."

There was a brief pause, then the voice – or was it a different voice? – said, "Mr Ormond, the girl isn't dead. If you think this is a murder charge, you're wrong. You're looking at an assault charge, probably not more than a fine at the moment. You may have discharged your weapon accidentally,

Unethical Practices

fearing intruders. Just toss the weapon outside and come out. We can sort this."

"*Liar!*" Victor screamed. She was dead. He'd killed them. He knew it. There was only one way to pay now.

Minutes ago as he loaded the gun, placed it in his mouth, put his finger on the trigger, he'd felt as if he were moving in slow motion. Now, suddenly, everything was happening in one rapid movement. He ejected the bullets from the gun, moved to the door, yanked it open and stepped outside. Barely hearing the order to drop the gun, he raised it to his shoulder and aimed it at the police car.

In the explosion of gunfire which followed immediately, no one heard Sir Victor Ormond yell, "Do it!"

The first call to Ted at Cynthia's flat was to inform him that the butler at the Ormond house had cracked under caution and made a statement: Helen Ormond had indeed been brought to the house the previous day by Victor Ormond, but had left early that afternoon with her other uncle, Charles.

Even as Cynthia protested to Ted that this made no sense, that Charles lived in New York, that she still had no idea where Helen was, where Jamie could have gone to meet her, the phone rang again.

The second call, announcing Victor Ormond's death in a shoot out with police in Gloucestershire, stunned them all.

Roger had been so engrossed in cross referencing the information Cynthia Werring was giving them with the dates Ted had for possible assaults that he'd barely noticed how much he wanted a cigarette or a drink. When Ted broke the news of Ormond's unexpected death, Roger reached into his pocket for his Silk Cuts and lit one without thinking. Only as he exhaled did he register the complete absence of anything which looked remotely like an ashtray. He mumbled an apology to Cynthia.

"Oh, please," she said, lifting one of the tea cups and handing him the saucer. "May I?" she asked with a nod towards the cigarettes he still held in one hand.

Roger handed her the pack and then reached across the table with his lighter.

"Oh, Christ," said Ted. He grabbed the pack and lit up, too. For some time, no one spoke.

Cynthia inhaled deeply and attempted unsuccessfully to come to grips with the fact that Victor Ormond could never frighten her again.

Ted wondered how getting a warrant issued for Sir Victor Ormond's arrest was going to screw up his already well screwed career. As far as he was concerned, there was no question of 'if'.

Roger tried to figure out why the news didn't make him feel jubilant.

It was Cynthia who finally broke the silence. Stubbing out her cigarette, she stood up and said, "I need a drink." She looked enquiringly at her visitors.

"What the hell," said Ted. "Scotch, if you've got it."

Roger couldn't think of anything in the world he wanted more than a very large Scotch. But, just as he was about to nod in agreement, the image of Sally Carpenter's bruised and battered face appeared in his mind. One Scotch would quickly become two, two then three, three then four. For Sally's sake and Polly's and Meg's and all the others, he had to stay sober for a little while longer.

"No, thanks," he said, standing up and collecting his notes. "I've got a story to write."

Ted began to protest immediately. "Roger, for Christ's sake, I don't know how this is going to play out. You can't write anything yet."

Roger shook his head. "Not once today did you say the words 'off the record' or 'in confidence' to me, Ted. I've been in on this from the start. Christ, *I* started it. I've got a story to write."

"Roger – "

"No, Ted."

"All right, all right. But you can't take those notes. They're police evidence." Ted held out his hand. Roger, after the briefest show of resistance, handed him the notes. "At least tell me where you're going to be in case I need to get hold of you. Your old rag?"

Roger's laugh was bitter. "You must be joking. No chance. Trendy lefty all the way for me, mate." He turned to look at

Cynthia, who was staring at him, her hand, holding a decanter above a tumbler, frozen in the air. "There is absolutely no need for me to say why he attacked these women. He's dead. It won't go to court now. Your name will never come up."

The smile she bestowed upon him lit up her entire face, the beauty of which, in that moment, was almost breathtaking. In that moment Roger could understand how it was possible for Victor Ormond to become so obsessed with this woman.

"Thank you," she said.

"Don't mention it." He turned to go, then added, "You might ring Tilly and let her know what's happened."

Cynthia nodded, then glanced at Ted. "Will you still join me in that drink, sergeant?"

"Christ," said Ted, "try and stop me."

CHAPTER NINETEEN

"So, what happened?" Charles asked, turning back to face Helen after the brief telephone conversation which had interrupted her story.

She smiled at him, nodding towards the phone, and said, "Who thinks they're going to gaol?"

Charles returned her smile with a dismissive gesture towards the phone. "No one," he said. "Just a pal of mine in New York who's about to be audited by the IRS. He knows he's going to get caught out in a major tax fraud. He also knows he needs to fess up before he's found out." He crossed over to the sofa, sat down beside her and repeated, "So, what happened?"

It had all been so simple, she told him. Yesterday was Arthur's birthday. All Helen had to do was show up at the VACO building in Kent first thing in the morning with a present and a card. She'd be reminded by the receptionist that her father was in Singapore, hand the present and card over, then drop her shoulder bag on the floor. Jamie would be on hand in the lobby to pick up her bag and hand it to her – after he'd inserted the envelope. Then all she had to do was jump back into the waiting taxi, get to the station and meet Tilly Arbuthnot at Waterloo.

Helen paused, her gaze wandering to the big picture window overlooking Covent Garden market. An Ella Fitzgerald CD, one of Charles' favourites, was playing in the background. He had opened a bottle of Cote de Rhone and poured her a glass, which she had so far ignored. She reached for the glass now and took a sip, before continuing.

"About 20 minutes after the train left, my phone rang. Jamie told me that his fiddling in the computer had set off some sort of alarm and that all hell had broken loose. I'd stupidly told the receptionist I had a taxi waiting to take me to the station. Jamie heard a security guy on the phone with Victor saying I'd been in the building and was probably on my way to London. Then he said, yeah, it might be worth trying to get to the junction before the train. By that point the junction was the next stop. I didn't know what to do. The carriage was full of all these self satisfied looking stockbroker types. I looked in the next carriage and there was this harmless looking guy reading a *Guardian*. I didn't even think. I just scribbled down Tilly's name and address, and shoved the envelope at him, hoping for the best."

Helen paused for another, more generous, sip of wine. "I should've just stayed on the train and tried to brazen it out with him, but I didn't want him to get anywhere near the envelope, so I got off and Victor grabbed me. Tilly must've got the material, because Victor got it back from her somehow."

Just talking about Victor made her shudder. She'd been trying ever since Charles rescued her not to think about the note Victor had left for her on his pillow. But she could ignore it no longer. She had to know if there was even the remotest possibility that Victor Ormond was her father. If anyone other than her parents knew, it would be Charles. She looked at him, but she couldn't force the words out of her mouth.

Charles reached over and placed his hand over hers. "God, Helen, you're like a block of ice." He enclosed her hands in his and began to rub them vigorously. "What is it? What's wrong?"

Helen couldn't look him in the eye. She turned her head and stared blindly out the window. "Victor claims he's my father," she said between clenched teeth.

Abruptly letting go of her hands, Charles stood up and crossed the room. He, too, stared out the window, his back to her, fists thrust deep in the pockets of his trousers. "Christ," was all he said.

"It's not true, of course," Helen said, more to herself than him. "It can't be." When Charles said nothing, her tone became more urgent. "Tell me it's not true, Charles." Still nothing. "Tell me."

He turned then, spread his hands helplessly and sighed. "I don't know, angel. Your mother had a lot of difficulty conceiving. Arthur went for some tests. There was a problem with his sperm. When she finally did get pregnant, Vic maintained he was your father. Your mother denied it. I chose to believe her. I don't know who Arthur believed."

"Oh, God." Helen slumped forward on the sofa, her hands covering her face. "He must have believed Victor. Why else would he have made me stay in that house when he knew how much I hated Victor and how much I wanted to be with my mother?"

Charles was across the room in seconds, sitting down on the sofa, slipping his arms around her. "Hey, hey," he said, pressing her head against his chest. As Helen began to cry, he stroked her hair gently. "I didn't say it was true, angel. I said Vic thinks it is. And we both know Vic's quite mad, so I wouldn't worry about it too much."

Helen breathed in a snotty breath and looked up at him, her eyes still brimming with tears. "He's not that mad. For him to think he's my father, something must have happened between them. Oh, God, I can't bear it."

Charles withdrew a handkerchief from his pocket, wiped her cheeks and handed it to her. She blew her nose noisily, then tried to look away. Charles cupped her chin in his hand and turned her head back to face him.

"God, I still can't believe how beautiful you are," he said, leaning towards her and reaching with his free hand for the sash of the silk robe she'd put on after her bath.

"No, Charles." She wrenched her head away from his kiss, just as he wrenched the sash loose.

"Yes, Helen." He slipped his hand under the robe. "Come on, angel," he whispered in her ear. "You can finish with me if you want, but you have to say goodbye properly."

"Charles, no," she said again, but even as she spoke, she could feel her body responding to his touch. Moments later her feeble efforts to push him away ceased. Suddenly there was nothing, no thought of Victor or Jamie or Bowinda or famine, nothing except Charles. The groan which escaped her lips was not of pleasure, but of acknowledgement. For Charles did possess her and had since that first night in Paris. He possessed her now and he always would. Happy families was a game she could never play and it had been crazy to think she could, for always, with anyone else, there would be something essential missing. There would be no Charles. The most important thing in her life would be missing. With a shudder, she gave in.

A new track started on the CD and Helen realised that Ella was now singing about that old black magic having her in its spell. Yes, she thought, groaning now with the pleasure only Charles could give her, that's what it is, black magic.

At precisely that moment, Jamie rang the bell.

"Jesus," she said, her wits regained instantly. Charles offered no resistance this time when she tried to push him away. Helen swung her legs off the sofa and stood up, clutching the robe closed at her neck. "I've got to get dressed."

Charles stood up slowly, looking inordinately pleased with himself. "You do that, angel," he said. He reached over to an end table and switched on a Tiffany lamp, which cast a rosy glow on the room, then smiled and tilted his head towards the bathroom. "Go on. I'll let your friend in and give him a drink."

Inside the bathroom, Helen scrambled into her jeans and T-shirt, both badly wrinkled from time spent crumpled up on the floor, but a glance in the mirror told her the state of her clothes was the least of her worries. Her eyes were still slightly pink from crying, but nowhere near as pink as the rosy pink of her cheeks. Her hair was so tousled it was almost impossible to run a comb through it. She stared in the mirror and knew that, despite everything, she was positively glowing.

There is no escaping the fact that I look like I've just been fucked, she thought. She quickly splashed cold water on her face. It didn't help. She was still glowing.

Charles was right, and had just proved it. There would never be anyone else for her. She must have been mad to think even for a moment that sweet and gentle Jamie, as much as she loved him in so many ways, could ever make her happy. Perhaps years ago, if she'd had the wit to realise Jamie loved her. Perhaps in those innocent days there would have been a chance for them. But there was no hope now. Charles had put paid to that. Charles owned her as surely as if he'd bought and paid for her. She could live without him, yes, but it would be a half life. The thought of never again being with Charles quite simply could not be born.

Helen grabbed the green silk jacket Charles had bought for her during their last holiday in Italy from the hook on the back of the door, slipped it on, then glanced at the bathroom mirror one last time. "You," she told her reflection, "are in serious trouble, my girl."

CHAPTER TWENTY

Tilly had just got off the phone with Jack Conquest, recently arrived at Waterloo and on his way to meet her, when Cynthia Werring rang with the news of Victor Ormond's death. She was so stunned she didn't even think to ask if anyone had heard from Helen or Jamie. It wasn't until Roger arrived in the newsroom ten minutes later that she remembered.

Gus, realising it might be hours before the Gloucestershire police made an official announcement about Ormond's demise and ecstatic at the thought of scooping the other papers, had put Roger immediately to work in his own office. He gave Tilly a filthy look when she pushed open the door, then demanded to know where the hell her scientist was.

Tilly ignored him and spoke to Roger. "Has anybody heard anything from Helen?"

Roger didn't even bother to look up from the computer screen as he said, "She's fine. She's with her other uncle, Charles."

"And?"

Roger finally looked at her. He shrugged. "And nothing, Tilly. That's all I know." Before she could ask him anything else, he went back to work.

Tilly walked back to the desk she'd been using, her expression thoughtful.

Charles Ormond. Charles Ormond. She sat down, placed her elbows on the desk and rubbed her palms against her eyelids. "What the hell do I know about Charles Ormond?" she muttered to herself.

"He's drop dead gorgeous and an absolute swine." Tilly's head shot up, looking for the source of the answer she hadn't expected to the questions she'd just ask. Three desks down,

Lynn, the business reporter was grinning at her. "But don't quote me on that."

Before Tilly could ask her to expand on this interesting remark, they were both diverted by the shouting coming from the news editor's office. "Gus," she could hear Roger bellowing, "for Christ's sake, you know this is bollocks. You can't let them get away with this."

Tilly stood up and walked to the threshold of Gus's office. "What is it?" she asked.

Roger groaned. "Gus just got a call. Gloucester fucking CID held a press conference about five minutes ago to announce that officers responding to reports of gunfire arrived at the house of Sir Victor Ormond to discover there'd been a terrible accident. Ormond was dead and they suspect one of his hunting guns must have gone off while he was cleaning it." He looked around the room for something to hit, considered the computer screen, then punched his right fist into his left. "Bastards. It's a total fucking whitewash. And Gus here isn't sure he can run the truth."

Tilly looked at the news editor, who was in the process of chewing his way through a pencil. "Gus?"

He threw the pencil across the room and sighed. "What have you got?" he asked Roger. "And I mean rock fucking solid."

Roger held up a hand and began counting off on his fingers. "Three women who will swear they were brutally assaulted by Sir Victor Ormond. One of them willing to admit she was paid off by Ormond." He left out the fact that the other two had yet to be shown a photograph of Ormond to make an identification. "Me sitting beside the policeman in charge of the investigation when he received a call saying Ormond had come out of the house with a shotgun raised at police officers, who had no choice but to shoot at the bastard, although they probably weren't supposed to kill him." He thought about his promise to Cynthia Werring, momentarily considered breaking it, then decided instead to give up his hold over Sir Geoffrey Bloody Middleton and kiss his job at *Sweetie* goodbye. "And I've got proof that one of the tossers who gave Ormond an alibi fifteen years ago was lying."

Gus shook his head. "It's not enough, Roger, and you know it."

"Jesus Christ, Gus," said Roger. "Victor Ormond has been beating up women for two decades. Don't they deserve something? They'll never get their day in court now. At least give them some acknowledgement. Isn't this supposed to be the paper of social conscience? Power to the fucking poor and downtrodden? Well, these women are as downtrodden as it gets, mate. Where are your bloody principles now?"

Gus pointed an accusing finger at Roger. "Don't give me that load of old wank. You don't give a toss about principles or the downtrodden. Victor Ormond wrecked your life and you want revenge." As Roger began to protest, Gus held up his hand for silence. "I don't blame you, Roger. In fact, I'd like to help you drag his name through the mud. But you've got to give me something solid. So far, I've got your word about the prostitutes and your word about how Ormond died. It's not enough. Your copper may have misunderstood the call. Even if he didn't, you're right, there's some sort of cover up and he's going to be muzzled now. I can't run this story without some corroboration."

"What the hell *do* you want?" Roger asked.

The piercing sound of a police siren cut off Gus's reply. He crossed to his window overlooking Farringdon Road, and peered out. Tilly and Roger were close behind. As they watched, a police car pulled up to a sudden stop on the double yellow lines in front of the building. The driver climbed out of the car, slammed the door and headed for the entrance.

"Ted!" said Roger.

"Your copper?" asked Gus. Roger nodded. The news editor grinned and rubbed his hands together. "*That*, Roger," he said, "that is what the hell I want."

A moment later the phone on Gus's desk rang. He picked up the receiver, listened briefly, then said, "Yes, yes, for God's sake, send him up." After slamming the receiver back into the cradle, he looked at Tilly and Roger and grunted. "I don't fucking believe it. There's no one on the desk when a pair of suspicious characters like you turn up, but when a fucking policeman arrives, they won't let him in."

As one, they exited Gus's office and began to make their way towards the lifts. Ted met them half way across the newsroom. "We need to talk," he said to Roger.

"My office," said Gus, after Roger had performed the introductions. Everyone filed back into Gus's office. Tilly, whom Ted had ignored, leaned against the wall to observe, as Gus sat down behind his desk and motioned to Roger and Ted to sit down in the chairs opposite him. Neither did. Roger perched his bulky frame on the front of Gus's desk and watched Ted pace around the room.

"Are you going to tell me what the hell's going on?" Roger asked Ted eventually.

Ted spun around and stared at Roger. "Nothing's going on." He almost spat the words out. "Nothing at all. Fucking Ormond's gun was empty and now Gloucester CID are shitting themselves. This," he said, pulling a crumpled piece of fax paper from his pocket, "is what they've dreamt up to cover their asses." He straightened up the piece of paper and read: "'A tragic firearm accident tonight claimed the life of Sir Victor Ormond, chairman of the board of VACO Industries. Sir Victor was apparently cleaning – '"

Tilly had been staring morosely at the floor as Ted began to read the fax, but when she heard the words "chairman of the board", her head shot up. All day long something had been niggling at the back of her mind, and now it came rushing to the fore. She thought back to the memo on the computer, the memo from the CEO's office to General Radad.

Like everyone else, she'd taken CEO to mean Chief Executive Officer and, like everyone else, she'd automatically assumed the memo was from Victor Ormond, largely, she had to admit, because she wanted it to be. But Victor Ormond had never, to her knowledge, used the title CEO. He had always been the chairman of the board or just the chairman. If the memo hadn't been written by Victor Ormond, then who had written it? Who at VACO was conspiring with General Radad?

Oh, shit, she thought, as she pushed past Ted and hurried back to the desk she'd been using in the newsroom. She grabbed the phone and quickly punched in Cynthia Werring's number.

"What," she asked, after assuring Cynthia she hadn't heard from Helen and guiltily ignoring the strain she could hear in the other woman's voice, "is Charles' middle name?"

Unethical Practices

"Edward," Cynthia replied. "Why on earth do you want to know?"

Tilly sank back in her chair. Charles Edward Ormond. CEO. Oh, God, she thought, we've been chasing the wrong brother. It was Charles, not Victor, who'd made the deal with Radad. Charles, who, like Victor, had been in love with Cynthia Werring and might, like Victor, use her name as a password for his computer. According to the police report from the Ormond butler, Helen was with Charles, and, Jamie Mortimer, the man who had what might be the only proof of the Bowindan deal, had gone to meet Helen.

Cynthia's voice broke into this horror-filled hypothesising. Forcing herself to sound calm – there was, after all, no point in needlessly alarming the other woman – Tilly said, "What? Oh, sorry, no there's no problem, I just needed to check his middle name for the story. Thank you for your help." She thought of something else. "Does Charles have a flat in London?"

"Not that I know of. Why?"

"No?" With some effort Tilly kept the disappointment out of her voice. "Oh, I was just wondering where he and Helen would have gone."

"So have I. I've been ringing hotels to see if he's registered anywhere. No luck, but I'll keep trying. I'll let you know if I hear anything." There was a moment's pause. "And you will do the same, won't you? Ring me if you hear anything?"

"Yes, yes, of course," Tilly assured her before ringing off. She felt dreadful about not sharing her suspicions with Helen's frantic mother, but that's all they were – suspicions, which were only poorly formed in her own mind.

While she was still considering what to do next, Gus appeared in the doorway of this office. "Brilliant," he called out to her, once again rubbing his hands together gleefully.

"What?" Tilly asked.

"Ted Beauchamp's just handed over a stack of documents to Roger – everything he's got on Ormond. He's giving Roger a statement right now." Gus walked towards her, lowering his voice, grinning. "It seems the sergeant's already being blamed for Ormond's death and he's decided to hand in his resignation over it tomorrow. He refuses to take part in the old boys' cover up."

Tilly took this information in, although she was barely listening. Time enough tomorrow to help Roger celebrate. She looked away from Gus, staring blankly at her computer screen. Think, Tilly, she commanded herself, *think*.

Charles Ormond. According to Cynthia, he was a cheerful charmer who charged to her rescue at a moment's notice. Yet, by Cynthia's own admission, Charles had played a role in the development of Victor's obsession with her and he'd been surprised that she wouldn't go off with him when her marriage to Arthur ended. It was clear Charles had a fairly hefty axe to grind with Victor. How far did it go?

Until that day, Tilly had known very little about the youngest Ormond brother beyond the fact that he ran the company's New York office.

"Oh, my God," said Tilly, smacking herself on the forehead. New York! Of course. Charles Ormond lived in New York. The U.N. was in New York. General Radad had been feted at the U.N. no more than two weeks ago. And at some point during his stay had undoubtedly had dinner with Charles Edward Ormond, C.E.O. of VACO.

Again, she recollected the look of astonishment on Victor Ormond's face when she'd presented the evidence she'd amassed for her VACO India story. At the time she'd put it down to surprise that she'd laid her hands on such solid proof. Now she began to wonder if he'd known anything at all about the deal before her story ran. What if Charles Ormond was making rogue deals? Was he trying to ruin Victor? Was this an elaborate scheme for revenge against his brother? Was he trying to oust Victor and take over the company himself? Or was it simpler? Was it just straightforward greed? Was the money going straight to him?

Out of the corner of her eye, Tilly was distracted by a movement. Lynn was standing up, shrugging into her jacket, her oil spill story obviously finished. Tilly nodded a cursory goodnight in the business writer's direction, but received no nod in return. Instead Lynn walked the few paces needed to be standing in front of the desk facing Tilly. "Look," she said, tilting her head towards Gus's office, "can you tell me what all this is about?"

Tilly shook her head. "Sorry, I can't."

Unethical Practices

Lynn bit gently on her lower lip, from her expression clearly not sure what, if anything, to say next. After a few seconds, she placed her hand on the desk, leaning closer to Tilly. "Okay, listen," she said quietly, "Charles Ormond *does* have a flat in London." She held up her other hand to silence Tilly before she could demand more information. "Please don't ask me how I know, even though what I'm about to say will make it pretty obvious. It's in Covent Garden somewhere. Don't ask me exactly where. I went there in a taxi after drinking too many champagne cocktails at a reception at Café Royal." She paused, ran her fingers through her tawny hair, thinking. "It's in an old converted warehouse and has a big window overlooking the market. That's all I remember."

Tilly grabbed for a phone directory sitting on the desk beside her.

"Don't bother," said Lynn. "I tried that a while ago. The number's ex-ex-directory." With that, she raised her eyes, smiled a self deprecating smile and sauntered out of the office.

CHAPTER TWENTY-ONE

"Ah, well," Helen heard Jamie saying as she exited the bathroom, "the system can over ride individual passwords, if you know what you're doing. That wasn't the problem."

"Oh?" Helen could see Charles raise an encouraging eyebrow. She could also see his mouth twitching in an effort not to laugh at the earnestness in Jamie's tone. Despite the frenzied response he had so recently and easily elicited from her and not for the first time in the past four years, she decided that Charles really wasn't a very nice man at all.

"No," Jamie was about to continue when he caught sight of Helen. He turned towards her, beaming. "Helen," he said, grasping both her hands, "thank God. I've been so worried about you."

A big smile froze halfway to her lips when she noticed Charles intently following their exchange.

"Darling," Charles said, his tone chiding and affectionate – and the fact that he never called her 'darling' lost on neither of them – "you really must stop dropping your clothes wherever they fall. You're looking quite rumpled. I do hope you hung your robe up." His turn to beam, albeit malevolently.

Jamie immediately dropped her hands. His eyes moved back and forth between Helen's face and Charles', his expression confused.

What the hell are you playing at? Helen thought as she shot Charles a warning look, which he clearly intended to ignore. "Yes, Uncle Charles," she said, "I did hang it up. Thank you for lending it to me." She smiled at Jamie. "Charles, as I explained on the phone, rescued me from Victor. When we got here, he insisted on lending me a lovely silk robe, so I could have a bath."

Jamie nodded, as if understanding, although his expression indicated he clearly did not.

Charles led the way to the seating area at the far end of the room. Crossing to the antique rosewood sideboard, he removed two crystal snifters. "I suggest Armagnac all round," he said, nodding towards the snifter he'd already poured for himself.

"I don't think so, Mr Ormond." Jamie shook his head. "I'd rather have a mineral water, if you've got one."

For a moment Charles looked as if he might argue. Instead, he pulled out a whiskey glass, which he filled with Perrier. After adding some ice from the bucket, he handed the glass to Jamie.

"What about me?" asked Helen. "I could do with an Armagnac." Although she'd barely touched the bottle of wine Charles had opened earlier, she was feeling in need of something much stronger.

Charles replaced the two snifters in the sideboard without glancing at her. "Have some later," he said. "Drink your wine."

When Jamie sat down on the sofa, Helen quickly curled up beside him, leaving Charles to take one of the chairs. As he did so, Charles reached over to the end table and scooped up a carving, which he held up to admire.

"That's a nice piece," said Jamie.

"Yes," Charles agreed. "I bought it for Helen. It's an Eskimo carving."

If Jamie wondered what a present for Helen was doing in her uncle's flat, the only comment he made was, "Actually, they're not Eskimos. That's quite an insulting term. They're Inuit."

"Really?" Charles placed the carving on the arm of his chair. "I sit corrected." He smiled brightly at Jamie. "So, how long have you two known one another? Helen's never mentioned you before. And I," he glanced in Helen's direction then, "thought she told me everything."

Jamie was facing Charles. Helen could sense rather than see him blushing. "Oh, there's not much to tell. We've known one another since school." When he turned to look at her, his face was every bit as flushed as she'd thought it would be.

Poor Jamie, she thought. "That's right, Uncle Charles," she said. "We've been *friends* for years."

"Old friends." Charles stared at Helen. "How sweet."

"Well, actually, we haven't seen that much of one another for the past few years, have we?" Jamie, warming to his theme, smiled at Helen, his high colour fading. He turned back to look at Charles. "I did my doctorate in California and she seems to have been avoiding me ever since I came back and told her I'd been offered a job at VACO. I'm surprised she talks to you, seeing as you work for VACO, too."

"Yes." Charles raised his arms slowly, laced his fingers together and, placing his hands behind his head, slid down lazily in his chair. Stretching his long legs out on the coffee table, his brown eyes observed Helen through practically closed lids. "Why is that, Helen? Why did you cut poor Jamie dead and keep talking to me?"

Helen's turn to blush. "You're family," she muttered, reaching for her wine and refusing to meet his highly amused gaze. "I can't avoid you."

An involuntary guffaw escaped from Jamie. When she shot him a questioning look, he shrugged an apology. "Sorry, Helen. It's just that, well, you've done a remarkably good job of avoiding Victor for years and he's family, too."

"Quite," agreed Charles, abruptly abandoning his languorous position and leaning, elbows on his knees, towards Jamie. Small talk over. "Which is, of course, why we're here. Victor. Now, Jamie, I think you had better finish telling me what you know."

"Yes, of course." Jamie swallowed half his Perrier in one long gulp. "But I wish you would ring the shipping people and tell them to put a stop on the order."

"I will," Charles assured him, "as soon as you convince me there's something to stop. So far all I've got is Helen's somewhat garbled story about some bloke waylaying you in a car park. The guy might have been mistaken. I rang earlier and no one knew anything about any shipment to Bowinda. Before I give orders for them to start tearing the place apart, I've got to have a bit more to go on. So, could you please tell me what this evidence is that you claim to have laid your hands on?"

As Jamie raked his fingers through his hair, trying to focus

Unethical Practices

on his narrative, a thought flitted through Helen's mind. When had she told Charles where the shipment was going? He'd also mentioned Bowinda when she was still in the bath, yet she couldn't remember saying anything about General Radad.

"All right," Jamie was saying. "I knew I might only have a short time, so I ran a very specific check using the keywords Radad and Bowinda and the product number seventeen eight seventy-two. Only one thing came up. I saved it on a disk and printed a copy. It wasn't until I looked at the print out that I realised it had been saved in wingdings."

Helen glanced at him sharply, the question forming in her mind momentarily forgotten. *Wingdings?* her raised eyebrows asked. Jamie smiled. "It's a symbols font," he explained. "A lot of people save things in it, thinking it will just look like gibberish if someone gets into the file. I recognised it straight away."

Charles leaned even further towards Jamie. "So you weren't able to read what the document said?"

"Not all of it, but enough," Jamie told him. "I converted it and was just starting to go through it when there was a little blip on the computer. I thought it might be an alarm I didn't know about, so I just grabbed the disk without saving it in Times, shut the computer off and dashed down to reception to slip the envelope to Helen."

Charles leaned slowly back in his chair. He picked up the carving and stared at it for a moment before speaking. "And what exactly were you able to read?"

For his part, Jamie looked extremely proud of himself, like a conjuror who is about to pull an elephant, rather than the anticipated rabbit, out of his hat. "It was a memo from Sir Victor to General Radad, outlining the terms of payment for the shipment of seventeen eight seventy-two." He grinned triumphantly, first at Charles, then at Helen.

"You're sure?" Helen asked. After everything Victor Ormond had put her through in the last day, not to mention all their previous history, she was beside herself with excitement at the thought of finally bringing him down.

"Oh, yes," said Jamie, "definitely. The memo started with 'CEO's Office, VACO'."

As soon as the words were out of Jamie's mouth, Helen's world began to topple. She grabbed Jamie's arm. "Are you sure it didn't say Chairman's Office or Chairman of the Board's Office?"

Jamie clearly couldn't see what difference it made. Sir Victor Ormond was the head of VACO, whatever title he chose to go by. "Yes," he said, smiling at her curiously, "quite sure. It said CEO's Office."

It was such an old joke. She'd lost track of the number of times she'd heard Charles say Victor might be the chairman of VACO, but he, Charles, was the CEO. Charles Edward Ormond. CEO of VACO. Christ. She turned her head and looked at Charles, willing him to shake his head, to laugh, to say how ironic that Victor had decided to start using the title.

But Charles did none of those things. Instead, while Jamie continued to stare with concern at Helen, before she could open her mouth to force out a warning, Charles raised his arm and brought the soapstone carving crashing down on Jamie's head.

CHAPTER TWENTY-TWO

Perched on the edge of the desk in Gus MacPherson's office, his foot bouncing up and down impatiently, Ted Beauchamp spoke in sharp tones to the person at the other end of the line. "You're sure? No Charles Ormond or C. Ormond or C. E. Ormond?"

Although he hadn't been able to see what the hell Victor Ormond's younger brother had to do with the price of beer, Ted had responded to the urgency in her voice when Tilly came storming into Gus's office, demanding he stop everything and use his soon-to-be-over role in the Met to check for an ex-directory listing in Covent Garden. Putting his hand over the receiver, he shook his head at her, shrugged and mouthed the word "Sorry".

Tilly's shoulders sagged at reaching this dead end. Of course, it had been a long shot. Lynn hadn't said when she'd been to this flat. He might have sold it. Or she might have been wrong. It might not have belonged to Charles at all. He might have borrowed it from a friend.

But he was somewhere and she had to find him. He had Helen. He had Jamie. And, clearly, at least to her, they were the only two people standing in the way of Charles Ormond making a huge profit from selling a famine to General Radad. The last she'd checked with the radio news folks, Jack's rescue team were still locked on to the gates at VACO, although it wouldn't be much longer before the police cut through the kryptonite – or whatever the Superman-sounding metal was that they used – and hauled everyone away. The shipment could still go. Hell, the shipment might have left before the protest started.

"Are you sure?" Tilly half heartedly asked Ted.

Before he could answer, he was spinning away from her,

facing the desk and grabbing a pencil. "Why the fuck didn't you say so?" he demanded of the person at the other end of the line. He scribbled something down, then slammed the receiver into its cradle. "Jesus Christ," he muttered, "I thought the bloody service was supposed to improve when they privatised. I swear to God they've still got the same bunch of gormless prats who've always been there."

He looked up at Tilly. "Honestly. How bloody literal do you have to be? I make it very clear that this is urgent police business, that I need an ex-directory listing for Ormond in Covent Garden and just because I said Charles or C it takes them five fucking minutes to decide to tell me there's an H Ormond with an ex-directory number in Henrietta Street. Christ almighty."

Roger and Tilly exchanged glances. "Your friend Helen?" he asked.

Tilly shook her head. "It can't be. Her mother told me quite definitely that she lives in Camden."

"Well, do you think it's a coincidence?"

As Tilly opened her mouth to tell Roger that she very much doubted it could possibly be a coincidence, Ted interrupted. "Would one of you please tell me what the hell is going on?"

Gus, who had been standing behind his desk, peering over Roger's shoulder as he rapidly typed up his notes for the Victor Ormond story, looked up then. "Yes, Tilly, what the fuck is going on? Where's your scientist? Where's your goddamn story?"

"Oh, fuck off, Gus," said Tilly, a statement which startled them both. She had, of course, sworn at and been sworn at by Gus frequently over the years, but always in drinking establishments of one form or another at the end of long, tense days and long, argumentative, drunken evenings. At work, Tilly was a professional. Although she had sworn at many an imbecilic editor in her time, Gus was no imbecile. It was difficult to tell which of them was the most astonished at her outburst. "Sorry," she said automatically. Then she added, enunciating each word slowly and precisely, "I am afraid that if I don't do something about it, the story will be dead."

Ever practical, Gus simply smiled. "Well, you'd better bloody do something about it, hadn't you?"

Unethical Practices

"Look," repeated Ted, "what the hell is going on?"

Tilly sank down onto the couch in Gus's office and began correcting what she now perceived to be her earlier mistake. She shouldn't have kept Ted out of the loop about the Bowinda shipment and was ashamed of the cavalier manner in which she had determined that she and she alone should be allowed to break that story.

Ted gave her a hard look, before saying, "Proof?"

Tilly sighed. "If it exists now, Jamie Mortimer's got it. And, if I'm not mistaken, the man responsible for the Bowinda deal has Jamie Mortimer."

She outlined her suspicions, holding up her right hand and counting each point off on her fingers. Sir Victor Ormond never, ever referred to himself as the chief executive officer of VACO. Charles Edward Ormond's initials spoke for themselves. The butler at the Ormond estate said Helen arrived with Victor and left with Charles. Jamie Mortimer said he was going to meet Helen. No one had heard from either of them since. Tilly had reason to believe Charles Ormond had a flat overlooking the market in Covent Garden. There was an ex-directory listing for an Ormond in Henrietta Street, which overlooked the market.

"It still doesn't mean either Helen or her friend are in any actual danger," Roger pointed out.

Tilly looked hopefully at Ted, who shrugged and said, "It's not much to go on, is it? We have no idea if a crime's actually been committed."

She wasn't sure if it was a case of them not believing her or not *wanting* to believe her when she said they'd been after the wrong Ormond.

Both Roger and Ted wanted too badly for it to be Sir Victor – the icing on their cake – the man devoid of humanity who beat women must also be the businessman devoid of ethics who sold misery for a profit. Looking around at the sceptical faces of Ted, Roger and the impatient Gus, prompted Tilly into another outburst. "Oh, for Christ's sake, all right. It's a hunch. Don't tell me none of you have ever run yourselves ragged chasing a hunch?"

After only the briefest pause, all three men had the grace to nod that, yes, of course they had.

Tilly leaned eagerly towards Ted. "Please, Sergeant Beauchamp. Just come with me to Covent Garden."

Roger, his attention torn between Tilly and the computer screen, looked at her sharply. "Oh no you bloody well don't, Tilly Arbuthnot. Ted's mine. I need him to finish my fucking story."

This time everyone except Tilly was shocked when she turned to Roger and, at the top of her lungs, yelled, "Fuck your fucking story!" As various efforts were made to reposition the various jaws which had just dropped, Tilly reached past Ted and grabbed the piece of paper upon which he'd scribbled the Henrietta Street address. "Oh, to hell with the lot of you," she said, standing up abruptly. "I'll go by myself."

She barged through the door of Gus's office and, pausing in the newsroom only long enough to retrieve her bag, battered hat and ancient Mac, made her way across the room, shoving the swinging doors with such force her gaping audience were astonished that neither door flew off its hinges.

The lift doors opened a moment after she'd pushed the button. Tilly, not even looking where she was going, walked straight into considerable bulk of Jack Conquest. "Whoa," he said, putting out a hand to steady her as she bounced off him and into the wall. One of his bushy black eyebrows shot up. "Weren't we supposed to be meeting here?"

Christ, she'd forgotten all about arranging that on the phone. Cynthia's call had sent it completely out of her mind. She nodded. "Sorry. Something's come up."

"So I see." Jack was still holding the lift door open. Clearly the lift didn't like being detained. Bells began ringing. "Anything I can help with?"

Tilly considered for a moment. A burly bloke might be very useful indeed, as she had no idea what she was going to find when she got to Covent Garden. On the other hand, she might find nothing. This might be yet another wild goose chase. What she really needed was help getting the story finished in time for the morning's paper.

"Yes," she said, nodding and pointing to the doors into the newsroom, which were still swinging on their hinges. "Get in there, convince Gus MacPherson you know what the hell you're talking about and get him to put you on the computer I was using. Check my copy, make sure I haven't completely fucked up the science, and write a side bar explaining Arthur Ormond's research."

Jack grinned. "Good thing I do know what hell I'm talking about." He let go of the lift door, which began to slide shut. Jack's hand, then arm suddenly shot into the space between the doors. The alarm bells got louder as the doors slid back open. "Here," Jack said, reaching into his jacket pocket, "you might need this." He extracted a mobile phone and tossed it towards her.

Tilly surprised herself by actually catching it.

CHAPTER TWENTY-THREE

"Jesus Christ, Charles. What the hell have you done?"

Jamie's head had fallen back against the sofa, his face rapidly draining of colour. Helen leaned towards him, not knowing what to do. Tentatively, she raised a hand to his neck and felt, unsuccessfully, for a pulse. She reached for his right hand and turned it palm upwards, pressing a finger against the vein on the inside his wrist. She hadn't realised she was holding her breath until the relief of finding a pulse allowed her to let the breath go. Why on earth had she never learned more about first aid? Basic mouth-to-mouth during swimming classes at school, that was her lot. Was Jamie's pulse all right or was it as faint as she thought? At least there was a pulse.

She looked at Charles, flabbergasted. "What's wrong with you? You could have killed him."

"I take it," he said, removing a silk handkerchief from his pocket and using it to rub the surface of the carving, "I haven't killed him, then?"

"No, thank God. But we need to get him to hospital." Helen started to stand up, intent on ringing for an ambulance. Cursing herself for once again curling up with her feet underneath her, she fell back against the sofa as pins and needles shot through her numb legs. Before she could right herself, Charles had shot out of his chair, crossed the room and yanked the phone loose from its connection in the wall.

As horrified as Helen had been at the realisation that Charles, not Victor, might be the perpetrator of the Bowinda atrocity, as shocked as she had been to see him bringing the carving down on Jamie's head, she hadn't until that moment been afraid. Now she was terrified.

"Charles?" She tried to keep her tone soft, level, but it was

Unethical Practices

difficult to get any words past the lump in her throat. "Charles, why?" Of course there was more than one question involved. Why had he hit Jamie was an obvious one, but so, too, was why would he sell General Radad those cursed seeds? She had no doubt whatsoever that Charles was the CEO in the memo. She'd seen the acknowledgement in his eyes when they'd met hers for an instant before he brought the carving crashing down on Jamie's head.

Watching Charles pace around the room as he tried to decide what to do with the phone, watching him place it down the side of his chair, then calmly reseat himself, cross his legs and smile at her as if they were conversing about the weather, Helen finally and belatedly realised that not all the evil she'd sensed in the Ormond household had emanated from Victor.

"Why?" Charles repeated, his tone perfectly natural, his expression quite bland. "He should have had an Armagnac, self righteous prat."

"What?" Whatever answer to whichever why she'd expected, this piece of nonsense wasn't it.

Charles seemed surprised that she didn't immediately grasp his point. "If he'd drunk the Armagnac I offered him, sweetie, he'd be falling asleep by now and I wouldn't have needed to hit him."

Jesus. She grasped the point now. He'd even said it again. Sweetie. Only her father called her sweetie. Last night – this morning? when had it been? – as strong arms lifted her out of the chair in the cellar, she'd heard him, her father telling her everything was okay, sweetie. Except her father, the man she'd always thought was her father, was in Singapore and couldn't have carried her out of the cellar. Until this moment she'd forgotten those murmured words. The shock of Victor putting her in his bed and leaving that awful note had driven the words from her mind. Except, of course, she now realised, it hadn't been Victor.

"It was you. You drugged me. You put me in Victor's bed." Again the question. "Why?"

Charles reached across the coffee table for her untouched wine glass and took a sip before answering. When he did, it was with the same bland, nothing out of the ordinary going on here expression. "I had to make sure you didn't go running to your mother or the Arbuthnot woman. I had to make sure you stayed with me until I found out who helped you and what he –" Charles shot Jamie a disdainful glance "– knew."

As if on cue, a low moan escaped from Jamie. There was a slight fluttering of his eyelids, as though he were struggling to regain consciousness, but the struggle, if such it had been, was lost. Helen reached for his hand again, pressing her fingers into the back of his wrist, trying to find his pulse. Jamie's lips seemed to be turning blue. There was a pulse, but Helen was convinced it was much weaker than it had been.

"Please, Charles," she said, her tone beseeching him to do something for Jamie while there was time. He responded with an almost imperceptible shake of his head which was clearly final. She turned her head and looked towards the solid metal door of the flat. What she wanted to see wasn't there.

"Oh, angel," said Charles, "you didn't really think I'd forget that, do you?"

In the building's warehouse days, the enormous storage rooms which had been converted into flats, were secured with ancient dead bolts. The key was needed on either side of the door to operate the lock. Some of the new owners had found the system irritating and changed it. Too easy to pull the key out of the lock without thinking, put it down somewhere and not be able to find it when one wanted to leave or admit guests. The authorities had warned that, unless the key was left in the lock at all times, it might be life threatening in the event of a fire. They advised changing the locks and many owners took the advice. But Helen loved the weight of the old key. She made sure it was always in the door, in case of fire. Charles, when she'd raised the issue with him, had said he would gladly risk the fires of hell to have her in his bed, and would not, therefore, worry overly about the fires of earth.

The key was not in the lock. Unless she could find her bag, she – and Jamie – were trapped.

"Don't bother, angel." Charles, when she turned back to look at him. "I took the keys out of your bag while you were in the bath."

◇ ◇ ◇

Half an hour after Tilly's hasty departure, Ted's curiosity

got the better of him. He got another, equally unhelpful operator on the line. Fortunately, this time he knew what question to ask and several moments later had the ex-directory number for the Henrietta Street flat.

"Well," he said when Roger, impatient to finish his story, raised his eyebrows, "it wouldn't hurt to ring and see if the Ormond girl is there. Let her know her mother's worried about her."

After fifteen rings, he replaced the receiver. "No one there. Your friend Tilly's on a wild goose chase."

The possibility that someone had disabled the phone did not occur to him. Why should it? That sort of thing, in his experience, only happened on *Columbo*.

CHAPTER TWENTY-FOUR

"Charles, have you gone completely insane?" Nothing else, Helen thought, could explain his cool, calm and collected demeanour.

He took no offence at the question. "No, angel, not yet, but, since you ask, I will. It's genetic. It positively gallops through the men in the family. Your grandfather was completely barking the last two years of his life. My father was apparently showing early signs before he threw himself off a mountain. The only one who seems to have escaped is your father, although I have my doubts about him. Vic's been half out of it for years now. I've been watching it and waiting all my life. I know the signs. The only thing that keeps *my* moods in check is fucking you."

He smiled at her affectionately. "So, you see, you really have been an angel of sorts. I figure I've got about ten years before I get as loopy as Vic. I *had* intended to spend them with you. I was going to use the jolly general's lolly to take you somewhere hot and sunny, and enjoy the time I've got left. And you would have come, wouldn't you? If it hadn't been for your stupid fucking interfering friend here." When she didn't answer, he raised his voice, "*Wouldn't you?*"

Helen's eyes darted uncertainly back and forth between the faces of her lover and her friend. Throughout this conversation, her hand had encircled Jamie's wrist. There hadn't been a sigh or a moan out of him for some time. She could barely feel his pulse now. But she knew there was no point in appealing to Charles. Somehow she was going to have to save Jamie. Somehow she was going to have to save them both.

She fixed her gaze steadily on Charles and took a deep breath. "Yes," she said. "Yes, of course I would've come – if I hadn't known where the money came from. And I probably wouldn't have asked. I wouldn't have wanted to know. There've been a lot of things I haven't wanted to know, haven't there?" She raised her chin an inch, and tilted her head slightly to one side, considering him. "I'm surprised you need to ask. Of course, I would have gone with you. It's what I've wanted for years, but could never imagine having." Her smile was sad, filled with regret. "I love you, Charles. I've loved you since that first weekend in Paris."

He raised the wine glass, quickly tossing back its contents, then looked at her and shrugged. "Not anymore, angel."

Tears, unbidden and unwanted, glistened in Helen's eyelashes. She knew he wouldn't believe her, that he'd think she was saying it to get around him, but, for her sins and they had been many with him, it was true. "Yes, Charles, still."

He shook his head. "Not the way I need you to love me, you don't. A week ago I would have stated with confidence that if your mother and I had been kidnapped by terrorists and you had to choose which one of us could live, you would have chosen me." He refilled the wine glass. "Not anymore."

It amazed Helen that she was able to appear so calm, when inwardly she was fighting not to scream. She could no longer feel even the faintest pulse in Jamie's wrist.

"Charles," she said, hoping against futile hope, "I will come with you and I will stay with you." She glanced towards Jamie's face, so pale the freckles stood out like a connect-the-dot birthmark. "If – "

Charles laughed with apparent delight. "Nice try, kiddo."

"Charles, he's going to *die*. I can't feel his pulse."

"Helen," Charles countered, no trace of amusement left on his face, "do I look as if I give a flying fuck? He tried to wreck my plans with Radad and he succeeded in wrecking my plans for you. It's his own fault."

"Charles – "

"No!" He waved her protests away impatiently with one arm, while glancing at his watch on the other arm.

It was fortunate that he had taken his eyes off her for in that moment not only did Helen begin to feel Jamie's pulse again, but Jamie himself managed a slight, but exquisitely important squeeze of her hand. When she looked at him quickly, his eyes flickered open for an instant, then closed, but in that instant she knew the most important thing in the world: Jamie was still alive.

She turned her face back towards Charles, hoping her expression did not betray her relief. But Charles' mind was not on her. After satisfying himself that the clock on the mantle agreed with the time on his watch, he said, "Sorry, darling, but the shipment's gone. In an hour the money will be in the bank and I'll be gone, too."

Keep him talking, she thought. "I don't understand. It was bad enough when I thought Victor was doing this to recoup some of the research investment. But the money's not even going to VACO, is it? You're taking it. Why? You don't need it."

This time there was little humour in his laugh. "Oh, yes, I do, young Helen. I've been divorced from a pair of vultures who've bled me dry. I neither can nor intend to live on what's left of my VACO salary after those supposedly liberated fucking cows took their cut."

"Charles, we don't need the money. We can go away together somewhere. Please Charles."

He stood up, walked around the coffee table, bent over to cup her chin in his hand. He smiled one of his incredible, light up the room smiles which had melted her heart so many times in the past. "Really?" he said, brushing his lips against hers.

Helen nodded. Believe me, believe me, she prayed silently. "Yes," she whispered.

Charles straightened. "Ah," he said, as if he could read her mind, "but I don't believe you." He sauntered away from her, over to the sideboard, once again removing a crystal snifter. After pouring a generous measure, he held the glass out towards her. "Come on, cherub, time for your medicine."

Of course, she thought, he must be remembering that Christmas in Kent when she'd been laid up in bed with some ailment or other and Charles had been the only one from whom she would take the loathsome medicine the doctor had prescribed. Was that why he was suddenly, after all these years, calling her cherub again? To remind her to be a good little girl?

Helen bit off a suggestion about exactly where he might put his medicine. While Charles might be remembering an old sick bed incident in Kent, Helen was remembering an evening three years earlier in an inn in Martha's Vineyard. It had started off as a pillow fight. Charles hadn't really wanted to play, but Helen kept bouncing the pillow on his head. Even when he tore the pillow out of her grasp and sent it flying across the room, she'd ignored the warning in his eyes. Instead, she made a grab for his sides, knowing full well that Charles hated anyone trying to tickle him. He told her to stop, but she wouldn't. She just laughed and darted round the other side of the bed to try to tickle him again. And then suddenly, he'd grabbed her. It had all happened so quickly. One moment she was reaching for him. The next moment both her arms were pressed up against her back and she was face down on the ground breathing in carpet fluff with Charles squatting over her back. He hadn't hurt her. In fact, moments later they were making love. But for an instant she'd been chilled by the knowledge of how easily and badly he could have hurt had he chosen to do so.

It alarmed her even more now. If it came down to a physical fight between them, she would lose. It was that simple. She let go of Jamie's hand, then stood up and crossed the room to where Charles stood. Near the sideboard. Near the bottles. Near potential weapons.

As Helen took the proffered snifter, she spotted the corkscrew, folded up neatly and resting on top of the sideboard where Charles had left it after opening the bottle of wine earlier. Folded into the corkscrew was the tiny knife he used to remove the foil from wine bottles. Not much of a weapon, but short of making what she knew would be an unsuccessful dash for the carving knives in the kitchen, it was the best weapon she was likely to lay her hands on. Now the question remained of how to remove it from the sideboard without Charles noticing. Of course, securing the corkscrew might be irrelevant. She held the snifter under her nose and breathed in the fumes of the Armagnac, then looked at Charles, eyebrows raised. "Is it poisoned? Are you going to kill me, too?"

Again he responded with a delighted laugh. Clever little

Helen. Just listen to what she's said this time. "Of course not, angel. I told you. All I was going to do was put you and Freckle Face to sleep for a few hours. It's the same stuff I gave you last night, except now it's in the Armagnac, instead of a carafe of Gewürz." His smile was quite sheepish as he indicated she should drink up. "I was a bit worried you'd suss me last night. I thought you'd recognise my salad dressing."

"Frankly," said Helen, surprised now that she hadn't, "there were other things on my mind – like being locked up in the dark, which you know I hate, by the man I used to think was my demented uncle."

"Oh, he is," Charles assured her. "Vic has completely flipped his silver lid. He's been close for a year now, but your little game pushed him right over the edge. I got there just in time."

"Just in time for what?" she asked, her tone sarcastic. Charles to the rescue, indeed.

His expression was suddenly very serious. He nodded towards the snifter. "Come on, angel. Drink up and I'll tell you all."

Helen glanced at the amber coloured liquid, wondering just how much it would take to knock her out. Obediently, she raised the snifter to her lips, tilted her head back and took a hefty swig. As Charles, content to see her obeying instructions, turned to ease himself back into his chair, Helen quickly spat most of the Armagnac back into the snifter and pocketed the corkscrew. She sat down, cross legged on the carpet in front of Charles, placing the snifter on the coffee table with her left hand, while keeping her right hand stuffed into the pocket of her jacket. Not for the first time in her life, but never more vehemently, she cursed her brittle, short fingernails. Prising the knife free from inside the corkscrew without Charles noticing was not going to be easy.

Meanwhile, she had to keep him talking. "Just in time for what?" she repeated sceptically.

"Just in time to stop him going back into that room and raping you, smarty pants. So wipe that smirk off your face."

The last instruction was hardly necessary. Helen recoiled, her back knocking into the coffee table so sharply some of the Armagnac spilled out of the snifter.

Charles sighed, withdrew a handkerchief from his pocket and wiped up the spill. "Yes, that's right, Helen. So, when I'm gone and you're thinking about how much you hate me, remember that I spared you what would probably have been the worst experience of your life. Be thankful I sent him off to find some tart to beat up. Because he called me afterwards and guess what? He'd lost it so completely, he killed her. Remember that when he gets sentenced for murder. I saved your life last night." He paused and shook his head. "Talk about fucking *deja vu*."

"What do you mean, *deja vu*?" The corkscrew, Jamie, everything else was momentarily forgotten as she tried to fathom his meaning. Had there been other times, times when she was still a child, that Charles had prevented Victor from harming her? Her father had never said so outright, but he'd made it clear when she was older that he'd sent her back to her mother because he didn't think she was safe around Victor. Had there been an incident? Something she'd repressed? "I don't remember – " she began, but Charles silenced her with an impatient gesture.

"Not you," he said, "although God knows what might have happened if Arthur hadn't sent you away."

"Who?" Of course, she knew the answer. Victor in the hallway, hurting her mother. Victor staring at her mother. Victor scaring her mother. Helen knew the answer, but she had to hear it. She pulled her hand out of her pocket and reached up to crush the fabric of Charles' immaculately pressed silk shirt. "Tell me."

Charles gently removed her hand and smoothed his sleeve, then laid his left hand on top of hers and squeezed gently, while leaning away from her, his right elbow on the other arm of the chair. After rubbing the side of his face, he brought his bearded chin to rest on his hand. And then he told her about the night, eight and a half months before she was born, when he came home to find Cynthia Ormond huddling in the hallway sobbing and Victor on the floor of Cynthia and Arthur's room, practically catatonic.

"Oh, my God." Helen couldn't bear to hear it. She tried to pull her hand away from Charles, but he gripped it firmly.

"He didn't succeed, thank God." Although a smile played

momentarily at the corner of his mouth, his expression was grim. "Victor always was a bit premature, if you know what I mean." Helen, swallowing hard, nodded to convey that yes, she understood what he meant. "I decided to take care of your mother before I dealt with Victor. I put her to bed in another room. When I got back, he was zipped up and on his feet and about to go looking for a fucking encore. Only now he was very angry as well as barking mad and he wanted to really teach her a lesson with his belt."

"Jesus."

"Indeed." He leaned towards her then, clasping her hand in both of his. "I couldn't let him hurt her, could I?" Helen shook her head mutely. "Of course not. And your mother wouldn't let me ring the police, even though it would have suited me nicely to get shot of the bastard, but she wouldn't have it. Thought it would kill your grandmother, which is probably true. Nor, for some reason, did she want your father to know."

"What did you do?"

Charles let go of her chin and relaxed back against his chair. "First, I took enormous pleasure in punching him in the face, then I made him pack a bag and go off to a conference I was supposed to be attending in Amsterdam. Then I told him there were plenty of blondes in brothels and bars and hanging around on street corners and that, if he couldn't control himself, he should try raping them."

His lips curled up into a smile of satisfaction. "It was a piece of advice he wholeheartedly embraced."

Helen remembered the awful pictures in one of the tabloids of the woman Victor had been accused of beating years ago. "That woman who had him arrested – ?"

"One of many, I fear." His smile became positively Cheshire cattish. "And last night, as I had hoped all along, his sickness finally did him in." More to himself than her, he added, "Irritating that I have to leave now, just when I could have finally taken over the company." For a moment he stared vaguely at the ceiling, as if weighing up his options. Then he looked back at Helen and said impatiently, "Angel, I really don't want to have to force that Armagnac down your pretty little throat, but I will if I have to. Now drink up."

Helen knew he wasn't lying, that he would, if necessary

hold her and force the Armagnac down her. She tried to remember how long it had taken the wine to knock her out the previous evening, but couldn't. She'd had no sense of time in the cellar. Praying she could stay conscious long enough to get Jamie to a hospital, she lifted the snifter to her lips and slowly poured the contents into her mouth. When the snifter was empty, she held it up in front of his face with her left hand, while she renewed her efforts to open the corkscrew with the broken fingernails of her right hand.

"I don't understand, Charles," she said. "If the Armagnac really isn't poisoned, if it really will just put me to sleep, I'll wake up eventually. And when I do, I'll scream until someone comes. And when they do, I'll tell them everything. I'll tell them," as she said it, she prayed it wasn't true, "you killed Jamie. I'll tell them about the seeds. Radad'll never be able to use them, so the plan will fail. You'll be arrested. You'll go to gaol for the rest of your life. I don't see how you can let me live."

"Oh, Helen." He seemed genuinely surprised that she should suggest such a thing. "By the time you wake up, I'll be long gone with Radad's money to a place where neither he nor the police will ever find me. Of course, you must live. If I killed you, they'd never know and I want them to know."

It was clear to Helen that Charles wasn't talking about the police. "Who won't know what, Charles?"

"You really don't get it, do you, angel?" He leaned forward and touched her cheek gently. "You're the prize. You're what everyone wanted." He smiled. "Vic, because he couldn't have your mother, so he had to develop his sick fantasy that he'd fathered you. Arthur, because he couldn't believe he *had* fathered you and he couldn't believe your mother would have him and keeping you was the best way to punish her for the sins she'd only ever committed in his mind. Your mother because you were all she ever wanted after your father's fantasies drove her away. When you got older and started looking more and more like her, Vic wanted you more and more. Everyone wanted you," his smile widened, "but I got you. And I want them all to know it."

He leaned even closer. "I want Vic in his prison cell thinking about me fucking you. I want your father, who thought Vic was the only one he had to worry about as far as your chastity was concerned, thinking about me fucking you. And I want your mother, who wouldn't have me after everything I went through to wreck her marriage, to think about me fucking you."

Through the horror of everything that was happening, through the increasing haze of the drugs, Helen's face registered surprise at this last remark.

"Ah," said Charles, smiling, his finger caressing her chin, "I guessed a long time ago that neither of you parents ever told you I was named as co-respondent in their divorce."

Although his finger on her chin had been the lightest of touches, Helen felt as if he'd just beaten her black and blue. The prize. Prize idiot, apparently, in a game which hadn't even been about her, but about her mother.

"Were you thinking about her when you were with me?"

"At first," he admitted, "but not for long. I'll tell you a little secret." He winked a good-natured, conspiratorial, just between us wink. "She was never as good in bed as you are. I've told you before. You're a natural."

"Am I supposed to be flattered?"

"Are you?"

"No."

"Ah, well. It was meant as a compliment, you know." He leaned back in the chair, resting his chin on his hand, observing her. "I'll miss you, Helen. I really will. Oh, I expect I'll find some beautiful, pliant, dusky young maiden to train as your replacement, but she'll never fit me like you do. That won't matter too much. Men can get by with a far from perfect fit. But after a while she'll bore me and then I'll have to shut my eyes and think about fucking you."

Charles talking about her as if she were some easily replaced whore, might have caused Helen more outrage, had she not at that moment finally managed to prise the knife free from its fold into the corkscrew. She'd seen Charles sharpening it often enough to know how easily it could cut through the foil of a wine bottle or the wax seal on one of his favoured bottles of cognac, but how useful was it really going to be as a weapon? Cautiously, her eyes never leaving Charles' face, she ran her thumb along the edge. She realised at once that she'd cut her thumb, but, unless Charles spotted blood seeping through the pocket of her jacket, a cut thumb hardly mattered. What mattered was that the blade was razor sharp.

She could feel the drugged Armagnac begin to take effect. Her head was slightly woozy, in need of support. She leaned to her left, rested her elbow on the coffee table, her chin in her hand, mirroring Charles' pose in the chair.

"And what about me, Charles? What am I supposed to think?"

The mirror effect ended abruptly as Charles sat up, leaning towards her, elbows on knees. "You, angel, are supposed to think what a pity it is that you had so many scruples, because if you hadn't had so many scruples, if you hadn't been such a good little girl, you wouldn't care what VACO does and you could have come with me." He leaned even closer, reaching out to cup her chin in his hands, his face inches from hers, brown eyes staring intently into aquamarine. "Instead, you will try to forget me. You will try to recreate what we've had with other men, but you never will. And when you make love with them, you'll think of me and how only I could make you feel. Won't you?"

Helen nodded, bitterly aware that it was true.

Satisfied with her acknowledgement, Charles smiled and moved his head the extra inch required for his lips to reach hers. With a sigh of regret, he kissed her.

That's when Helen stabbed him in the neck with the corkscrew knife.

CHAPTER TWENTY-FIVE

Charles let out a howl. His expression, as he reached for the corkscrew, utterly astonished. Blood spurted all over him, all over Helen. She tried to stand up, but the drug was taking hold firmly. Her far from steady legs nearly buckled beneath her, but she managed to right herself momentarily. Then Charles grabbed her leg. She fell on top of him. He wrapped his legs around her body and his hands, so gentle a moment before, closed around her neck. Despite the blood pouring out of the wound in his neck, his grip was like a vice. She clasped on to his baby finger and pulled as hard as she could, back until it was pressed against his arm, back until she heard it snap, but still she could not loosen his grip. She could feel the blood pounding in her head, knew that she would be unconscious any moment. Her frantic gaze fell on the Inuit carving, back on the end table, in its place beside the Tiffany lamp. If only she could reach it, but it was no use, the carving was infuriating inches too far away. Her hand fell limply on the table. Underneath it was the lamp cord. She closed her fingers around it. In what felt like slow motion when there was no time for slow motion, she pulled the cord until she felt the base of the lamp within her reach.

Charles was gasping for breath as loudly and desperately as she was, but still his grip stayed firm. She was pinned against him by his legs, unable to move her lower body, trapped by the merciless hands around her neck. She looked into his eyes, but there was no help or pity to be found. These were not the eyes of the man she'd loved, they were the eyes of a maniac. Helen pulled her right arm up, raised her hand to his face and, with what strength she had, began to press her thumb into his left eye socket. Please, God, she prayed, let him still be able to feel something. Her prayer, by luck or God, she cared little which, was answered. With another howl, his grip loosened enough for Helen to lift her head. Still the blood flowed from his neck. They were both drenched in it now. As Charles' left hand pressed against his eye, he grabbed a fistful of her hair with his right hand. Feeling as if her hair was being torn out by the roots, Helen raised the Tiffany lamp above her head and slammed it down on his forehead, slivers of coloured glass covering them both. Charles hand fell to his side, his head lolled back against the chair.

Helen scrambled away from him, collapsing in the middle of the carpet, gasping in painful breaths. She didn't know whether it was the drug or the near asphyxiation, but she knew she had precious little time before she blacked out completely. Crawling on her hands and knees, she retrieved the telephone from beside the chair. Steadying herself on the coffee table, she hauled herself into a semi-standing position and lurched across the room. Slowly, so she wouldn't topple over, she bent down to push the plug into the socket, only to realise the plug was still in the wall, the wire ripped from it when Charles yanked the phone from the socket. The phone was useless.

It was too much. The door was locked, the keys God alone knew where. The phone had been her last and only hope.

"*No!*" she screamed at the top of her voice as, with strength she would not have believed she still possessed, she hurled the telephone at the picture window.

The telephone was old and heavy, vintage 1940s, something Helen had purchased as part of her modern/antique decorating scheme. It crashed through the window, landing at the feet of Tilly Arbuthnot just as Helen, now completely spent, landed on the floor of the flat.

Tilly looked first at the telephone, then at the window from whence it had flown. "Well," she muttered to herself, "that answers that question."

She had arrived in a taxi minutes earlier, only to discover a number of frustrating things. The address Ted had written down did not include a flat number. There were dozens of flats in the old warehouse. Although there was a buzzer system, there were no names beside any of the buzzers. Undeterred, she had tried ringing them all and got absolutely no response. Stepping away from the entrance, she'd peered up at the building. There were lights in the windows of several flats, lights which didn't necessarily mean anyone was home – it was after all Friday evening – but did suggest someone might be. Either the buzzers weren't working or the tenants of this up market warehouse didn't like answering them. She decided to try them all again.

It was while she was doing this that she heard the first howl from above. Tilly had, in her time, been dangerously close to both soldiers and civilians who'd just lost some part of their anatomy to enemy artillery or land mines from some war long forgotten but still not over. To her the howl was all too familiar.

She spotted a callbox half way down the road and sprinted towards it, hoping no hooligan had been there before her to vandalise it, a fate which seemed to have befallen every callbox Tilly had tried to use in the past five years. She grabbed the receiver, then realised it was in no way attached to the rest of the mechanism. The wire had been severed. Tilly was about to start banging her head on the glass when she remembered the mobile phone Jack had tossed to her in the lift. Fishing it out of her pocket, she peered at the phone suspiciously. The on/off switch was easy to work. She punched in the number for Gus's office and got no response, belatedly remembering that Jack had borrowed the phone from someone in Belgium. Christ, she thought, dialling codes. The damned phone still thought it was in Brussels, so what code did she have to add to make a call from EU Central to London? It took her a moment to remember. God, she'd been deskbound in London for far too long. A few years ago she wouldn't have even had to think about it. She punched in the code and the number and put the mobile to her ear. It seemed to take an eternity to connect, but, just as she was about to give up, the phone at the other end finally started to ring.

"Put Sergeant Beauchamp on," she barked without preamble into Gus's ear when he answered. She was equally succinct with Ted when he came on the line. "I'm at Henrietta Street. Someone's being murdered. Get over here." Knowing there wasn't a policeman alive who wouldn't drop everything when he heard the word murder, she ended the call before Ted had a chance to speak and hurried back to the entrance.

At that moment she heard the second howl.

"Christ," she said, peering up again. The howl had definitely come from this side of the building. "But which flat?"

Then she heard a woman's voice screaming the single word, *"No!"* and a moment later a telephone came flying through one of the second floor windows, answering the question she'd just asked herself.

It was on her third try with the buzzers that she finally noticed the instructions for punching codes in before pushing individual flats. After several tries, Tilly heard a window open and a Hooray Henryish voice called out, "Roddy, is that you, you silly sod?"

She left the entranceway to peer up at the source of the voice, who looked every bit as gormless as his accent suggested.

"Are you deaf?" Tilly hollered at him. "Haven't you heard the screams?"

"Eh? Screams? What screams? Oh, do you mean a minute ago? I say, were they real? Thought it was some bastard's telly up too loud. Happens all the time, you know."

Tilly gave up her enquiries about his hearing and pointed to a window one flight up and two rows over from his. "What flat is that?" she demanded. "The one with the light on."

Henry or whatever his name really was, leaned some distance out his window and peered in the direction she was pointing. "The one with the broken window or the next one over?" he asked.

Give me strength, Tilly muttered under her breath. "The one with the broken window."

Henry glanced over his shoulder again. "Seven," he said.

"Thank you," said Tilly. "Now, will you please let me in?"

Henry stared down at her blankly. "Let you in? I shouldn't you know. If you want the people in seven, you should buzz them."

Tilly removed her battered fedora, so as to give Henry the full thrust of her most penetrating stare. "Young man, this is police business. If you don't get this door opened in ten seconds, I shall have you arrested for obstruction."

Henry's head disappeared almost immediately. Tilly began to tap her foot impatiently. Would he call her bluff? Was 'Henry' not quite dim enough to believe she was a police officer? Was he, in fact, ringing the police himself? The buzzer sounded and Tilly quickly pushed the door open. Thank God, he really was as gormless as he looked.

Although she was itching to get up the stairs, she realised Ted was going to need a way to get in the building. While he might prefer to just kick through the plate glass door, she doubted it. There was a large metal ashtray in the foyer, the sand in its bowl recently cleaned and buttless. Tilly dragged it over to prop open the door and used her index finger to print FLAT 7 in the sand. Hopefully, Ted would figure this out.

Then she took the stairs two at a time, wondering what the hell she was going to do when she got there.

In the end, the answer was: not much. She found Flat 7 and, never wondering if she were in any danger, began pounding on the heavy door until her fist ached.

She had been right that the police would take the word murder very seriously. The first thing Ted did after she rang off was put out a call to the nearest station which was only minutes away from Henrietta Street. Tilly was surprised to hear feet pounding up the stairs long before Ted could have possibly made it, even with siren blaring, from Farringdon Road. Four policemen, led by a uniformed officer, whose rank she recognised as inspector, appeared at the top of the stairs and hurried towards her.

"Did you call this in?" the inspector demanded of Tilly. She nodded. "Right then, what's going on?"

"There were two dreadful howls and a scream." Tilly said, feeling no need to elaborate.

"Two howls and a scream?" the inspector repeated. "That's it?" Tilly nodded again. "Discharge of weapons?" Tilly shook her head. Ten years ago, hearing that question in England would have astonished her. Sadly, it no longer did. "Crashing? Banging?" he asked hopefully.

"The telephone flew through the window. That's how I was able to identify the flat. I was watching the window and the entrance when I rang Sergeant Beauchamp and no one has come out. Someone is inside there and they're not answering the door."

"Oh, fuck," she heard one of the constables say, "it's another bloody domestic argie bargie, what do you want to bet? 'Piss off, officers, me and my black eye are just fine, no problem here.'" The other two groaned.

Tilly looked at the inspector. He'd also heard the constable's comment and was waiting for Tilly to tell him something to contradict the suggested scenario. "People," he said to her, "have domestic quarrels. Things get thrown, sometimes out of windows. There's no law says they have to open their door when concerned neighbours knock."

"In the first place," Tilly informed him, having fully caught his drift, "I am not a nosy neighbour, as Sergeant Beauchamp will inform you when he arrives." She drew herself up to her full five foot and ten inches, which gave her an inch on the inspector. "In the second place, my good man, I have covered wars on four continents and have heard and seen more people die than you will *ever* have hot dinners." She pointed at the door of Flat 7. "Someone in there is either dead or dying. If I find out they could have been saved if you hadn't decided to stand here arguing the toss, this information will, I assure you, be plastered over the front page of every newspaper in the country." When he still did nothing, she pulled a notebook and pen out of her pocket. "What is your name, Inspector? I want to make sure I spell it properly."

And, just as the Shah of Iran had once acceded to her demands, so, too, did the inspector. Without giving Tilly his name, he pounded on the door, identifying himself loudly as an officer of the law. When there was no reply, he signalled to the constables to go to work.

After some unsuccessful grunting and kicking, Tilly patiently pointed out to the inspector that it was a reinforced door with an extraordinarily good dead bolt. "Don't you have any tools for this sort of thing, Inspector?" she asked.

"Yes, of course we do." He nodded in the direction of the constable who'd been so eager to put forward his domestic dispute theory. "Go on, Brown. Get the stuff out of the boot."

Brown, rubbing the shoulder he'd made the mistake of

trying on the door, set off down the corridor, but had barely made it to the head of the stairs, when more heavy footsteps could be heard coming up at a run. A moment later, Ted Beauchamp appeared, brandishing an alarming-looking crowbar. One quick look down the corridor at the empty hands of his colleagues told him what he needed to know.

"Thought you might want this," he said, handing the tool to Constable Brown. Several seconds later, he was followed into the corridor by a panting Roger, who'd refused to be left behind when the call came.

Brown and another constable prised the monster crowbar between the door and its frame and applied their own heavy frames to it. A moment later there was a splintering of wood and the door flew open.

The inspector crossed the threshold first, followed by Ted. Tilly pushed past the constables, who in turn ensured they got inside before Roger.

"Jesus fucking Christ," said the inspector, moving into the sitting area of the large open-plan flat. He looked at the dark, bearded man, slouched in the chair, covered in blood and at the equally blood-drenched blonde woman lying on the floor. The geezer collapsed on the sofa didn't look too good, either. "Who the hell are these people?"

"Helen Ormond," said Tilly, crossing the room to crouch beside the young woman's motionless form. She gestured towards the bearded man in the chair. Even covered in blood she could see some sort of family resemblance to Victor Ormond. "I think that's Charles Ormond."

"Jesus," said the inspector. "Tell me they're not related to Sir Victor Fucking Ormond."

"Brother and niece," said Ted.

"Oh, Christ." The inspector reached up and rubbed his temple with his fingers. "I'm two years short of retirement. I don't need this." He pointed at the sofa. "And him?"

"Your scientist?" asked Roger.

Tilly glanced at the young red headed man on the sofa. He was so pale the freckles on his face stood out like spots on a leopard. She nodded. "I think so. I think his name is Jamie Mortimer." She looked back at Helen and fought the urge to weep. Ignoring the shouted warning from Ted not to touch anything, she reached out and placed her hand on the girl's bruised neck. Helen wasn't the first strangled woman she'd ever seen, but never before had the sight hurt so much.

And then the miracle. The pulse she felt, ever so faintly, throbbing in Helen's swollen neck, just as she heard Constable Brown, over near the sofa, say, "This one's still alive."

Another constable, the one who'd helped Brown with the door was bending over the chair. "This one's had it," he said of Charles Ormond at the same moment the inspector was radioing for an ambulance.

Jamie Mortimer revived briefly as the ambulance workers were lifting him off the sofa. He began to thrash about, calling Helen's name, Tilly hurried to his side. She squeezed his hand and promised him that Helen was alive, already on her way to the hospital. Jamie relaxed back against the stretcher, but did not let go of Tilly's hand. "Arthur," he murmured weakly, "coming from Singapore – stop shipment."

CHAPTER TWENTY-SIX

The following morning a national newspaper would run a front page story quoting Ted Beauchamp as saying that Sir Victor Ormond was responsible for a series of violent assaults on women and had not, contrary to officials reports, died by accident whilst cleaning a gun, but had been killed in a police shoot out.

Until that act of insubordination forced his resignation, Ted Beauchamp was still a bona fide member of the Metropolitan police force. He had no difficulty using these credentials to track down which flight from Singapore had one Arthur Ormond as a first class passenger.

"Oh, Christ," said Inspector John Smithers, relieved that that awful woman in the fedora had never taken down his name, "by all means, Ted, you go and break the news to him."

Cynthia Werring, assured by the hospital that her daughter was simply sleeping off the effects of a non-lethal drug and was in no danger, insisted on going to the airport with Ted.

Tilly, apprised by Jack that his eco-warriors had been removed from the gates of VACO, wanted solid reassurance that the shipment was not heading to Bowinda. So, she wangled her way into the back seat of the police car – Ted's objections quashed by Cynthia's insistence that she wanted Tilly's company.

Roger had, with Ted's blessing, gone to finish the story which would, in the morning, require Ted to hand in his resignation from the force. After twenty years on the job, he felt curiously light-headed and liberated.

The flight was due in at one in the morning and Heathrow, when they arrived, was virtually deserted. It was not, therefore, difficult for Tilly to spot the dishevelled figure of Roger's chief sub, slouched in a seat in the Arrivals area.

"Baldwin, what on earth are you doing here?" she demanded, the bark in her voice which so alarmed him more habit than intention.

Alec immediately leapt to his feet, his glance shifting uneasily from Tilly to a uniformed police officer to a glamorous woman who looked disconcertingly like the beautiful girl from the train. "No one rang to let me know what was going on," he said, choosing to address his scruffy plimsolls. "I tried to get in touch, but there was no answer at your flat."

"And?" prompted Tilly, forcing him to look at her.

He did so briefly, then his eyes darted towards the Arrivals. "I rang VACO, just when they were shutting for the day. I said I needed to speak to Arthur Ormond, that it was an emergency. I mean," he risked another glance in Tilly's direction, before returning his gaze quickly back to his plimsolls, "I gather from everything everyone said, that Sir Victor Ormond's beyond the pale, but I thought, well, you know, perhaps his brother's not so bad." He looked up again, his eyes darting from Ted to Cynthia to Tilly. "He has won awards, you know, for medicine."

Tilly did her best to smile encouragingly. "Go on, Alec."

"Well, this woman at VACO told me Arthur Ormond was on this flight back from Singapore and couldn't be contacted." Another reassuring look at his feet, before risking a glance at the man in uniform, the dreaded authority figure. "I expect she didn't realise there are phones on a lot of planes now."

Ted, barely able to conceal his astonishment that this was, in fact, the case, simply nodded. "Good man. So you rang him?"

"Well," admitted Alec, "you can't actually ring the plane yourself. But I called the airline and told them it was a dire family emergency, and that he must ring me." He glanced at Ted, inordinately pleased with himself. "And he did, about twenty minutes later. I told him about the seeds and General Radad and all that. Mr Ormond was awfully shocked. And really very grateful that I'd told him." Alec's age old problem with authority figures kicked in and he found himself unable to continue meeting Ted's steady gaze. Tilly's piercing blue eyes weren't much of an improvement. "He said he'd get on to HQ straight away and put a stop to it."

To Alec's complete and utter astonishment, the Arbuthnot woman threw her arms around his neck and said, "Oh, Baldwin, you're brilliant."

Ted, ever the copper – until the following morning, at least – hadn't finished ascertaining the facts. "Did Arthur Ormond tell you to meet his plane?" he asked.

Alec, emboldened by Tilly's praise, answered the policeman without looking at his shoes. "No, but while I was sitting in the office hoping someone might ring and tell me what was happening, I heard about his brother's death on the radio, I wasn't sure if anyone knew he was on this flight and would think to meet him."

The startled looks the three newcomers gave him and exchanged with one another as soon as he'd said the words 'brother's death' confirmed to Alec that, yet again, there was something he did not know.

"That was very nice of you, Baldwin," Tilly told him. "Do you, by any chance, know what he looks like?"

"Um, no," Alec admitted, "but I made a sign." He reached over to the seat he'd recently vacated and produced a piece of paper upon which Arthur Ormond's name had been printed so faintly in pencil that it would have been indecipherable to most of the tired passengers, assuming they'd been looking for it.

"Your sign won't be necessary," said Cynthia Werring, speaking for the first time. She'd spoken to Jamie long enough at the hospital to find out how much he and Helen had risked to prevent the shipment of those VACO seeds. She was grateful to this shambling young man that he had stumbled on a solution no one else had considered.

She bestowed upon Alec a smile more gracious and charming than she would have been able to muster had she yet been aware of the full extent of Charles' villainy. "I'll recognise Arthur, but please stay – " What had they called him? Baldwin? Alec? That couldn't be right. She was muddling it with the name of a film star. "My husband will want to thank you himself, I'm sure."

Soon afterwards the Arrivals doors burst open and the first of the passengers from Singapore began to issue forth. What was left of Ted's position, could have got him and Cynthia

Werring past security, but Cynthia, uncomfortable about meeting her ex-husband with only a police officer for support, had demurred. She'd insisted on waiting with the others.

When Arthur Ormond emerged, briefcase in one hand, flight bag in the other, and spotted Cynthia waiting for him, he couldn't believe his luck. Although she was with a number of other people, he saw nothing of them.

Unlike his brothers, who'd retained the full heads of hair and slim figures of their youth, Arthur's sandy hair was receding, and, like his mother, he was inclined towards a substantial spread in the middle regions. Although both these facts had bothered him slightly, neither had seemed particularly important over the years, because he was never going to love another woman again the way he'd loved his wife. Seeing her now, he sucked in his belly, but he did not smile. It was impossible to suggest the joy he felt. He must pretend surprise.

Because Arthur knew why she was there, although it would not do to let her know, or the policeman he now realised was with her. Or the others who seemed to cluster about her as she shifted her position.

Cynthia smiled at him. It was a hesitant, I don't know why I'm smiling, really sort of smile. Arthur forced himself to look surprised. Surprised *and* pleased. He kept his eyes on her and only her. His expression said, why are you here, my dear? What a surprise and a pleasure. But that wasn't quite right. Why would she be here after all these years? He adjusted quickly to feign concern. I'm surprised and delighted to see you, his new expression said, but I realise you wouldn't be here if something were not wrong.

She'd tell him in a minute, of course, her and the policeman and the extraordinary woman in the battered old hat. And who was the nondescript character with them? Could that possibly be the stuttering fellow who'd got through to him on the plane?

Well, God love him, if it was, because that was the phone call which had alerted the airline to his presence on the flight. If it hadn't been for that call, someone on the ground wouldn't have thought to radio through the news reports and the very kind co-pilot would not have sought him out in his first class seat. He could tell by the look on Cynthia's face that she was there to break the news. But he'd already heard it.

The older brother he'd hated for corrupting their father's company was dead.

The younger brother he'd hated for corrupting his marriage to Cynthia was dead.

The wife he'd always loved, but had allowed his hated brothers to drive away, was ready to return to him. He could see it in her face.

The company he'd always wanted was finally his and his alone.

"But Helen's all right," Cynthia was saying, beaming at him and slipping her arm through his. Arthur smiled back at her.

Thanks to that fortuitous in-flight phone call, he'd been able to contact the Butcher of Bowinda and cut a deal for an excellent retirement package. Of course, the 17872 shipment had to be cancelled, the general understood that.

But VACO had plenty of other products which would suit the General's needs.